little

SECRETS

A DARK MAFIA ROMANCE

USA TODAY BESTSELLING AUTHOR

KALLY ASH

Little Secrets

Cover design by Sly Fox Cover Design
Edited by Swish Design & Editing
Proofread by Swish Design & Editing

Disclaimer: The material in this book contains graphic language and sexual
content and is intended for mature audiences, ages 18 and older.
There is content within this book that may set off triggers.

For you know who...

PROLOGUE

Eighteen Years Ago...

I WAS LOSING MY BABY.

That was the only thought that echoed in my head…

Taunting me…

Tearing me apart.

I was losing my *baby*…

And there wasn't a thing I could do about it.

Desperate, I peered up at the bus station security guard from my hunched-over position in the metal chair in the depot waiting room. His name badge said Cox.

"Help m-m-me," I whispered. "Please."

He paled.

He recognizes me then.

"Miss… I…"

"*Please*. My baby is dying."

I didn't know whether it was my plea or the fact that blood was slowly dripping to the linoleum between my feet—giving him the visual he needed—but he nodded. Wrapping an arm around my back, he helped lift me from the chair, pausing when I moaned in pain. It felt as if a red-hot poker was being jabbed into my abdomen, then circled like someone was trying to make scrambled eggs out of my intestines. I tried to straighten—to lessen the pain somehow—but I cried out as a sledgehammer of agony was driven into my lower back.

Doubling over again, I attempted to relearn how to breathe, taking in shallow breaths through my mouth. The smell of blood coated the back of my tongue, overtaking the taste of diesel fumes that somehow still infiltrated the building from the forecourt outside.

"Come on, miss," Cox said, helping me stand once more. "We have to get you to the hospital."

I blinked, trying to get my eyes to focus on his face. He had to be in his forties with a gray-flecked beard and kind blue eyes.

My throat felt clogged, like I couldn't draw in a deep enough breath, but I managed to whisper, "Thank you."

The guard looked around—at who or what—I didn't know. The station was empty at this time of night. Well, except for the ticket seller who sat behind a long eggshell-colored counter. She stared at me when I'd first entered but had studiously ignored me after that.

"Come on, miss," Cox urged again. "My car is parked out back."

I shuffled beside him, each step agonizing. Behind me, a line of blood followed in my wake, a macabre breadcrumb trail. He pushed open the door that led out to the forecourt. Cold Michigan air slapped at my senses, making the tears streaking down my face freeze. I tried to draw in a deep breath of air through my mouth again, my eyes scrunching up tight when another wave of pain hit me.

When I was younger, I remembered watching news footage of a hurricane hitting Belize. They'd showed the waves demolishing the small boats that had been anchored offshore with such force that they were found at the top of palm trees ten miles inland.

That's what I felt like now.

The boat.

The waves of the storm my pain.

I clutched a hand to my rounded stomach and sent up a prayer that I wouldn't be found battered and broken after the storm surge—that I would be whole and holding my baby in my arms.

Out of the harsh glare of the station's lights, cleared asphalt gave way to small snow drifts.

"My car is just over there," Cox said, his breath puffing out in front of his mouth. "Not much farther."

I nodded, pressing my lips together once more when my lower back spasmed. I drew to a stop, eyes squeezed shut, a deep frown forming between my eyes.

"Just breathe through it," he said. "My wife and I have four kids. I've been through this before."

I gave him a watery smile. "You have four kids?"

"Yes, miss. Frank Junior, Celeste, Nickolas, and my youngest is Chantelle." As he spoke, he urged me forward once more. "If my Marie got through four deliveries naturally when she was in her thirties, you'll have no problems with delivering your baby."

God, I hoped he was right.

We'd arrived beside his early-model Toyota, and while he unlocked it, I leaned against the window, taking a moment to collect myself. My gaze tracked the bright red spots on the snow, marking where we'd walked.

Frank took me gently by the arm. "Come on, in you go."

He settled me into the back seat, slammed the door, and got into the driver's side, gunning the engine. I watched the buildings pass us by, biting my lip to stop from crying out in pain. With one hand firmly on the door handle, I had the other one curved around my belly, praying to a God I didn't believe in anymore to save my daughter.

The scent of blood suddenly got thicker and something hot splashed between my thighs. Reaching between my legs, I touched my fingers to the place where I felt all that moisture. When I brought my fingers into the light, they were bright red—coated in too much fresh blood. My vision went fuzzy then, my hearing dropping in and out.

"Oh, God."

Frank peered over his shoulder at me every few seconds as he sped through the empty late-night streets. Whatever he saw in my face, made the color drain from his. "I'm only a block away. Just hang on."

My eyes began to shut, but I jerked them open again when I felt the car lurch to a stop. Frank got out, leaving his door open. I knew cold air was barreling through the interior of the car, but it felt warm to me. The dome light above my head came on and a pair of feminine hands were there. It was a nurse. She was speaking to me—I could see her mouth moving—but all I could hear was the ringing in my ears.

"What's... name?" the woman said. She ran her index and second finger along my neck. "... weeks pregnant?"

"I..."

Pain rendered me speechless. Sightless. Deaf. I was the boat being carried inland.

I smiled.

At least there would be no more pain…

I WOKE SLOWLY, MY SENSE OF HEARING THE FIRST thing to come back online. There was a machine beeping somewhere behind me, a hush of air conditioning and the soft murmurs of people not wanting to disturb anyone. My eyes fluttered open, and I blinked at the fluorescent lighting above my head.

There was a numbness to my body that I recognized. I was on a lot of pain medication, and I wondered why. Surely giving birth didn't warrant that. Slowly, I moved my hands to my stomach, expecting to feel my baby moving beneath the stretched skin, but she wasn't there. My new reality forced my eyes to stay open this time as I peered down the line of my body.

My stomach was flat.

My baby was gone.

I jerked into a sitting position, sucking in a hissed breath and clutching at the stabbing pain just below where my baby should have been. My mouth parted on a pant as I tried to figure out what had happened. I'd been at the bus station, intending to leave Michigan behind when…

Blood…

There'd been so much blood.

There was a choked mewling sound, and it took me a moment to realize I was the one making it. Cupping one hand over my mouth, I breathed heavily through my nose, the sensation of falling dizzying and terrifying.

"Oh, God," I whispered, swallowing back bile. My wild gaze bounced around the cubicle that was shielded on three sides by blue curtains. Where was my baby?

"My baby… where…" A ragged gasp escaped me, and I screamed, "Where's my baby?"

My words echoed around me, but still nobody answered.

A familiar scent was suddenly in my nose—leather, gun oil, and Boss Bottled. It was as familiar as it was terrifying. Outside the curtain, there was a scrape of shoes, and my gaze shifted to the stiff blue fabric that was my only defense against the world. A hand speared through the center, parting the two sides with agonizing slowness. My heart lurched in my chest. My pulse jumped up into the back of my throat.

"Aidan." His name came out as a whisper. I pulled the thin blanket a little higher up my body. "What are you doing here?"

His dark blue eyes tracked the movement of my hands like a tiger stalked its prey. It was almost with a casual nonchalance, but I knew deep down he was cataloging everything. Like he always did.

"Hello, Seren," he said in a smooth, cultured voice—nothing like the typical midwestern accent I was surrounded with in everyday life. His expensive British boarding school upbringing meant he never mispronounced his Ts as Ds. He stepped fully into my space, leaving the curtains open.

I repeated, "What are you doing here?" This time my voice sounded steadier. "Where's my baby?"

He arched a brow. "Don't you mean where's *our* baby?"

I squeezed my eyes shut for a moment, but I couldn't escape the truth. Aidan was my baby's father whether I liked it or not, although it hadn't ever been my plan to get knocked up by the only son of the head of the Irish-American mafia.

Aidan and I had a tumultuous relationship at best—a downright invective one at worst. A relationship based on violence, vitriol, and desperation. I slept with Aidan because he could keep me safe. I stayed with Aidan because, without him, I'd be back on the street, back on drugs and probably dying in a gutter somewhere.

"Where is she?" It was a question I would keep repeating until I got the answer I needed to hear. "Where's Sloane?"

He cocked his head to the side, but I wasn't prepared for the next word to come out of his mouth. "Dead."

All the air in my body came out in a rush, my lungs crushed under the meaning of that one word. I began shaking my head, unable to believe it. "What..." My hands curled into fists as I stared at my blanket-covered legs. When I was finally able to look at him again, I asked in a whisper, "What do you mean... d-d-dead?"

The ends of Aidan's dirty-blond hair slid against the starched collar of his business shirt as he glided farther into the room. Under his arm, I caught a flash of the gun he kept holstered there. It was a 500 S&W Magnum, and the only reason I knew this was because the image of him pressing the muzzle of that gun into the temple of my only friend was burned into my memories. Every time I blinked, I saw Lucy's terrified eyes, her stiff shoulders... her last pleading words as blood and bits of brain were splattered on the carpet at my feet.

His top lip curled off his teeth in a sneer. "*You* killed her."

"I..." I glanced down to avoid the accusation in his eyes. My chin was suddenly captured in his strong fingers, my head yanked up where I met his midnight-blue eyes.

They were cold—a dead stare.

"Where were you going, Seren?" he asked in a low drawl.

Feeling like a rabbit caught in a snare, I tried to keep the fear out of my eyes, but I knew he saw it there. Bare. Raw. "I don't know." My words came out in a broken whisper, and I thought, *how poetic is that?* I felt broken now. Insubstantial as a whisper.

With a disgusted snarl, he released my chin, but I didn't rub away the pain of his grip—no matter how much I wanted to.

When Aidan next spoke, his voice was devoid of emotions. "Do I need to take care of you like I took care of Lucy Stern?"

The fine hairs on the back of my neck prickled in warning. Yes, Aidan had taken care of Lucy—my only ally inside the impenetrable Kavanaugh empire. The only mistake she'd made was talking to a cop, but that had been enough. Her one and only chance. The Kavanaughs demanded complete and utter devotion. Nobody talked to the cops for any reason. End of story.

I was the only witness to Lucy's murder. She was shot in the head—execution-style while she was still on her knees after sucking Aidan's dick. I was seven months pregnant at the time, and Aidan had worried about hurting the baby if we fucked. So, he used Lucy instead, since her only role was to sleep with whoever Aidan and his father, Killian, wanted her to. She was passed from man to man, sometimes to sweeten a business deal. Sometimes—most times—it was simply to humiliate and degrade her.

"My father has ordered your execution."

My eyes widened, and my heart thundered in my ear. "What?"

"You've seen too much... *know* too much. He can't trust you anymore. *I* can't trust you anymore," he continued conversationally. I flinched as he reached out a hand and stroked my hair, something like regret passing over his features. "But you did carry my daughter inside your body." He ran his thumb along my bottom lip, pulling it down slightly. "In my own way, I do love you, Seren, but your betrayal..." He shook his head. "Your betrayal is unforgivable. Did you think you could just leave Detroit... leave *me*? You don't get to leave. Once you're in, you're in."

Casually, he pulled the gun from under his arm and leveled the muzzle at my head.

Instinctively, I curled in on myself, shut my eyes and waited. I waited for him to pull the trigger and end my misery.

A tense minute ticked by then another.

"But I'm going to give you a choice, Seren. To prove my love for you, you have one chance. Leave now and never come back."

I blinked. Aidan wasn't known for giving second chances to anyone. "What?"

"Call it grief, but I'm giving you to the count of three to decide. Leave now and live or die in this bed."

Death would be a relief. I wouldn't have to feel again.

"One."

But I couldn't give in. I couldn't give up. My father had taught me better than that.

"Two."

I stared at Aidan, wondering whether this was all real.

"You're running out of time, Seren," he drawled, flicking the safety off and pressing the barrel flush with my temple. "Choose. Now."

1

Dagger

ONE YEAR AGO...

WARM WATER SLUICED OVER MY HEAD, SHOULDERS, and chest. The stream running down the drain in the center of the shower floor was pink with blood.

None of it was mine.

The liquid donation had been made by the unlucky bastard currently handcuffed to the chair in my office just outside the bathroom door. I'd left Hawk Montana blubbering to himself five minutes ago after I'd brought him in for my boss—Bane Rivera—to see.

Bane was the owner of the largest gentleman's club in LA. The Dollhouse was one of three legitimate arms of his business. The others were real estate in and around Los Angeles, as well as a part share in a restaurant owned by his sister.

His less-than-above-board business involved Colombia's finest white powder and being the head of what some people might call the mafia. The reality was what he did was more closely related to an organized crime syndicate. Far less familial than the mob.

And Hawk was a mid-level dealer for Bane.

The fucker had dropped off his profits from the week of selling coke earlier in the day. Now, normally, that wouldn't be a fucking problem. But what was a problem? The fact that it was fifty large lighter than it should've been.

And Bane didn't like it when people stole from him.

Shutting off the water, I stepped from the stall and toweled off quickly. I pulled on the clean pair of slacks I had hanging on the back of the door then tugged on the navy-blue button-down shirt. The Heckler & Koch MP5K I'd left by the sink was the final thing I'd picked up as I opened the bathroom door.

Hawk Montana whimpered as I stepped into the office, his wide blue eyes darting from my face to the H&K.

"I'd be more terrified of Bane," I told him, a sardonic grin twisting my lips. "A bullet is quick. Bane prefers to drag out death."

"Please," he said. "Oh, God, *please.*"

My expression was level, my stare cold. "I'm not your savior." I undid the cuffs and slid my hand under his arm to lift him from the seat, noticing a puddle of piss hitting my hardwood.

"Fuck me," I muttered, shaking my head. "What kind of grown-ass man pisses himself?" Grabbing a handful of the back of Hawk's shirt, I opened my office door and pushed him through it. At the base of the stairs, I stopped when someone else came down. It was Kandy. She was dressed in black lingerie that barely covered her. Her legs looked lean and long in the black pumps.

"What's doing, girl?" I asked.

"Just getting the boss a drink." She winked at me and stepped back out into the club. I swore 'getting a drink for the boss' was fucking code for a blow job, but Kandy's lipstick hadn't been smeared so maybe Bane had turned her down.

"Get your ass up the stairs," I growled to Montana.

When he reached the top, he hesitated, shifting from one foot to the other. His wide eyes were darting between the bottom of the stairs and Bane's office door. Before he could bolt, I spun him around and pinned him to the wall, the muzzle of my H&K pressed into the base of his skull. "You should know I have a hair trigger." It was an idle threat. I hadn't even loaded the damn thing. Not that Hawk would've noticed.

Keeping my gun in place, I knocked on the office door.

"Come in," came the barked reply.

"Stay," I told Hawk then opened the door.

Bane's dark eyes traveled the length of my body, no doubt taking in my clean clothes and wet hair. "Did you get him?"

"Yeah, he's out here pissing his pants for you."

A smile pulled at the corners of his mouth. "Just the way I like it. Send the fuck in."

I stepped outside then pushed Hawk into the room. The bastard tripped over his own feet and ended up sprawled in front of Bane.

How fucking fitting.

When he tried to get up, Bane drove his foot between Hawk's shoulder blades and shoved him back down. Reaching into my pocket, I slid a magazine into the MP5K and hovered it above our dear mathematically challenged dealer's head.

"Where's my money?" Bane asked in a bored drawl.

"It was all there," Hawk replied. "I counted it. Twice."

"Then I'd say you need to go back to school, Hawk, because it wasn't all there. *I* counted it twice, and you were at least fifty grand short."

All the color drained from Hawk's face as sweat started to form on his brow. "*Fifty* grand?"

Bane held out his hand, fingers outstretched. "This many, times ten, asshole, unless you can't count those up without the help of a calculator."

"I counted it twice," Hawk muttered, more to himself than to me. "Jesus, Bane, I'm sorry. It was all there when I dropped it off. I swear!"

Bane looked over at me, silently asking whether I was buying the steaming pile of horseshit. But that wasn't the only question. The more pressing one was should we just kill the guy now and make an example of him, or did we take the path less traveled and give him another chance?

I shrugged.

Bane crouched in front of Hawk. "How about I make you a deal, Hawk. I give you two weeks to come up with the cash you owe me, and you deliver it to me like a good little boy. If you can't do that, then I'm afraid our working relationship is over... as is your heart's relationship with beating in your chest."

When Bane rose to his feet again, he jerked his chin in my direction, dismissing me. I hauled Montana up and held him still so Bane could deliver one last, piss-pants-inducing proclamation.

"And to make sure you understand just how serious I am, you now have one week to get me my cash." His dangerous gaze shifted to me. "Rough him up a little before sending him on his way."

I gave him a nod and directed Hawk from the room. He spun

around, attempting to plead with me. "A week isn't enough. I counted it twice."

I shut the office door.

"I counted it twice. Please," he begged.

"You're lucky, kid. If it were me, you would've been dead the moment you started pissing on my office floor."

AN HOUR LATER, I STEPPED FROM MY PRIVATE BATH-room for the second time that night. There was a towel slung over my shoulders, and water dripped steadily from the ends of my hair, dropping onto my bare shoulders and going lower. I stood buck-naked in front of the closet in the corner and pulled a black business shirt and black slacks off their respective hangers. I always kept at least half a dozen changes of clothes here, but the dry-cleaning bill was a bitch.

After I slipped my boots back on, I left my office and went out onto the floor of the Dollhouse. One of my jobs here at the club was to keep everything running smoothly, keep the trouble out, and manage the Dolls. I scanned the space, looking for Syndy out of habit. That girl was nothing but trouble. She was too attached to Bane. She thought she was more than just someone to suck his dick, and that kind of thinking could get out of hand very quickly.

I walked the perimeter, making sure everyone knew I was there. Trouble among the patrons wasn't something I had to worry about. They all paid enough money to come to the Dollhouse to know to keep their hands to themselves and their dicks in their pants in the public areas. It was the cashed-up spawn of rich daddy that came in most nights hoping to get more than a dance from one of the Dolls without paying for the privilege.

It was those nights I enjoyed the most.

"Hi, Dagger," someone said, and I turned my head to see Mandy waving at me nervously. It was something a little girl would do—wave like that—but with her dressed in lingerie, it was hard to put those two images together.

"How are you, Mandy?" I asked, watching her approach. I'd taken her in my office last night—a quick fuck to take the edge off. I thought we'd understood each other. It was just sex. There were no repeat performances.

She swayed her hips as she walked toward me, circling her arms around my waist and bunching my shirt in her hands to hold me close. Reaching behind me, I uncurled her fists and set her back a step.

She frowned. "I don't understand."

"We just fucked, Mandy. Nothing more."

A confused smile graced her lips for a moment before that smile turned into an erotic promise. She finger-walked her way up my chest. "I can make it worth your while."

"I can assure you, you can't. I don't do relationships, Mandy."

"You wouldn't even want to try?"

I shook my head. "Not even to try. It's nothing personal, sweetheart. I'm just not built for long-term shit."

Crestfallen, she nodded and wandered off, taking a seat in the lap of a man whose net worth was triple what mine was.

"Well, if that wasn't so sad, that would've been funny to watch." I looked over my shoulder to see Rachel wiping down the bar, her straight black hair sliding over one shoulder. "It always takes the new ones time to learn that lesson."

"Better she learns it now."

"Yeah, I guess so." She stopped wiping and stared at me. "You looking for the boss?"

"You seen him?"

"He took Syn to one of the rooms then went up to his office afterward."

"How long ago was that?"

She shrugged her slender shoulders. "Fifteen minutes?"

"Thanks." Scanning the crowd, I found Syndy grinding on the lap of an investment banker, who had joined the Dollhouse as a member a couple of months ago. Syn was rubbing her tits in his face when she noticed me. Her mouth was red—swollen—from sucking Bane's dick. He never let them do any more than that. I didn't know how he did it. He'd have to have a will of fucking iron.

Syn said something to the banker then slid from his lap, moving in a sinuous way that only women seemed to be able to. She was dressed in black lingerie, complete with garters and fuck-me heels. Moving with purpose, she approached me and folded her arms under her breasts, pushing them up.

My eyes dropped. Lingered.

"Why won't Bane fuck me?" she demanded.

My gaze returned to her face. "I beg your pardon?"

"Bane," she said. "He only ever wants a blow job. Why won't he fuck me?"

"That's something you're going to have to ask him."

"I have. He said he doesn't shit where he eats."

"Smart man," I murmured.

Syndy popped out her hip, anchoring one hand on her waist. "How can I make him change his mind?"

"You can't, Syndy. Deal with it."

"But—"

I put my finger up to silence her. "No. No *buts*. If Mr. Rivera wanted more from you, he'd get it."

"But—" she tried again.

"If you pursue this, Syn, I'll have you replaced. Mr. Rivera doesn't need this shit." She finally shut her mouth, but it didn't stop her from glaring at me. "Go and earn your tips."

Turning, I walked away before she could protest again. If she continued like this, she'd be working her last shift sooner than she thought she would.

After checking in with a few waitresses, I started toward my office when I drew to a stop. There was a blonde woman in a thin tank top and cut-offs marching my way. She looked like she could castrate the next guy who spoke to her with her bare hands and be fucking happy about it. I watched her leave the club then turned my attention to the office window above. Bane's gaze was fixated on the blonde, his expression clouded in concentration and pure desire.

Going up the stairs two at a time, I opened his office door. "Who was that, boss? A new Doll?"

He smiled like the cat that got the canary. "Hawk Montana's big sister."

"What did she want?"

"She wanted me to forget about the fifty thousand he owes."

"In exchange for what?"

"Nothing. She came in here with no fucking bargaining chip *at all*." He added, "I want you to find out what you can about her."

I kept the surprise off my face. Bane had never shown this kind of interest in a woman before. "You got it."

2

Cox

THIS WASN'T THE WAY I WANTED TO SPEND MY Thursday night. As I approached the yellow police tape flapping between the low chain-link fence in the hot LA breeze, I wondered whether this was going to be another kid gunned down all because they'd made some pretty bad life choices. Or could it have been a drug deal gone bad? Gangbanger? Or maybe, just maybe, it was some innocent bystander who had been caught in the crossfire.

I showed my badge to the uniformed cop guarding the tape, and he lifted it for me to step under. The gold cross around my neck swung free, catching and reflecting back the blue and red lights of the cop cars that had arrived at the scene.

Night time in LA rarely felt like a true night. Light pollution made it impossible for the oppressive blanket of darkness to fall. It was suspended in a perpetual state of darkening twilight where the full effect of the stars was lost in the velvety stillness.

Even though the sun had gone down a couple of hours ago, there were people crawling around the perimeter of the scene, trying to get photographs of a dead body. Ignoring the rubberneckers, I walked across the cracked asphalt that served as the parking lot for the residents. An EMT was attending to a woman in the back of an ambulance. She didn't appear to have any visible injuries, so I figured it was just shock that she was being treated for. That was never a good sign.

"Detective Cox," I said to the cop standing guard at the bottom of the stairs that led up to the second level of the apartment block. He was tall—at least a few inches past six feet—with skin the color of dark chocolate. His name tag read Franklins. He stared at my badge for a moment with his dark eyes.

When he refocused on me, I asked, "What are we dealing with?"

"A teen male was shot in the chest, point-blank. It appears it happened when he opened his apartment door."

"Anything missing from the apartment?" If there was, it would indicate a burglary. Burglary wasn't uncommon for this side of town, but the fact that the guy opened the door for his killer? That didn't sound right to me.

"Not that I could see."

"Who called it in?"

He jerked his chin in the direction of the ambulance. "The woman being treated right now."

I glanced over. The woman was staring blankly over the shoulder of the EMT treating her. I turned back to Franklins. "Who is she?"

"The kid's older sister."

"Has anyone spoken to her yet?"

"We were waiting for you."

I looked up the steps and exhaled sharply. "All right, I'll go check out the scene then speak to her."

When I stepped onto the landing at the top, I noticed metal bars covering the windows, along with security doors. Single light fixtures were fitted above each door, all of them functional except for the one above the second apartment in the row. The door was open, and through the gap, I could see the soles of the shoes of our victim.

The photographer, who was busy snapping pics of the victim, glanced up at me.

"Single GSW to the chest. Probably a .40 or .38."

"Same as last month then."

He nodded. "Yup." Sweat was beading on his dark skin, and he wiped it away with the back of his hand.

I pulled a couple of nitrile gloves from the box on the ground and approached the body.

The entry wound was small and neat—a straight shot through his heart. Blood had bloomed, covering his whole chest and saturating his baby-blue basketball shirt. His eyes were still open, his dark pupils looking sightlessly up at the ceiling. There was a trickle of blood coming out of the corner of his mouth, the color of it darker than it should've been on account of his dark complexion.

He looked young. Too damn young—a goddamn waste of life.

Rising to my feet, I walked into the apartment. The air was thick with the scent of cigarette smoke. Stale heat felt like a blanket pressing against my skin, making sweat dot my brow. It looked like a frat house. Empty beer cans littered almost every surface—empty food containers riding shotgun. In the living room, there was a low, rectangular coffee table, and on it was two bricks of cocaine.

I looked at the distance from the door to the living room. It was only maybe fourteen feet of unimpeded line of sight. The shooter would've seen it, so why in the hell were drugs left behind?

Ella Murdoch, the lead for our CSI team, approached me. "What are you thinking, Detective?" she asked. Ella was a veteran in the forensic sciences. Like cops, there was a limit to how much death they could see before they needed to transfer to another department or choose another profession. Not Ella. She'd been working with the LAPD for the last fifteen years and showed no sign of slowing.

"Clearly, the kid's a dealer," I told her, jerking my chin in the direction of the coffee table. It was too much coke to ignore. "Maybe, he encroached on someone's turf and got popped? Or maybe it's just a message." I shook my head. "No. That doesn't feel right. What are the chances that two dealers get hit while drugs are left sitting, untouched, and in plain sight? All within the space of a month."

Ella shrugged. "It's LA. Everyone is trying to get a better life. I'll dust the bricks for prints and see if we get any hits."

I didn't say it, but I knew the only prints they'd find were the vic's. "What's his name?"

"Malachiah Smith. Twenty-one-years-old as of last week."

Jesus *fuck*.

I took another look around, trying to see what the shooter would've seen. Two bricks of coke that he could sell without having to answer to a bigger fish. Walking back to the coffee table, I turned one of the bricks over and studied it. There was a crown stamped onto it. The drugs belonged to the same person Tiberius Zaire had been dealing for, but I had no idea who that was. Nobody—not one of my sources—was willing to talk.

"Well, if it isn't the fucking golden girl herself."

My shoulders tensed, and I turned to find Tom Bridey standing just inside the doorway. He'd worked his way up to detective in less than six years. I knew he was in his late twenties, but he looked fresh-faced and straight out of high school. He worked it to his advantage.

"Don't tell me you already know who the shooter is," he taunted, stepping into my scene.

I ground my teeth together. The guy suspected me of using less-than-honest methods to get my information, but I was careful. I wanted to help people, no matter how I had to do that. "What are you doing here?"

"Was in the neighborhood. Thought I'd come by and check things out."

"I've got it covered." My words were bitten out. "Thanks."

Bridey whistled through his teeth. "If I didn't know any better, I'd say this looks uncannily like the hit last month. What was that kid's name? Zaied or something?"

The bastard knew I never forgot a victim, so him getting it wrong on purpose pushed me into the cool zone of my rage. "Zaire," I corrected. "Tiberius Zaire."

Bridey crossed his arms over his chest and leaned against the nearby wall. He was here for the long haul, but the thought of him breathing down my neck irritated the fuck out of me.

"Get the fuck away from my scene." The words were spoken with heat—a lashing of flame to get the bastard to back off.

He held his hands up in surrender, a smirk on his face. "No need to get testy, Detective. I'll go."

Once he was out the door, I let out a harsh breath. Ella caught my eyes, giving me a long stare. That stare asked whether I wanted to talk about it or not.

I didn't.

After I shook my head to tell her as much, she got back to work again. Jesus, I needed to get out of this apartment. Stepping outside, I took off the gloves, dumped them in the trash bag and stepped away from the scene. Dragging in a deep lungful of slightly less hot, humid air, I stared at Malachiah's sister still in the back of the ambulance looking shaky and pale.

I made my way down to her. Pulling back the side of my jacket, I showed her my badge and gave her a sympathetic smile.

"I'm Detective Cox. What's your name?"

"Shanice."

"Shanice, I'm sorry you were the one to find your brother." I leaned against the side of the ambulance. "Can you tell me anything about what you saw or heard here today?"

Her dark, unfocused eyes flickered to my face then away again. "Talking to cops gets you killed."

"Is that what you think?"

Her gaze sharpened and turned intense. She'd seen some shit in her life. That one look screamed *jaded*. I knew it because my eyes still held that cynicism. "It's what I *know*."

I drew in a deep breath through my nose and let it out through my mouth. I had to be patient with her, otherwise she'd clam up just to spite me. "I want to get justice for your brother, Shanice, but in order to do that, I need your help."

When she looked at me again, she really looked at me. "What the fuck do *you* know about justice for the black man?" she spat.

"This isn't about race. Or economic status. This was about your brother getting killed before his time. This is about a life being taken away. I want to help you, Shanice, but I can't do my job without you."

She stared at me for a long time. For a moment, I thought she wouldn't talk at all, until...

"I was asleep in the bedroom when Malachiah started hammering on the front door."

"Wait, this is your apartment, not his?"

"It's mine, but he crashed here most nights."

"What time was that?"

"Around midnight, I guess."

"What happened after you let him in?"

"I went back to bed. I start work at five, and I was pissed that he'd forgotten his key." She lifted a shaking hand to her forehead and wiped away a bead of sweat. "I woke up about an hour later when I heard raised voices. Then there was the gunshot."

"Do you know who he was talking to?"

"No. I didn't recognize the voice. Malachiah never brought his friends around here. I told him if he did, I'd take away his key and report him to the cops myself."

My brows rose. "Report him for what?"

"He was dealing. I told him I didn't want that shit in my house."

"Had he brought drugs here before?"

Shanice shook her head, her voice raising as she said, "That boy knew I'd whoop his ass if he did."

"But you saw the two bricks of coke on the coffee table." It wasn't a question.

She frowned. "I didn't see no drugs."

I wasn't surprised. She probably went into shock the moment she saw her brother dead on the floor.

"Do you know who he was working for?"

"I don't ask no questions about that shit. The less I know, the better." She tilted her face in the direction of her apartment. Malachiah's body—now in the body bag—was being brought down the stairs.

"My brother died for that shit, and for what?" Anger had hardened her eyes, and lowered the timbre of her voice. Looking at the EMT, she asked, "Can I go now?"

"Where will you go?" I asked.

"I got friends," she replied, but I doubted it.

"I can send a crew here tomorrow to help clean the scene." It was an offer I made to every member of a victim's family, especially the less-than-privileged ones in LA. Shanice wouldn't have the option of moving, but living in an apartment that was the site where her own brother had been killed was a tough fucking gig.

"I don't need or want your charity."

"It's not my charity. It's on the LAPD," I lied.

That seemed to placate her because she said, "Well, if the Pigs are paying, you can bet I'm taking it."

Reaching into my pocket, I pulled out my business card and handed it to her. "If you hear anything or remember anything of the conversation your brother had with whoever had come to the door, please reach out and give me a call."

I nodded to the EMT, giving them the go-ahead to release her if she was medically sound. Walking away a few paces, I stopped and turned back. Shanice was stepping from the back of the ambulance. She crushed something in her palm and dropped it to the ground—my business card.

Shaking my head, I turned when I heard the door slam on the coroner's van. Well, that was it. I had a dead kid, an angry sister, and no fucking clue how two bricks of cocaine had ended up on the coffee table.

I ducked under the police tape and stepped away from the press of the crowd. Six feet away, my phone rang.

"Cox."

"Detective, I finally got a hold of you."

Rubbing my forehead, I remembered to take a beat and ease back on the bitchiness that was about to come out of my mouth. "Marjory, what can I do for you?"

Marjory Fuller was one of the dispatch operators who always made a comment about me working late or on weekends. I'd told her that I didn't have time to meet anyone nice, hoping that would be enough to get her off my back, but the woman was fucking relentless. She'd mentioned setting me up on a date with her nephew. I'd been doing my best to screen her calls, but I guessed my time was up.

"My nephew, Charlie, said he'd love to take you to dinner."

"Marjory," I began, but she steamrolled over me.

"He's already made a reservation for you and him at Rivera. Eight o'clock next Tuesday."

"Marjory—"

"Wear something other than black, Detective. A man likes to see a woman dress up a little too."

"Marj—" I tried to interrupt, but she was still waxing lyrical about her nephew. I made it to my car. I unlocked it but didn't open the door. I tried again. "Marjory, I—"

Beep. Beep. Beep.

I pulled my phone away from my ear to see another call was coming in. Shit. This was the call I was always waiting for.

"Fine," I bit out. "Eight o'clock." I ended that call and picked up the other. "Dante?" My voice was high—frantic—and I swallowed to loosen some of the panic that was making its way up my throat.

Dante's throaty voice came over the line. "Seren."

My eyes closed at the sound of my birth name. He was the only one who called me that.

"Have you seen her? Is she okay?"

"From what I've seen, she's fine."

I slumped against the side of my car, not sure my legs would be able to hold me up. Relief flooded me. My daughter was okay. She was okay.

"Sorry it's been so long between calls. I'm embedded right now."

"I understand." Dante was working a human trafficking case in Detroit, going undercover with the Savage Hunt Motorcycle Club. "When did you see her?"

"Two days ago. She was with her father."

I felt myself go very still at the mention of the man who had convinced me my daughter had died at birth. It was only a little less than two years ago that I found out the bastard had lied—that my Sloane was alive and well, and he had raised her himself. There were days when I worried about what sort of poisonous lies he'd dripped into her ear about me. He probably told her I abandoned her, that I didn't want her, when that was as far from the truth as it could possibly be.

My free hand curled into a tight fist until I felt my fingernails digging in the meaty part of my palm.

"Aidan is becoming more erratic," Dante added. "Unpredictable."

"His father was the same," I murmured. "He was a dangerous man."

"Yes." Dante's breathing was steady on the other end. "I'm doing my best to get eyes on her, but it's getting harder and harder. Something's happening. I don't know what, but something. I might not have anything for you for a while."

"Okay," I whispered, hating that one mention of Aidan had reduced me to the scared little girl I once was. I'd worked so hard at building myself up, to turn myself into ice—a cold-hearted bitch who didn't take shit from men.

Dante hung up, and I was left staring at the backlit screen for a full minute before it winked into darkness once more.

Numb.

I was so fucking numb.

I got into my car and drove home.

THE NEXT AFTERNOON, I FOUND MY INFORMANT, JAY, on his regular street corner. He was in his mid-thirties, a junkie who had seen enough and heard enough to know everybody. Unfortunately, everybody knew him too, but it didn't stop him from talking to me.

I tossed him a brown paper sack, which he caught eagerly. Pulling apart the top fold, he peered inside then looked up at me.

"All your favorites, Jay, but we need to talk."

He crumpled the top of the bag in his fist. "I got nothing for you, Detective."

"Come now, Jay. You're holding out on me."

Having a twitchy addict as a reliable source was an oxymoron, but Jay and I had an understanding. He helped me, and I helped him eat regularly. With him blowing any cash he did find on a drug he pumped straight into his vein, food wasn't high on his priority list. Besides, people said all sorts of things around an addict who they assumed was going to be high ninety-nine percent of the time.

He sat on the stoop of a nearby building and opened the bag. Reaching inside, he pulled out the foiled-wrapped burrito and carefully extracted the silver coating away. The scent of black beans, spice beef, and tortilla fragranced the air as he took his first bite.

Jay made a sound down low in his throat that was a combination of pleasure and ravening hunger. I wondered how long ago he'd eaten. Judging by the fresh track marks in his arm, it had been a while. Feeding his addiction before feeding his body seemed to be his preferred MO.

"I put a pack of clean needles in the bag, too, Jay. I want you to use them only once, okay. I can get you more."

I doubted he heard me. He was too lost in masticating.

"Why do you help me, Detective?" he asked after swallowing a mouthful.

I couldn't tell him the truth—that I saw parts of myself in him. That I'd known a dozen other guys on the streets just like him. They were all dead now, but they probably wouldn't have been if someone—*anyone*—had given a fuck.

"We help each other, Jay. Now that I've held up my end of the bargain, it's time for you to hold up yours."

He stopped mid-chew to look at me. His brown eyes were sunken and hollow—void of any real life. His skin had taken on a grayish tint that I usually associated with cadavers, and I knew he didn't have much longer. In the very near future, his next hit was going to kill him.

"What do you need to know?"

"Dealers are getting hit. Do you know anything about that?"

As soon as the question left my tongue, his whole demeanor changed. He stopped chewing and dropped the burrito back into the bag. Wiping the back of his hand over his mouth, he muttered, "I don't know nothing about that."

I'd been working with Jay long enough to know that he meant the opposite. He knew something, but he wasn't willing to talk. Yet.

"Where are you staying right now?"

He blinked at me, jarred by the change in subject. It was easy to confuse him sometimes, not that I did it on purpose. It was simply that his brain was so addled from prolonged drug use that it was an easy thing to do.

"In that abandoned supermarket on East 6th."

"What about that share house I got you into?" About a year ago, I'd discovered a small, non-profit shelter that operated out of a two-bedroom apartment in Skid Row. Run by a drug and alcohol counselor and attended to by a private nurse, it was a safer alternative to living on the streets. Last month, they offered Jay one of the rooms.

Unlike a halfway house, there wasn't an expectation that the residents stayed sober while there—they just weren't allowed to bring drugs onto the premises.

He shook his head and pulled out the burrito again. Whatever had caused him to drop it was now clearly forgotten.

"Got kicked out."

"What for?"

"They found drugs in my room."

"Jesus *fuck*, Jay. How hard is it to keep that shit on the streets?"

He looked up at me, a flicker of anger in his brown eyes. "I don't control it, Detective. You know that."

I wanted to tell him that was bullshit. People could dig themselves out of this shitty life if they wanted to. He just wasn't ready to do it yet. Drawing in a breath through my nose, I let it out through my mouth and said, "I know, Jay. I also know you're not telling me the whole truth about these dealers."

He gave me a crooked smile. He'd lost one of his front teeth in the time between visits. "I ain't saying nothing more."

"Why? What's going to happen to you?"

He darted his eyes around the street, then gestured for me to lean in a little closer. Out of instinct, I put my hand on the butt of my sidearm. "They'll kill me if I talk about this."

"*Who* will kill you, Jay?"

He sighed, and his breath smelled like chemicals, burritos, and tooth decay. Shaking his head, he backtracked. "No. No. I can't tell you."

Leaning back, I studied him, making sure he felt the weight of my gaze. "You can. You're just choosing not to."

He shrugged and peeled down more of the foil. "Sorry, Detective."

I turned away, but before I left, I told him, "You'll be seeing me again soon, Jay."

He heaved another sigh, his voice was resigned. "I know I will, Detective."

3

Dagger

ANGER SINGED MY VEINS AS I LISTENED TO JACK 'Dolla' Cooper tell me Malachiah Smith was dead. Shot in the chest when he opened his apartment door. We were at the basketball court on East 6th and Gladys, watching a game of hoops. Some charity had a table set up where they were serving food to the myriad of people who called Skid Row home. The clang of their metal spoons hitting the huge serving trays punctuated the air every now and then, competing with the sound of the bouncing ball.

"The cops were crawling all over the building last night." Dolla wanted to be a part of the dealing crew, and although he was a smart kid, he was too young—barely fourteen-years-old. People grew up quicker in this neighborhood. "I saw it, man. They were everywhere."

"Who's investigating the case?"

A basketball came bouncing Dolla's way, and he lobbed it

back to one of the guys playing. "Some fine-looking bitch."

I tried not to roll my eyes at the pubescent gangbanger-wannabe. Really, I did. "Did this bitch have a name?"

"I heard her say Cox. Chanrell, maybe?"

"Chanrell Cox?"

Dolla nodded like he'd just done good. "Yeah, Chanrell Cox."

It probably wasn't Chanrell. More likely Charmaine or Chantelle. "Anything else you heard?"

"Yeah," he replied, drawing out the end of the word. "Rumor is his supply was left inside."

My brows rose. "Smith got touched and the shooter didn't take the drugs?"

Dolla shook his head. "That's the word."

Fuck. It was just like what happened with Tiberius Zaire last month. Bane was going to be fucking pissed. Zaire had been shot when he'd opened his apartment door. The cash had been taken, but the drugs had been left. Bane hadn't thought anything of it, and honestly, neither had I. Dealers sometimes piss off the wrong people and get capped. Now, the execution made sense. This was a message.

I glanced at the ballers then back at Dolla. Sweat was trickling down the side of his face, and he wiped it away with a bandana from the front pocket of his overshirt. The kid was carrying a weapon—which was the only reason for the thick flannel shirt over his T-shirt in this hellish heat.

"Call me if you hear anything else." I rose to my feet, and Dolla followed. He offered me his fist, but I only stared down at it impassively. When my eyes met his face again, my expression was blank. He dropped his hand and played it like he'd meant to do that.

Turning on my heel, I walked past the table where food was being served, then out through an opening in the tall gates. Digging inside my pocket, I pulled up a contact and dialed.

"Wolverton," came the answer when the call connected.

Fox Wolverton—AKA Devil—and I had served in the same unit in the Marines. We both got out at the same time, but instead of sliding into civilian life like I had, he became a merc for a couple of years. Now, he had his own private security firm with at least two guys from our old unit.

"It's Dagger."

"Master Guns," he replied warmly. "Two calls in as many days. What can I do for you, sir?"

"I need information. The kind of information government departments don't share."

"My boy, Hex, can get anything you want as long as it involves a computer."

"There's a detective working with the LAPD. Goes by the name Cox."

I walked along the pavement at a fair clip but stopped when a young woman emerged from a sidewalk tent. She was crying and her shirt was torn. She jumped when the flap of the tent opened behind her, and her fear was as astringent as the smell of vagrancy around me.

"Yo, bitch, come back here!" the homeless man yelled. "We ain't finished."

"L-leave me alone," she told him, her voice soft—feeble. She hugged her upper body, curving in on herself.

"Give me a sec," I told Devil. Still holding the phone, I grabbed the man as he lunged for the woman and threw him backward. Weak from malnutrition, he toppled into his tent, but the thin nylon did very little to hold his weight. It collapsed under him, and he started swearing as he staggered to his feet.

"I'm gonna…" His eyes widened, his words dying on his tongue when he realized who he was talking to.

"You're going to do what, huh?"

"Sorry, Mr. Dagger. Didn't see you there."

My gaze slid over to the woman, whimpering as she held her shirt down over her waist.

"How old are you?" I asked her.

"F-f-fifteen."

Fuck.

I rounded back on the guy who thought he could take advantage of a minor. "You think it's okay to rape little girls?"

"No, Mr. Dagger. No. She told me she was eighteen."

"Well, she lied." In one swift movement, I pulled out a dagger from the sheath hidden beneath the sleeve of my shirt and pressed it to his groin. "You and me, we're going to have a little talk."

Holding the knife in place, I put the phone back to my ear. "You still there?"

"Keeping the peace?" Devil asked in an amused drawl.

I pressed the tip of the blade a little harder against the guy's groin. "Something like that. Can you get me the information?"

The girl made a little sound. She was going to bolt, but one look at my face, and she stood very still, her eyes shifting to the ground.

"What do you want to know?"

"Everything."

"Give me a sec."

The line went dead, but only for a few minutes then Devil was back.

"Full name is Chantelle Cox. She transferred into vice about eighteen months ago. She lives alone. According to her credit card details, she eats a lot of Thai food. No dependents listed. Want her social security?"

Chantelle Cox. I rolled the sound of her name around in my head for a moment.

"No. Her address."

The sound of clacking computer keys filled the line. Devil read the address to me and I committed it to memory.

"Please, Mr. Dagger."

My eyes flickered to the guy whose dick was meeting the business end of my blade.

"Anything else?" Devil asked.

"No. Thanks, Wolverton." I ended the call and repocketed my phone. My nose wrinkled when the smell of warm piss hit me. "Jesus *Christ*."

The guy had wet himself. What the fuck was it with these pieces of shit pissing themselves? Pulling a business card from my pocket, I handed it to the girl along with a hundred-dollar bill. "There's an address on the back. Go there. Now."

She bobbed her head and started running, not looking back. Good for her.

"Start walking," I barked to the guy, directing him to an empty parking lot behind a shutdown wholesale business.

"Please don't hurt me," he whimpered.

"You should've thought about that before you raped a fifteen-year-old girl."

"She told me she was legal."

"And you believed her?" I shook my head. "Fucking delusional motherfucker."

In the cover of shadows, I slammed him against the wall so hard I heard what was left of his teeth clatter.

"Please," he begged, spittle gathering in the corners of his mouth. "Please. I didn't know."

"I'm going to call bullshit on that one. Even if you did know, you wouldn't have stopped. And men like you won't ever stop."

Sliding the tip of my blade into the elastic waistband of his sweats, I twisted. The sharp edge of the blade bit into the fabric, slicing it in two. It fell to his feet. He grabbed for his manhood, cupping it protectively in his hand.

I clicked my tongue disapprovingly. "Now, now," I started in a taunting tone. "There's no reason to be shy." Running the flat of the blade along his knuckles, I tapped them, then added in a soft voice, "Let Mr. Dagger see what he's working with here."

The sick fuck only clutched tighter, and I'd had just about enough of this shit. I sliced downward on the back of his wrist. The cut was shallow—superficial—but the guy howled liked I'd cut his fucking hand off.

"Shut the fuck up," I growled into his face. "You don't know the real meaning of pain yet."

His eyes widened. "Please."

"You didn't show any mercy to that kid. What makes you think you'll get any from me?"

I pried his hands away from his dick with the knife, and he finally grew a brain cell and did as I wanted. A fine tremor was working its way through his fingers, and I breathed in the scent of his fear. I rolled that motherfucking aroma around my mouth then bit into it.

"I don't like men," he whimpered, and my gaze darted to his face.

"You think I want some kind of sexual favor from you?" I let him see the disgust in my eyes. "Lift up your dick."

He blinked. "W-what?"

"Lift up your dick..." I repeated slowly, "... or I can use the tip of my blade to do it if you prefer."

In hurried movements, he lifted the offending appendage. As much as I wanted to remove it, the likelihood of him bleeding out before anyone discovered him was pretty good. I didn't want to kill the guy. I just wanted to make him hurt for a little while.

"What are you—"

A strangled sound escaped his throat when I grabbed one of his testicles and sliced through the skin and connective tissue with one stroke. Shoving my hand over his mouth, he screamed into my palm, his eyes wide and wild. His blood spattered on the ground between us.

I lifted the dismembered testicle, holding it in front of his face where he could see then growled, "The next time you even *think* about raping a young girl, I want you to reach into your pants and touch your balls." I barked a laugh. "Sorry, I meant ball." I threw the fleshy sack over my shoulder, and he followed it with his eyes.

Wiping my hands and the blade on his shirt, I stepped back then released his mouth. I thought he was going to scream for help, but he only dropped to his hands and knees and scurried to the dumpster. He reached underneath it, groping around in the putrid puddles for his nut.

With a smirk on my face, I started back in the direction of the street.

🔫

I WALKED INTO THE LOBBY OF THE APARTMENT BLOCK

Bane owned on the edge of Little Tokyo, rapping my knuckles on the concierge desk, saying hello to Liz behind the counter as I passed.

"How are you, Mr. Harrison?"

"Great, Liz. Has this one been any trouble?" I jerked my chin in the direction of the kid. She was huddled on one of the cherry-red couches in the seating area, looking completely out of place and uncomfortable.

"Haven't heard a peep from her."

The girl watched me approach, a spark of... *something* in her eyes. Defiance, maybe.

I perched on the edge of the coffee table in front of her. "What's your name?"

"Sierra."

"Sierra what?"

"Storm. Sierra Storm."

She was skinny, her body not fully formed. Small breasts, but she hadn't gotten the hips yet. "You're fifteen? And don't even fucking think about lying to me."

"Fourteen." Her unwashed blonde hair fell over one shoulder as she dropped her gaze back to the floor.

With two fingers under her chin, I tipped her face up. "Why are you on the streets? It's a dangerous place for a kid."

"My boyfriend's mom kicked me out of their house."

"What was wrong with your house?"

Sierra's blue eyes slid off to one side, unwilling to meet my face. When her gaze returned, it was like I was staring at a completely different girl. "Mom is a crack addict. Living anywhere else, even if it's on the streets, is better than living with her."

I felt my hands begin to curl into fists, but instead of letting my anger get the better of me, I stared at the photograph above the couch. It was of the inside of a barrel of a wave. There was something calming about that—the photographer capturing the stillness of something that by its very definition was power and energy.

When I looked down again, Sierra was holding her hand out to me . Crumpled in her fist was the Benjamin I'd given her. I shook my head. "That's for you."

She stared at the bill then returned her blue eyes to me. "You want to sleep with me too?"

Easing back a little, I gave her my best blank look. "That's not why I'm helping you."

"Then why are you?"

"Because I can. Do you know who I am?"

She shook her head.

"Name's Dagger. I run security down at the Dollhouse. Have you heard of that place?"

A nod this time. She chewed on her bottom lip like she wanted to say something.

"What is it?"

"You want me to be a stripper?"

"No, Sierra, I don't. My boss doesn't employ jail bait to work the poles. I was thinking of a more janitorial role."

One of her pale brows winged up. "Excuse me?"

"A cleaner. We have a professional team who clean during the day, but we need someone small and invisible to clean our... *discreet* rooms."

"I don't understand."

"The Dollhouse has five kink rooms. They need to be cleaned after each use."

Sierra made a face. "You want me to clean up other people's jizz stains and ass marks?"

I stifled a smile. "You'll be paid well for an honest day's work."

"How well?"

I eased my elbows back onto my knees. "How much would you want?"

She seemed to think about that for a moment, then asked, "How much do you earn?"

I liked this kid. "More than you ever will."

She rolled her eyes like the true fourteen-year-old she was. "I don't want the same as you. I just need a yardstick."

Seemed fair. I told her. Sierra let out a long breath—a steady stream of air as she settled back into the deep couch.

"You could probably ask for five percent of that and get it."

Her eyes sparked with hope, and I liked seeing it there. "Five percent of your wage? That's how much I could get?"

I nodded. "Make it two and a half percent, and I'll fix you up with a place to stay too. The club will pay your rent and utilities. You just need to pay for food. Internet. Whatever the fuck else you want."

She nibbled on her bottom lip again, and I knew I had her. "How do I know this is legit?"

Pulling my phone from my pocket, I scrolled through my contacts and found the name I wanted. "Chas, Dagger. You home?"

"Hey, Dagger. Yeah, I am. Am I needed at the club or something?"

"No. But can you come down to the lobby for me?"

"Ah, sure," she replied, sounding a little confused. "See you in a few."

I hung up and balanced the phone on my knee. Sierra simply stared at me. I stared right back.

We both sat there motionless, wordless, until the *ding* of the elevator car drew Sierra's attention. I knew it was Chastity who walked out because Sierra's mouth popped open in awe.

Yeah, Chas was a fucking knockout. Her red hair was in a high ponytail today. Dressed in yoga pants and a loose T-shirt, her face was clear of makeup but if anything, that enhanced her natural beauty.

"Sierra, this is Chastity. She's a Doll down at the club."

"A Doll?"

"A dancer," Chastity replied with a smile. "Mr. Rivera calls us his Dolls."

"Sierra is considering joining the cleanup crew. I want her to make an informed decision."

Chastity's eyes lit up. "Oh, you'll love working for Mr. Rivera. He's a great boss. Kind. Generous."

"How much do you get paid?"

Chastity smiled and leaned in, cupping her hand around Sierra's ear. Whatever she whispered, it made the girl's eyes widen and her mouth pop open.

"Think I could earn that much?"

"One day, Sierra. Maybe. But you're young. You should start with clean-up. Work for a few years then make a decision about your future. This isn't a job I'll be doing forever, but it is a job that's changed my life for the better."

"What else would you be doing right now?" she asked.

Chastity smiled serenely. "Nowhere as nice as this." She gestured to the lobby. "I'd probably be about three blocks from here living in a tent."

Sierra swallowed hard then looked at me.

I stared steadily back at her. "It's your chance to make it, kid."

Once again, she drew her bottom lip into her mouth and chewed. In about three or four years, that gesture would make a man part with his money, but for now, she was just a skinny kid. When her eyes locked on mine, I knew what her answer was going to be.

"Okay."

"Okay." I rose from the coffee table and strolled to Liz. "Got a furnished studio available?"

"Yes, Mr. Harrison, we do," she said after typing something into the system.

"Set it up under the club. A kid called Sierra Storm will be living there."

"Yes, Mr. Harrison."

Fuck, that had to be my favorite sentence.

"Here are the keys." She slid a set of metal keys along with a swipe key over the counter. "Should I charge the bond to the club?"

Reaching into my pocket, I pulled out the roll of hundreds and counted off what I needed. "I'll pay cash up front. Can you send me the paperwork? I'll sign it later today."

"Yes, Mr. Harrison."

She smiled. "I'll have it ready for you this afternoon."

"Thanks, Liz."

I took the keys over to the girls, who were chatting like they were old friends. "Chas, would you mind keeping an eye on Sierra for the rest of the day?"

"Sure."

"Bring her in on Monday afternoon when the club's shut, and

I can give her a rundown."

Her smile was bright. "Sure, Dagger."

I handed Sierra the keys to her new apartment, but as she grabbed them, I held on tight for a moment. Making sure I held her gaze, I told her, "Don't mess this up, kid. You have one chance here. Teenage angst doesn't fly with me... it never has. Sass me and you're gone. Screw it up and you're gone."

She swallowed. "I understand. I won't let you down."

4

Cox

WALKING DOWN EAST 6ᵀᴴ STREET IN SKID ROW during the day was dangerous. Pounding the pavement after dark brought its own special kind of risk. The chances of getting mugged, maimed, or killed rose exponentially. I had an FN 509 under my arm—the latest duty weapon for the LAPD—and grim determination straightening my spine.

Even now, I felt the eyes of hidden people on me, watching me. Stalking me. Throwing my shoulders back, I projected the confidence that I knew exactly what I was doing and where I was going.

As I passed the corner of Ceres, I drew to a stop. There was a dealer standing on the opposite side of the street, and begging at his feet was Jay.

"Shit."

I started across the road, my jacket flapping open as I walked. The dealer took one look at the gun, kicked Jay out of the way, and took off running.

I let him go.

Crouching down beside Jay, I helped lift him to his feet. There was blood trickling from a split lip. "Are you okay?"

He shoved me away, sliding backward until his back hit the brick wall of the nearby building. He was staring at me with wide eyes, like he really wasn't seeing me at all. His fingers were rapidly tapping against his knee, a kind of manic state I'd seen before.

"Jay?" I asked again, hoping to break through the agitation that was a sign of the onset withdrawal of heroin. "*Jay?*"

Sweat dribbled down his brow. The weather had cooled somewhat with the setting sun, so this sweating was definitely withdrawal. He looked at me, his eyes darting away just as quickly.

I tried one last time to gain his attention. "Jay, it's me."

His lids shuddered shut and when they reopened, they looked more focused.

"Jay?"

"Detective," he replied in a strained voice, running the back of his filthy hand over his bleeding mouth. He stared at the blood like he didn't know where it had come from. "What are you doing here? It's not safe for a woman to be here at night."

"I can take care of myself."

His tongue darted out and moistened his lips. "What do you want?"

I glanced in the direction the dealer had taken off. "Did you make a buy?"

He was quiet for a long moment, before saying, "No."

But he'd wanted to. I could see it in the set of his shoulders. In the way he was sweating. In the agitated movement of his fingers.

He shook his head. "You should go."

"Not until I find out what I need to know."

His fingers flexed then resumed their tapping. "I don't know nothing."

"See, that's what I don't believe. You talk to me, Jay. You've been giving me the information I need without question. What's different this time?"

He pressed his lips into a hard line and shook his head. His dull, dark, greasy hair slid across his forehead. Jay's eyes matched his hair. Once upon a time, he might have been quite good-looking, but years of drug abuse left him a shell of his former self. His fingers were still tap-dancing across his thigh, and I noticed his whole body was twitching—all his muscles vibrating under his skin in tandem.

"How long since your last fix, Jay?" I asked, keeping eye contact with him.

His upper lip twitched with beading sweat. "Don't know."

"You were fine yesterday afternoon."

"Yesterday," he repeated, scratching at his arm. "Yesterday." His foot started tapping, but I doubted he had control of the action. Turning his head, he looked up and down the street, but what he was looking for, I didn't know.

I sucked in a breath. I needed to know what was inside Jay's head before he figured out where to get his next high. He'd probably sell his soul to whoever gave him what he so desperately needed.

I stared at him steadily, then asked slowly, "Jay, if I get you a fix, you'll owe me, right?"

Jay's eyes widened ever so slightly, and he licked his lips. "You'd get me a hit?"

"Only if you tell me what I need to know."

This kind of shit could land me in hot water, but I didn't care. I needed to find out who had taken the lives of these two kids, and I would stop at nothing to do that.

"What do you want to know?" he asked in a small voice.

"Which supplier has a crown on their product? Who are their dealers?" He blinked up at me, and I wasn't sure he was still tracking the conversation. "Do we have a deal, Jay?"

He wiped some more sweat off his brow. "I'll tell you whatever you want. I just need another hit." The last statement came out as a pitiful moan.

I glanced around the neighborhood. The sensation of being watched was still there.

"Stay here," I told him. I rose to my feet and walked toward Kohler Street. I buttoned up my jacket to stop flashing my gun, and as I rounded the corner, I found exactly what I needed. A dealer nicknamed Vapor was leaning against the dark-painted wall of a closed-down Mexican restaurant, a couple of his crew surrounding him.

They watched me approach, his two lackeys pushing off the wall to circle behind me. I peered at them quickly over my shoulder then refocused on Vapor.

"What's a pretty bitch like you doing here at this time of night?" he asked, flashing a gold grille at me. The other two at my back chuckled.

"I want to buy." I reached into my pocket and flashed him a Benjamin. Vapor's eyes alighted on my hand, his grin growing.

He approached, his hungry gaze roving over me. "You look too well dressed to be in this neighborhood."

"I'm visiting a friend," I lied, spinning around when one of the men behind me trailed his fingers down the center of my back and over the shoulder holster. If they knew what I had on under there, I was in trouble. I turned back when I felt Vapor's hot breath on my neck.

He was standing less than six inches from my body. He smelled faintly of Axe body spray and weed. I had a heartbeat to decide how to play this. I could see the gleam of rape in his eye. A single heartbeat to go for my gun before the two men at my back grabbed my arms. I moved without thinking, unbuttoning my jacket and reaching under my arm to pull out my gun. Vapor backed up a step with his hands up, and I spun away from the trio. The two lackeys raised their hands.

There was a sound behind me, and I turned to find another man stepping from the shadows.

Keeping the weapon trained on the newcomer, I turned my head to look at the other three. Vapor had a Glock pointed in my direction. My eyes darted to the other two. One held a length of chain. The other a knife.

Time seemed to be suspended as I worked through all the scenarios. I was outnumbered. Outgunned. Out of fucking luck.

"Put your gun up, and we'll be *real* gentle with you, bitch," Vapor said with a smile. The other men laughed darkly. Vapor knew he had me, but I wasn't ready to roll over and let him rape me.

I looked back at the guy standing behind me. He had moved a step closer while I wasn't looking—maybe only four feet away now. A shot at this distance would blow his head off. I lowered the muzzle down slightly and to the right.

I let out a breath and squeezed the trigger. The slug took him in the shoulder as I'd planned, knocking him off his feet. I spun to get off another shot, but chain grabbed my outstretched arm, the links biting—then tightening—around my wrist. My jacket saved me from sustaining any serious damage. I dropped the gun, catching it in my free hand and shooting him under my outstretched arm.

Chain guy dropped, blood blooming from the stomach wound. Moving fast, I raised the gun again, pointing it at Vapor and Knife Guy. I was fucking lucky Vapor hadn't pulled the trigger while I was taking out the other two guys.

Vapor's eyes were on his two guys currently bleeding out on the asphalt. When his gaze returned to me, anger flickered in their dark depths. "You bitch. For that we'll cut you up a little while we fuck you."

"I don't think so," I replied.

"How do you think you'll walk away from this one, huh?" he asked, still cocky even though I'd halved his backup in a matter of seconds. "Eddie?"

Knife Guy—Eddie—came at me. Bringing a gun to a knife fight was just bad. I couldn't stop and get a steady shot. I jumped back when he swiped the blade across my middle, barely dodging the biting edge by less than an inch. He ran at me again. Eddie outweighed me by at least a hundred pounds but being the biggest didn't always mean having the advantage. When he was close, I took a knee and slammed the butt of my gun into his quad muscle as he passed. A Charlie Horse wasn't exactly my finest tactical move, but I would fight tooth and nail to survive. His leg buckled beneath him, sending him sprawling to the ground behind me.

I spun. Bringing up the gun, I put a bullet into the same quad, his scream echoing and bouncing off the buildings around us.

I was trying to skirt away from him, sliding in an unbalanced half-crouch when Vapor wrenched me from the ground and shoved me against the opposite wall. The move made me lose my grip on the gun. The back of my head slammed into the red brick. Black roses bloomed in front of my eyes, my world dimming to velvet shadows around the edges. I knew a concussion when I felt one.

Vapor tore at the waistband of my slacks, popping the button and yanking down the zipper. I tried to shove him off, but he was stronger than I'd anticipated. After undoing his own pants, he shoved his hand down the front of my panties. I bit my lip to keep from screaming, knowing that if I did, it would only get him off more.

Flashes of my past started to assault my frontal lobe—things from a lifetime ago that I thought I'd forgotten. There was a small whimper, and I realized it was me. The sound was small and pitiful, and I was dragged kicking and screaming back to when I was fifteen and unable to defend myself.

"I think I might kill you after I fuck you, bitch," Vapor told me in a hushed whisper that seemed to be in complete opposition to the violence he was about to commit.

"Fuck... you." I spat in his face, hoping my bravado was believable.

"I'll be the only one doing the penetrating tonight." He tore my panties off, and I knew what was coming next. Humiliation. Pain. Rage.

I froze.

Out of habit or survival, I didn't know. But I froze as he shoved aside his boxers.

"How about *I* penetrate *you* instead?" someone asked in a dark voice.

My eyes sprang open, and I stared at the newcomer. Partially hidden in shadows, he was tall, but other than that, his features were indistinguishable.

Vapor bared his teeth. "Stay out of this, man. This bitch pulled a gun on my boys. She deserves everything she's about to get."

I felt the weight of his gaze as it shifted to me. I didn't know whether he was friend or foe. He could just as easily help me as help rape me.

"Get outta here, mother—" Vapor paused mid-sentence, his lips parted like he was crying out soundlessly. Blood dribbled from the corner of his mouth, and his knees folded beneath him. He landed in a heap at my feet, and all I could do was stare at him for a moment. He had a knife shoved into his back, the hilt kissing the fabric of his shirt.

My gaze landed on the stranger who had saved me.

He studied me closely, holding out his hands to show me he wasn't armed. My pulse felt like it was trying to crawl out of my throat. Blood whooshed around in my head, making the world sound muffled and soft.

"You okay?" he asked, taking a step closer. Leaning down, he pulled the blade free, wiping it clean on the leg of Vapor's jeans.

Green.

His eyes were green.

Green like evergreens.

Green like waxy leaves.

"I'm fine."

His gaze was heavy—an almost physical caress against my skin—as he put away the weapon.

"I'm fine." I figured if I repeated it enough, it would be true. I'd survived things like this before—*worse* than things like this.

"You shouldn't be here at night," he told me in a bass drawl. "Lots of bad people around." After one more lingering look, he turned around and walked back down Kohler, where I assumed he'd come from.

My hands were shaking as I took off my jacket and wrapped it around my waist—the fastenings on my slacks were gone, and the tails of my shirt didn't hide shit. I picked up my gun and reholstered it then pulled out my phone and called in the scene.

5

Dagger

RETREATING BACK INTO THE SHADOWS OF THE building, I watched Detective Chantelle Cox take off her jacket and secure it around her waist. Aside from the small tremor in her hands, she was rock-steady. With practiced movements, she reholstered her weapon before making a phone call.

Those few actions right there said it all.

She was a woman who prided herself on being in control.

If anyone was going to get to the bottom of the dealer slayings, it would be her.

Her hair was pulled back into a tight bun, sleek and shiny, but a few whisps of hair had come undone during the scuffle. In the ambient light, it looked light brown, but it could've been blonde.

The white blouse she had on under the jacket was crisp cotton and starched to within an inch of its life. It molded to her upper body, following the line of her big tits and slim waist. She had it buttoned all the way to the top, and a sick part of me wanted to run the tip of my knife under each delicate button and slice them away to reveal what was underneath.

The trousers were black, and she'd paired them with heels that I wouldn't mind seeing wrapped around my waist at some point in the near future. My body stirred as I looked at her, wondering whether she was a screamer and that buttoned-up look was a front, or whether we would fight tooth and nail in bed. I was hoping for the latter.

I wanted to follow her a little longer—see where she went—but any plans of that were destroyed when my phone started vibrating.

I pulled it from my pocket. "Yeah?"

"Dagger, it's Rachel."

"What's going on?"

There was screaming in the background, then Rachel said, "Syn's gone crazy."

"You'll have to give me a little more information." Syndy was one crazy bitch. Was this one of her normal episodes, or was it something more?

"She's demanding to know where Bane is."

"His whereabouts isn't her goddamn business."

"I know," Rachel replied softly. "She's starting to make a scene, though."

"Fuck." I scrubbed a hand through my hair. "Send her up to Bane's office. We need to keep a lid on her."

I hurried back to the club, going through the side door and straight up the stairs. Syn was pacing the thick carpet like a caged lioness.

I shut the door behind me. "Bane's not here right now."

"I know!" she shrieked. "He's with *her*. That *bitch* who stole him from me."

"You have to leave."

Her jaw tightened. Her nostrils flared. "Not until I see him. Not until he hears what I have to say!"

I gave her a flat look. "If what you have to say involves you flashing your cunt at him, I think he doesn't want to hear it."

Putting a bullet in her skull would be fucking easier, but she was a commodity to the club.

She lunged at me. The stupid bitch telegraphed her move though, so I had time to wrap my arms around hers and pin them to her sides, her breasts pressing against my chest. For a heartbeat, we stared at each other from only inches apart. We shared the same air. I saw the crazy glint in her eye. Why the fuck had Bane gotten involved with this one?

As gently as I could, I shoved her away from me, then pulled out my phone.

"If you call the cops," she said in a rush. "I'll tell them that you raped me. There are no cameras in here. No witnesses to say you didn't."

Cold anger crawled through me, turning my blood to ice. If there was one thing I didn't appreciate, it was talk that I would even *consider* raping a woman. I may be a cold killer, but my moral compass was still firmly set to true north.

"Careful, Syn. You know what I'm capable of. How good I am at my job."

She swallowed hard as the color drained from her cheeks.

I dialed Bane's number.

"Yeah?"

"Is that Bane?" Syn demanded in a desperate tone, reaching

around my shoulder to grab the phone from me. I shoved her away again. She stumbled backward, slamming into the edge of the desk and sending the lone pen on the blotter rolling.

Returning my attention to the call, I told him, "You need to get down here. Syn has lost the fucking plot."

There was a pause, then, "On my way."

"You pushed me!" Syn screamed, righting herself and swiping up the letter opener from the desk. With an inarticulate scream, she ran at me. Holding out my arms to catch her again, the little cunt ducked under them and slammed the sharp end of the opener into my thigh.

"Fucking bitch," I hissed. Staggering back until I hit the wall, I slid to the ground, holding the handle of the letter opener with one hand and compressing the wound with the other. Gritting my teeth, I pulled the blade free and threw it across the other side of the room.

She retreated away from me—her eyes wild like she couldn't believe what she'd just done.

Well, that made two of us.

Syn whispered in a small, tremulous voice, "Why doesn't he want me?"

Blood wet my hands, running through my fingers, and dripping onto the floor. For such a small wound, it sure as shit was bleeding a lot. I just hoped she hadn't nicked an artery. "Because you're batshit crazy," I bit out between my clenched teeth.

She shook her head and picked up the paperweight from the sideboard, weighing it in her hands. "No. You're wrong. We're meant to be together."

I had the fleeting thought that she was trying to figure out whether it was heavy enough to be a killing blow.

The office door burst open, and Bane marched into the room. Syn made the wrong fucking decision and threw a paperweight at him, and when that one missed, she threw an empty crystal tumbler. Moving faster than a snake, Bane grabbed Syn around the waist and turned her, so her back was to his front. When he had his arm over her chest, pinning her in place, his dark gaze scanned the room. His eyes finally landed on me.

"What the fuck happened?"

Syn bucked wildly against his hold, trying to break free.

I shifted my leg, letting out a hissed, "She's fucked up. She came here looking for you. I told her you were out. She started yelling something about some bitch you were seen talking to earlier, then she hopped on the crazy fucking train and broke the brakes."

"Like I fucking need this right now?" he bitched at me. I could've said something about not letting the Dolls suck his dick more than once, but I kept the thought to myself. He was already pissed off enough.

He forced Syn onto the floor, straddling her waist and pinning her arms above her head. "Wendy!" he shouted. Using her real name seemed to snap her out of her rage, and she blinked up at him with wet eyes.

She whimpered. "Why, Bane? Why don't you want me?"

I watched Bane's expression shut down. He was closing all the doors to his emotions. Hell, he may be even better at that than I was. "You know I don't date."

"I don't want to date you, Bane. I just want you to fuck me and only me."

"You know that can't happen for exactly this reason." He gestured to the trashed office, then to me, bleeding on the rug.

"But I love you."

"You don't love me. You only think you do."

"But I've given you two blowjobs in as many days."

Fuck, her logic was twisted.

Bane replied, "Because you were there, Syn. Lips around my dick are all the same."

"But I love you," she whispered again. Like saying the words were going to make them any truer. "We're meant to be together."

Bane glanced over at me and shook his head. Wincing, I tried to stand to throw her out, but my leg buckled beneath me. More blood flowed too easily from the wound.

"Stay the fuck down, you stupid bastard," Bane snarled before turning back to Syn. "I'm sorry, baby, but you're fired. Effective immediately."

The color drained from her face. "You can't fire me. You can't fire me…"

Transferring Syn's wrists to one hand, Bane dug in his pocket for his phone.

"Rach," he said when the call was answered. "Can you call the doc and get him to swing by. There's been a situation in my office… Nah, he's the only one on the door. Just call the doc."

"I can't be fired," Syn was saying softly to herself. "I love you, Bane. I love you so much. How could you do this to me?"

"YOU NEED STITCHES."

I stared at the doctor as he inspected the wound on my thigh. "Do whatever you have to do."

"I don't have any ability to numb the area. You can go to the hospital if you'd rather?"

I shook my head. Going to the hospital would be easy. Everyone knew who Bane was, and in turn, they knew who I was. I simply didn't have the energy to drag my ass over there.

Bane handed me a bottle of vodka, which I grabbed with a stiff nod of thanks. I took a big gulp of the clear liquid, let out a breath then said to the doc, "Do it."

As the doc readied the needle and thread, I drank a few more mouthfuls of the vodka then put the bottle down on the desk. The doctor started without warning, and I sucked in a breath. In comparison, this wound had nothing on the injuries I'd sustained in Afghanistan. It was more embarrassing than anything else.

"Where's Syn?" I asked Bane.

"Andy took her home." He ran a hand through his hair, exhaling sharply. "Fuck, this is my fault."

"You didn't know she'd react like this."

"No, but I knew she was unhinged. Fuck!"

"He's lucky the wound wasn't a few millimeters to the left," the doctor said, not taking his eyes off the sutures. "The blade only barely missed the nerve. Stitches would've been the least of your problems if that had happened."

"How long until these need to come out?"

"Five days, at least. But I want you to stay off this leg. No vigorous exercise."

"I'll make sure he rests," Bane said, giving me a look. There was no fucking way I was resting. It just wasn't in my nature.

The doc finished up the stitches—six in total—then dressed the wound with a non-stick dressing. As he packed up his leather bag, he repeated, "Stay off the leg."

"Yes, doc. Scout's honor."

He simply shook his head and replied, "Why don't I believe you?"

"We don't pay you triple your exorbitant fee to believe us," Bane said.

The doc stared at Bane for a long, weighted minute. "Fair enough."

Bane walked the doctor out, leaving me in the office staring at the bandage.

6

Cox

I MET SANDERSON AT HIS GALLERY IN BROOKSIDE. AS soon as I stepped into the building, I felt out of place. Polished concrete floors revealed flashes of silvery aggregate as I walked over it, the surface so highly polished that the lighting overhead was bouncing right back into my eyes. Artwork hung on the clinical white walls on either side of me, none of which I would have called *art*. If there was one way to describe it, I would've said *aggressive*.

It was aggressive in the use of color and the technique to apply the paint.

Aggressive in the subject matter.

"You must be Detective Chantelle Cox," a man said. "Thank you so much for meeting me. I'm Mr. Peter Sanderson."

I glanced over in the direction of the voice. Peter Sanderson looked like everyone's least favorite uncle. At least a hundred pounds overweight, he wore an ill-fitting suit paired with a red tie. As I got closer, I realized there were little paintbrushes on it like he'd been given the tie as a gag gift, yet he genuinely liked it. He wasn't the refined upper-crust man I was expecting. Collecting art denoted some sort of affluence. Poor people couldn't buy expensive pieces. It was a fact. They had to spend their hard-earned money on essentials like food, rent, and utilities.

When I was standing in front of him, he offered me his hand, then with his other, he gestured to the walls. "What do you think of this collection?"

I turned so he couldn't see the blank look on my face. "Bold," I told him after a minute.

Sanderson nodded. "The artist is new on the scene. He has a lot of anger."

"I can tell." I returned my gaze to his face. "Why did you ask me to come down here?"

"As a concerned citizen, I have something to report to you."

"We have a phone number you can call to report crimes."

After giving me a searching look, he turned, striding to one of the artworks hanging closest to us. It was a slash of red on a black background. Some of the canvas had been torn in what I assumed was a designed way too. My gaze flickered to the price tag underneath it.

Seventy thousand dollars.

Jesus Christ.

"This one is entitled 'Rage.'" Sanderson turned to me. "Do you like it?"

"No. What do you want, Sanderson? I'm working a case right now."

"I know you are, Detective, which is why I called you down here."

My eyes narrowed on his homely face. If he was married, I'd be shocked. "Do you have information about the case?"

"I heard there were drug dealers being shot." He raised his brows—a silent inquiry.

Only Tiberius Zaire's murder had made the news, but Malachiah Smith's wasn't public knowledge yet. His death indicated that we were dealing with something a little more serious.

"Who'd you hear that from?"

He shrugged casually, a pleasant smile appearing on his lips. "I hear a lot of things from my artists."

"Let me put that burning curiosity to bed then. There was one dealer last month. He was a victim of gang violence."

"And what of the kid at Courtland Avenue?"

"Unrelated crime."

He tutted me gently, and it struck me that his manner of speaking did not match how he looked and dressed. "You know that's not true, Detective."

Folding my arms across my chest, I said, "I didn't come here to debate criminal activity with you. Tell me what you know, or I'm leaving."

He took a step nearer to me, moving his face closer like we were sharing a secret. "You need to look at Bane Rivera."

"The guy who owns the Dollhouse?" I asked, surprised.

"That's the one."

"What would he have to do with dealers getting hit?"

"You should ask him that."

I eyeballed the art collector and knew that something was up. "Why?"

"Why, what?"

"Why the tip-off?"

He opened his hands wide. "Like I said… concerned citizen. Now, if you'll excuse me, my next appointment is here."

He brushed past me, greeting a couple with a chihuahua-a-piece under their arms. Only in fucking LA.

"Concerned citizen? Yeah, right," I muttered under my breath as I left the gallery.

The sun was beating down on me as I returned to my car, but I turned back when I felt eyes on me. Peter Sanderson was standing in the doorway to his gallery, staring at me with a cold, dead expression. When he realized I was looking right back, some warmth spilled back into his eyes—resuming his good-old-boy appearance.

He said, "Rivera."

It was one word, but it felt like a bullet firing from a gun. He retreated back inside.

I returned to the precinct and immediately started researching the databases for any information on Peter Sanderson and Bane Rivera.

Sanderson's past didn't show me much more than I already suspected and some things I didn't—he was an art dealer and occasional philanthropist. He paid his taxes. Had been married twice and had one kid from his first marriage who he got on weekends.

Bane Rivera owned the Dollhouse as well as a few other properties including an upscale restaurant and some apartment buildings in the city. He never had any trouble with callouts by the police, and was actually lauded as the most eligible bachelor three years running.

I pulled up a photo from a news article that ran when his club was opened. Rivera was standing in front of the club wearing a three-piece suit. His hands were in his pockets, and his face was serious. He looked more like a drug dealer than Sanderson had, but I knew from personal experience that appearances could be deceiving.

THE SUN WAS ON ITS SLOW DESCENT IN THE SKY AS I walked down Figueroa Street in South Los Angeles, scanning the faces of the girls who sold their bodies in order to survive. I was looking for one in particular—Harper Stephenson—also known to her Johns as Paris L'Amore. I'd met Harper while I was a beat cop before I transferred into vice. Despite her life choices, I'd taken an instant liking to the girl.

She reminded me of Lucy.

Prostitutes heard a lot while they worked the streets, but I knew Harper had more than one regular who was in the dealing game. I was hoping she would be able to shed some light on the questions I had.

I approached a couple of girls.

"I'm not into girls, but she'll do you," the one on the left said. Her skin was dark, like there'd never been mixing in her genetic history. The friend was as white as you could get, but her eyes were dull. She'd seen too much in this life.

"I'm not interested in buying. I'm looking for someone."

"Ain't we all," the first woman said, laughing. Her friend didn't laugh, though. She looked like she was ready to break.

"Paris L'Amore. Have you seen her?"

The woman glanced around before returning her eyes to me. "Paris got picked up by the cops about half an hour ago."

Shit. "Okay. Thanks." Digging into my pocket, I handed them

each a twenty-dollar note. "Make sure you eat tonight. And stay safe."

The pair stared at me, mouths open. The quiet one looked directly at me for a full minute before she said, "Why?"

"I know you're both here not by choice, but by circumstance, but that doesn't mean you should starve."

She looked down at the money and crushed it in her hand. "Thank you."

Turning, I walked back to my car, then headed to the station.

I found out Harper was in the cells at the precinct, so I took a trip down to the basement to speak to her. It was a Saturday night, and the holding tank was full of drunk or drugged-out people. Most of them looked like staying overnight in a police cell was a fucking godsend, while others were impatiently pacing, waiting to get out.

"I need to see someone," I said to the cop on guard.

"Who?"

"Girl called Harper."

He checked his records. "We don't have anyone by that name."

"What about Paris?"

He flipped a sheet of paper on the clipboard. "Yeah, we got a Paris. Last cell."

Nodding my thanks, I wandered down the long hall until I got to the end. Harper was sitting on the solid metal bunk. She was wearing perhaps the most conservative outfit I'd ever seen her in—a skin-tight black dress that showed off her breasts. There was a tattoo done in a cursive script over her décolletage, the curving letters spelling out the word *Monster*.

She glanced up, then stood when she saw it was me.

"Detective."

"I went out looking for you, Harper."

She shrugged, giving me a carefree smile.

"Have they charged you yet?"

"Not yet."

I leaned my shoulder against the bars and folded my arms. "A misdemeanor crime, you might catch some jail time. Maybe just a fine."

"How big of a fine?"

"A thousand *if* you're charged."

A grin spread over her mouth. She was twenty-five and still had the beauty to demand larger fees from her Johns. She didn't have a pimp—which was an oddity—so everything she earned, she kept. A grand was chump change for a woman like Harper. A grand was the equivalent of one John for her.

She pushed a slice of her honey-blonde hair behind her ear. "Why were you looking for me?"

"I've hit a wall on a case I'm working. I was hoping you could help. I'll get any pending charges dropped if you agree to cooperate."

She cocked her head to the side and watched me. I let her, meeting her stare. Eventually, she nodded and said, "If I can, I will."

The great thing about Harper was she had no loyalties to anyone out there. She was an entrepreneur. A businesswoman. She knew what was good and what was bad for business. Being in jail for any longer than a night was bad. Helping me was good.

I called the guard over.

"Let her out. I need to interrogate her."

He looked at me with that blank cop stare. "Who authorized this?"

Fuck, this guy was a stickler for the rules. "I did. She's a witness in a goddamn case, now open the fucking door."

With one final scathing look, he opened the cell door, and Harper strolled out, swinging her hips and catching the guard's—Smitherson—attention. He must've been a rookie because his attention was fixated on Harper.

I hooked a hand around Harper's arm then said to Smitherson, "Get back to your desk. If Captain Holt sees you away from your post, he's going to tear you a new asshole."

Smitherson hurried off, and I directed Harper to a small interrogation room.

"What do you need to know, Detective?" she asked when she sat down, crossing her legs elegantly.

"Dealers are getting hit. Have you heard anything about that?"

She tapped a perfectly manicured fingernail to her mouth as she thought. "I was told that the kid who got popped on Thursday night belonged to Bane Rivera."

That was the second time today I'd heard that name.

"Rivera is a member of a drug cartel?"

She shook her head. "He's the fucking lord of a drug cartel."

I shifted on my feet. I hadn't known any of this. Eighteen fucking months, and I had no idea that he was even involved in LA's seedy underbelly. "Where's his territory?"

"It's the space between Manzetti's and Sanderson's."

"*Peter* Sanderson?" At her nod, I asked, "I thought he was just an art dealer."

"He is an art dealer, but he also supplies a third of LA with their drug of choice."

There'd been nothing in the database about that. Either he was incredibly good at keeping his hands clean, or Harper had it wrong.

"Can you tell me anything else about Rivera?"

"I have a friend who works for him. She says he's a great boss—kind in his own way. He set her up with an apartment when she started at the Dollhouse. Rivera takes care of all his Dolls."

"Why haven't you ever approached him about a job?"

"I like how much money I make on my own. Plus, my friend says if you don't want to fuck any of the men there, you don't have to, but I do enjoy fucking." She said 'fucking' with a sly grin. It made me wonder what else she enjoyed doing.

I sat back in my chair. "Is there anything else you can tell me?"

"Yeah. Bane loves getting his dick sucked so if you're looking for information from him, you might want to start on your knees."

I let my face go blank. The smile of Harper's face dimmed then vanished. Wrapping her arms around herself, she said, "Can I go now?"

I pulled a card with my personal cell number out of my pocket and handed it to her. "Give me a call if you have any more information."

"Will do."

I took care of the paperwork then walked her out of the precinct. By the time I was done, it was almost eleven-thirty.

Shutting down my computer, I left, intent on speaking to Bane Rivera.

7

Dagger

THE CLUB WAS ALMOST FULL, AND I KNEW IT WAS only going to get fuller. Saturday night in the Dollhouse was stuff of legend. Every pole was in use, a shower of bills laying like abandoned inhibitions on the stage at the performing Doll's feet.

I glanced down when two pale arms wrapped around my chest, and the warmth of someone's chest pressed against my back. A sickly-sweet perfume edged with sweat hit my nose.

"When are you going to take me into your office and bend me over your desk, Dagger?"

Circling my fingers around one delicate wrist, I tugged on the arm, bringing Isobel around so I could see her. A petite woman, she had dark curly hair and eyes. She was an exotic addition to the Dolls, and one that had proved lucrative. Half French and half Mexican, Isobel oozed sexuality, which in her line of work, was a necessity.

I pinched her chin between my thumb and forefinger, raising her face to mine. Her lips parted on a sigh. "Why don't you go and use that line on one of the clients, Iz? Now isn't the time to flirt with me."

A smile pulled at her mouth. "That's not a 'no,' is it?"

"No, not a no," I replied, releasing her chin. I'd been waiting for Isobel to approach me for a while now. It looked like all that time had finally paid off.

I needed to let off some fucking steam. Ever since coming to Cox's rescue, I'd been semi-hard and horny as fuck. That woman exuded confidence, and if there was one thing I liked, it was confidence in a woman. Besides, I'd found out she had a reputation for being a ball-busting bitch, and I always enjoyed bringing women like that to their knees.

Isobel turned her head to the side, and I followed her line of sight.

Bane was heading this way.

He lifted his chin in greeting as he drew to a stop. "How's the leg?"

My leg? I'd completely forgotten about Syndy's attempt at surgery on my thigh. "Fine." But where the fuck was he going?

The question must've showed on my face because he replied, "Heading out for the night. Make sure everything runs smoothly. Call me if shit gets hectic."

"Will do."

He clapped me on the shoulder and left the club.

This was the second time Bane had left the club early in as many days. What the hell was up with that?

Isobel raised up a little on her pleasers to put her mouth against my ear. "Fuck me tonight?" She lowered back down onto her feet.

"Think you can handle my brand of fucking?"

"Oh, yeah. Terri told me about what you did to her."

I nodded. Good enough for me. "Come to my office on your break."

Isobel beamed at me then sashayed through the crowd to perch on the rolled arm of a nearby chair, running her hands over the shoulder of the man sitting there.

"Boss?" I heard in my ear.

I looked away from the temptation, and touched the earpiece. "Go ahead, Kingston."

"I've got a detective out here looking for Mr. Rivera."

Goddammit. "I'm coming now."

I made my way to the door, anticipation making me twitchy. It could be only one person. As I came to stand beside Kingston, Cox's cold, gray gaze shifted to me. Her eyes widened slightly before she roved them around my body, starting at my shoulders and working her way down. When they returned to my face, she seemed to shake herself. Brushing her jacket away from her hip, she flashed the badge—and the butt of her gun—to me, like I assumed she also did for Kingston.

"LAPD, I need to speak to Bane Rivera."

Ah, so we were pretending we hadn't met before.

I took a moment to stare at her badge, taking a long fucking time to get back to her face. Unlike last night where she had buttons done all the way up to her throat, her blouse was open in a deep V tonight. A white lace bra cup skirted the edge of the fabric, drawing my gaze to her breasts. Her nipples hardened.

Fuck. Me.

Forcing myself to stop looking, I asked in a drawl, "Got a

warrant?"

"I don't need one to ask your boss questions."

I folded my arms, feeling the seams in the shoulders of my jacket start to strain. "He's not here."

"Are you sure?"

Mentally, I stripped her down to nothing but her panties. They'd match her bra, which would mean Detective Cox was playing the virgin with all that white. When I finally looked back at her face, I knew I'd taken a little too long to look, but fuck it. Cox had a body made for fucking. She was lean—a runner, maybe—but still had more than a handful when it came to tits, her hips flaring almost violently before tapering down for her strong, long legs.

"What questions do you need to ask him? Maybe I can pass them along."

"I'd rather ask him myself." She shoved past me, and I let her. She was in my world now, which meant my rules applied.

Cox came to an abrupt stop on the other side of the coat check. I looked past her, trying to see what she was seeing. The Dollhouse was a velvet and leather haven, one that smelled of expensive cologne, whisky, and sex. Music throbbed like an erotic pulse, just as it was designed to do. Gorgeous women dressed in lingerie worked on the poles, while others sat in the laps of men who were lapping—no pun intended—up the attention they were getting.

She seemed to take in a deep breath, then started walking. I followed her, wondering whether she would go left or right at the end of the bar. Right it was. Without hesitation, she pushed against the door that led into the employee area. After scanning the space quickly, she went straight up the stairs.

I followed her into the office, startling her when I spoke. "How did you know this was Bane's office?"

She spun around, arrogance making her mouth twitch. "A man like him would want to be higher than anyone else."

I conceded her statement with a nod. "And as you can see, Mr. Rivera isn't here right now." But I was. I was already semi-hard from the chase, and I let her see the heat in my eyes. Reaching out behind me, I shut the door.

It closed with an ominous *click*.

Her cool eyes darted between the now barricaded only way out and my face. She dropped her gaze to my hips, her mouth opening a little as she exhaled hard. She was scared and that was a fucking turn-on. I took a step forward. She lifted her foot to ease back but obviously thought better of it because she held her ground.

"What do you think you're going to find in here, *cara*?" Standing this close, I thought I would smell her perfume, but she wasn't wearing any. Honestly, I think I fucking liked her more for it.

"Don't call me that," she spat.

I smirked. "What should I call you then?"

"Detective Cox."

"And you can call me Dagger." I took another step, putting us so close that if she inhaled deeply enough, her breasts would rub against my chest. I bet her nipples would be as hard as diamonds. She didn't step away, and I said, "You aren't afraid of me."

"Why would I be afraid of you?"

"Most people are."

Her eyes were a pale gray in this light. "I'm not most people. I've seen things that would send most people screaming to their mommies."

"Me too."

She shook her head. "This isn't a dick-measuring contest."

Running my gaze down her body, I imagined what I could do to pleasure her—how I could make her scream. In a bass rumble, I said, "No, it isn't." But talking about dicks had made mine harder than a steel pipe.

Cox's eyes widened as she stared down between our bodies. She tried to step around me, but I followed. Now that I had her here, in private, there were questions I wanted answered. "Why were you talking to that dealer last night?" he asked.

"Who I speak to in an ongoing police investigation is *none* of your business."

I shook my head. "I saw you talking to Jay. You were going to buy him a hit, weren't you?"

She narrowed her eyes. "Like I'd admit that to you."

"If it were true, you could be thrown off the force. Buying drugs from a known dealer, giving them to a known junkie." I tutted. "If the guy had died, you'd have his blood on your hands."

Her eyes went cold—killer eyes. "You can't prove shit."

I pulled out my phone, loaded up the photographs I'd taken. Cox looked at herself from last night talking to Jay then going to the dealer. I'd captured it all.

When she looked at me again, anger flared and burned in her gaze. "These don't prove a goddamn thing."

I gave her my best blank face. "You've been a cop for at least the last ten years. You've been in vice division for less than a fifth of that time, and you've already cleared out and shut down at least three small-scale cooking operations, one large-scale, and arrested over thirty dealers. You always seem to know exactly where to go, who to speak to. Don't you think your captain would like to know *how* you get your information?"

"Having informants isn't a crime."

"No, but buying them drugs to keep them talking to you isn't exactly kosher either, is it?"

She backed up a step, her anger like a physical lash against my skin. She hated this, hated being hogtied by threats. "What. Do. You. Want?" She bit out each of the words with a snarl.

What I wanted was for her to figure out who was hitting Bane's dealers, but what I asked for was something purely selfish.

Taking another step closer, I forced her back until she collided with the edge of the sideboard in front of the long bank of windows. I pressed forward, grinding my cock against the cradle of her hips.

She let out a sharp breath but made no move to get away. She could have, though. She was wearing her sidearm. So easily, she could've pulled it out and leveled it at my head.

But she didn't.

Her body was warm against mine. She was only an inch shorter than me.

A good height for fucking.

"What do I want?" I asked, repeating her question to me and putting my face closer to hers. "I want a cop to owe me."

"You think because you killed Vapor before I could that I *owe* you?"

"You wouldn't have killed Vapor," I replied. Burying my nose behind her ear, I dragged in a deep breath then released it. "He was going to rape you, and you froze." I bit down on her earlobe, making her gasp. Still, she didn't move away. "How did you explain what happened anyway?"

"Unidentified assailant killed my attacker."

"Assailant?" I asked.

"The definition is correct." Her words were breathy as she tightened her fingers around my shirt. "What word would you have used?"

"Vigilante," I growled, nibbling her neck. I bit down on her thundering pulse ever so slightly. Her hands tightened—convulsed—and a whimper of pleasure escaped her.

Did she hate herself for enjoying this?

Maybe a better question was, did I give a fuck if she wasn't?

"You still haven't told me what you want." Her voice was soft, and I imagined that was what she sounded like when she was begging to be able to come.

I leaned back so I could see her eyes. They'd gone a little darker—more of storm gray. Her pupils were blown too. She was turned the fuck on.

I rolled my hips against her, biting back a groan. I needed to get inside her, but I didn't think it would be that easy.

So, I painted her a fucking picture.

"I want to use my knife to cut off every single button on your blouse then slice your bra off. I'll suck on your fucking perfect breasts until you're begging me to get inside you. When I know you're good and ready, I'll bend you over the arm of that couch, tear the panties from your hips, and sink so deeply inside you that you won't know where you end and I start."

"And if I said no? Would you rape me?"

My jaw clenched. If there was anything I hated more, it was rapists—men who forced themselves on women because they're the perceived 'weaker sex.' Women were fucking masters of pain control. "You won't say no to me."

"If you force yourself on me, I will fight you the entire time." Her words came out steadily. "And if you take a knife to me, I'll pull a gun on you."

I chuckled darkly. She had no idea she was tapping into a space inside me where getting a gun pulled on me in an intimate situation was a fucking aphrodisiac.

Fear and fucking danger.

"Do we have a deal?"

"We fuck and you keep your mouth shut about me paying addicts with their drug of choice in exchange for information? Do I understand that correctly?"

"Almost." I dragged my gaze down her body, slowly—thoroughly. "I want carte blanche on your body."

Her throat bobbed as she swallowed. "No."

I clicked my tongue, chastising her. "Carte blanche on your body or nothing at all."

She shook her head. "I won't agree to something like that."

"What are you afraid of... enjoying yourself?"

"I won't put myself in your power any more than I have to."

"How about I tell your captain that you're supplying drugs to a known user then? I'll tell him you're paying for your information with illicit substances. I'll tell him that you coerce, bribe, and bargain to get what you need from people. Now, they don't sound like good qualities for a detective to have."

A muscle slid in her jaw. "You're coercing, bribing, and bargaining with me right now."

"I'm not a cop," I replied with a smile. "Let me ask you a question. You dispense justice like a vigilante, but you hide behind the badge. What if I tell you I can take away that badge and all you'll have is your good intentions and blood on your hands?"

It was a long minute before she spoke again, "I have lines you can't cross."

"Like what?"

"No drawing blood. No bondage."

"Are they hard limits?"

"Yes."

"Anal?"

"Hard limit."

"Deprivation?"

She canted her head to the side. "I don't understand."

"Sense deprivation. Blindfolds. Earplugs."

Her cheeks actually flushed with color. "I don't know."

I think she liked that idea. "This is a business deal. We need to know the parameters. You need to know my expectations."

"A negotiation, you mean." A deep frown settled between her eyes. She shook her head, muttering to herself, "I can't believe I'm doing this."

"Believe it. I've told you what I want. You've told me three hard limits. Anything else I need to know?"

"Yeah. You breathe a word about this to anyone, and I'll put a bullet in your head."

"Not unless I put one in yours first."

We glared at each other for a long time. Neither of us broke. Fuck, this woman was something else.

"Deal. I can't wait to have your mouth wrapped around my dick, *cara*." I rimmed her lips with my finger, pushing a digit inside. "Suck," I commanded.

Baring her teeth, she refused.

Gripping her jaw, I applied just the right amount of pressure, unhinging her bottom jaw. "*Suck.*"

With fire in her gray eyes, she sucked, taking my index finger down to the third knuckle.

Fuck.

Me.

I was painfully hard for this woman. I was so distracted by her mouth that I had to know how she tasted. Removing my finger, I slammed my lips to hers, plunging my tongue into her mouth. She bit my lip. I jerked back, and she spat the blood onto my shirt.

It landed, wet and red, in the middle of my chest. With a shaking hand, she rubbed blood from her bottom lip. "I'll fuck you, but no kissing. Nothing intimate. This is fucking blackmail. Let's treat it like that."

Darkly, I said, "Have it your way, *cara*."

I STOOD AT THE BOTTOM OF THE STAIRS AND WATCHED Cox leave the club. My dick was straining to get out, to get used. I glanced at my watch. Isobel would be on break in ten. I could take my sexual frustration out on her.

I'd just opened up the closet to change over my shirt, when there was a knock on the door.

"Enter."

Isobel strode in like I'd fucking conjured her with my thoughts. She was wearing a black and red bustier with a sheer panel down the middle and lace up the sides. Black heels completed the outfit. She'd changed outfits since I'd last seen her, which meant she'd been busy in one of the private rooms.

Walking to the door, I locked it then turned back to face her. "Number five?" I asked her, referring to the most extreme of the BDSM rooms the Dollhouse had.

"One."

The voyeur's room then.

"I'm all hot and bothered, Dagger." Her voice was a sultry purr. There was heated anticipation in her eyes like it was fucking Christmas and all her festive wishes were coming true. "Come and put me out of my misery."

Like Bane, I regularly took what the Dolls offered.

Unlike Bane, I had no qualms about sleeping with them, but I only did it once.

No repeat performances.

Isobel crooked her finger at me. My semi-hard dick got harder. It didn't care that Isobel's curly black hair was the complete opposite of Cox's straight blonde hair. It didn't matter that her dark eyes weren't clear gray.

When I was standing in front of her, Isobel quickly undid the buttons on my shirt and slowly eased it off my shoulders. Her eyes widened a little when she saw the naked dagger holstered on my hip, but it wasn't fear that made her pulse race.

I brought the blade up, showing it to her.

All the Dolls knew about the knife play I enjoyed while I fucked.

"You want this?" I asked her.

Rolling her bottom lip into her mouth, she chewed on the delicate flesh and nodded.

"I have a safe word. Landslide. Use it if you want to stop. Understand?" I waited for her acknowledgment then added, "When I begin the edge play, you can't move. Tell me you understand."

"I understand," she breathed. "I promise I won't move, Dagger."

With my chin, I gestured to her outfit. "Are you attached to this?"

"No."

Her pulse was pounding against the side of her throat—hammering against her neck. She was turned on by the idea of cold steel against her soft skin. I'd find out soon whether or not she'd like the reality as much as the idea. Gripping the top of the bustier with one hand, I slid the tip of the blade against the fabric. Her eyes widened a little, fear crossing her face for a moment before she banished it.

She hadn't said stop, so I continued. The steel was sharp and melted through the satin and lace. It fell away from her body, leaving her standing in a black lace thong and heels.

Laying the blade down, I took off the holster and draped it on the back of my chair. When I was standing in front of Isobel once more, her heavy-lidded eyes roved the scars on my chest. With a tentative hand, she reached out to touch one.

"*Don't.*" The word came out thick with anger.

She paused less than an inch from touching me, her dark eyes intent on my face.

"Don't touch the scars." She didn't have the right. "No kissing either."

Isobel nodded. "I know the rules," she said softly.

If she'd known the rules, then she was trying her luck. She wasn't a fucking special snowflake. In a cold voice, I commanded, "Turn around and place your hands flat on the desk."

She did as I asked, hinging forward on her hips to lay her palms on the lacquered timber. Her ass was pushed out—an offering I would take advantage of soon. Wrapping an arm around her hips, I tugged them back further, exaggerating the curve of her spine, putting her in a position of vulnerability. With my palm in the center of her shoulder blades, I pressed down until her chest touched the top of the desk too.

She peered at me over her shoulder, her lips puffy from biting them.

Using the tip of the knife, I twisted it at a forty-five-degree angle against the top of her spine. She gasped, and I lifted the steel away. One wrong move, and I'd draw blood. One really wrong move and I'd sever something more vital.

"You said you wanted this." My tone was harsh, and yeah, I was pissed off that she flinched.

"I do."

"Then stay still."

She nodded, resting her face against the desk. I tried again, keeping that same angle, but instead of positioning it at her nape, I pressed against her hip. She yipped and shied away from the edge.

"Landslide," she whispered in a trembling voice.

Reaching over, I drove the blade—tip-first—into the top of the desk.

Frightened, Isobel tried to straighten, but I kept my hand pressed between her shoulder blades.

"No. Stay there."

"But—"

"What? Do you still want me to fuck you?"

"Yes," she whispered. "*Please.*"

My voice was hard when I replied, "Then stay there."

Undoing the zipper on my slacks, I freed my cock then dug in my pocket for a condom. After I rolled it down my length, I slid my fingers under the string-line waistband of her panties and pulled them down to her knees.

She whimpered, shifting her weight from one leg to the other.

"Do you still want this?" My voice was rimmed with anger.

"Y-y-yes."

I stepped back. "Say it like you fucking mean it, Iz. Do you want this?"

"*Yes.*" The word came out fiercely.

I had to make sure she wasn't going to turn around later and say I'd forced myself on her. That was not what I was about.

Pushing her ass out, she moaned, "Fuck me, Dagger. Fuck me hard. And rough. And without mercy."

Taking back my step, I skimmed my fingers through her cunt and found her wet and ready. Running my hand up my length, I positioned myself at her opening and slid home.

No foreplay.

You had to have feelings about someone to care whether they were ready or not.

I grabbed her hips, fingers curling over the delicate bones. Isobel moaned when I drew out then sighed as I thrust back in. A few more thrusts later, and she was clawing at my arms. Wrapping one hand into her dark hair, I pulled, torquing her shoulders back and exposing the delicate column of her throat.

Isobel's hands grasped at nothing but air as I ruthlessly pounded into her. Her inner walls clenched around my dick, her orgasm sending the muscles into spasm. She screamed out nothing but an inarticulate word, but I got the gist. She was fucking coming, and I was the one to get her there.

Leaning over her back, I bit her shoulder and pumped into her. My pelvis slapping against her ass was all I could hear until I emptied into the condom with a groan, the last of my thrusts growing quieter—slower. I felt about as empty as I did when we started, but like hell I was going to say that to Isobel.

I released my grip on her hair, and she lowered herself down to the desk, panting hard. Holding the condom at the base of my cock, I slid myself out of her wet heat and rolled it off, pitching the used latex into the trash can.

Isobel slowly stood, her dark eyes glittering with her orgasm.

"Terri was right."

"In what way?" I tucked my semi-hard cock back into my pants and zipped things up.

"You're a savage when you fuck."

Yeah, they all wanted to fuck a savage.

I scooped up my shirt I'd left crumpled on the floor. "Let yourself out, Doll," I told her as I shut the bathroom door behind me.

8

Cox

I'D SPENT MY SUNDAY HOLED UP IN MY APARTMENT, but being cooped up for more than fourteen hours staring at the walls was starting to take its toll on me. Dagger would come for me. Eventually. But the exact where and when weren't known.

Fuck. I needed to get out of here—to run off this nervous energy.

Changing into my running shorts and sports bra, I slid my feet into my Nikes and unhooked the apartment key from the bundle I kept by the door. My phone sat beside the keys, and I hesitated—looking at it. In the end, I decided to leave the apartment without it. Being left alone sounded like the best fucking idea I'd had in ages.

I didn't see anyone on my way down in the elevator—no one but me and my reflection. I didn't look at myself in mirrors half the time, but here in the silence, I stared at the woman who had agreed to sell her soul to save her career.

Blackmail.

Dagger had some incriminating photographs.

Were they enough to land me in hot water? Maybe.

I'd been warned in the past about my choice of informants. The information I got from Jay was solid, but Friday night hadn't been the first time I'd bought drugs as payment.

I'd had a partner when I first transferred into the unit. Henry Murphy had been a crooked cop. He took kickbacks from dealers in exchange for turning a blind eye to any crimes involving them. He was found dead in his apartment twelve months ago, a point-blank shot to the head that had gone in like a nickel and come out like a pizza, blowing out the back of his skull.

Despite his questionable methods, Murphy had actually taught me something. He taught me that there was a line I wasn't willing to cross, but I did nudge the fucking thing with my toe sometimes. Legally, it wasn't wrong. Morally, though? That was the bit I didn't seem to struggle with. Call it being a product of my environment growing up.

Stepping outside the lobby of my building, I thanked Frank, the doorman, and turned down West 8th Street, maintaining a jog as I weaved between the light foot traffic. Sweat immediately beaded on my face, the suffocating heat from the day yet to dissipate. Breathing in deep, the air felt as if it had been blasted in an oven, the aftertaste of exhaust fumes coating the back of my tongue.

I finally drew to a stop after running through MacArthur Park. The cars on Wilshire Boulevard whizzed by in a flash of lights and speed, the road bisecting the park ruining some of its city-oasis vibe. This was my halfway marker, so I turned around and started back to my apartment.

SECRETS

Frank waved me through once more, and I rode the elevator in silence. When I was outside in the hall on my floor, I could hear my cell phone ringing. Pulling the key from the inside pocket of my shorts, I opened the door and caught the call before whoever it was hung up.

"Cox."

"Detective?" a woman asked.

"Who is this?" I shut the apartment door behind me and locked it.

"It's Harper. You said to call if I had any information."

"Harper. I'm glad you called," I told her, pinning the phone between my shoulder and ear and pulling open the fridge to grab a bottle of water. I cracked the lid and twisted it off. "What's going on?"

There was a pause, and I pulled the phone away to see if the call had been disconnected by accident. "Harper? You there?"

"Yeah. Look, I've been thinking about telling you this since Friday night, but I wasn't sure."

I placed the bottle of water down. "You know the deal, Harper. You scratch my back, I scratch yours. What is it?"

She blew out a breath. "One of my regulars is a mid-level dealer for one of the Big Three."

"Big Three?"

"LA drug dealers. Anyway, he told me that he'd been tasked with making a hit on a kid in Pico-Union."

Pico-Union? My heart skipped a beat. "Did he give you the name of the guy he was supposed to hit?"

"No."

It had to be the Malachiah Smith murder. Aside from an attempted carjacking, no other crime had been reported in Pico-

Union on Thursday night.

"Why didn't you tell me this while you were in jail?"

"Because I wanted to get *out* of jail, Detective."

I moved around my kitchen, thinking. "So, this John of yours tells you he's going to commit murder, and you don't think to report that to the police?"

"I'm reporting it now, Detective. Like you said, I scratch your back, you scratch mine."

"I don't suppose you'll give me his name?"

"No."

"Who's his boss?"

"I can't tell you that either."

Fuck. "Has your John been asked to do any more hits?"

"We normally get together on a Sunday night, but he's canceled tonight's meeting."

"Do you think he's been asked to murder someone else?"

"Maybe," she whispered. "Detective, this shit can't come back on me."

"I understand, Harper. I can send a uniformed officer to watch you if you want?"

"No. No cops. I'll lose half my client list if they see a cop hanging around." She inhaled slowly then let it out. "I can take care of myself."

"Harper? Harper!" The line went dead. "Shit."

HALF AN HOUR LATER, I WAS IN THE SHOWER WASHING the sweat from my run off me when someone started pounding on my apartment door.

"Fuck."

Tipping my head back under the spray, I rinsed the suds from my hair then shut off the water.

Wrapping a towel around my breasts, I picked up my sidearm that I'd left on the closed lid of the toilet and held it down beside my thigh.

"Who is it?" I asked through the door, water dripping down my face and back from my wet hair.

When there wasn't an answer, I peered through the peephole. A dark figure was standing in the hall outside my apartment. It took me a moment to realize who it was.

"What do you want, Dagger?"

"You know what I want, *cara*." His voice was a dark crawl, easing through the door and caressing my skin. "I said I'd come for you."

There was a double entendre there.

"How'd you get past the doorman?"

He chuckled. "You think one man in a suit could stop me? Let me in."

Breathing in deeply, I let it out then said, "I need five minutes."

"I'll wait inside."

I shook my head even though he couldn't see it. "Alone. Five minutes *alone*."

There was a pause then he said in a voice so low it was almost inaudible, "Let me in, *cara*, or I'll force my way in."

I tapped the barrel of the gun against my naked thigh, indecision tearing me apart. I could lock the bathroom door while he waited in the living room. If I didn't let him in, he'd make a damn scene. Against my better judgment, I unlocked the door and drew across the slide. Dagger jammed his foot at the bottom of the door when I pulled it open a sliver, shoving it open wider.

"You have wet hair," he said, leaning against the jamb casually, his arms crossed like he had all the time in the world.

"You interrupted my shower."

"How about I join you?" He stepped into my apartment and shut the door behind him. I backed up a step, bringing up my gun and aiming at his torso. His brows rose, an amused smile twisting his lips. "Going to shoot me before we fuck? I didn't realize you had a blood fetish."

"We wouldn't be fucking after I put a 9mm Luger into your shoulder."

He took a step closer, making me slip my finger from outside the trigger guard to the trigger itself.

"Stop, or I will shoot." In fact, killing him would do away with my little blackmail problem. The question was, could I do that? Could I kill someone in cold blood? Dagger moved in a blur of speed, wrapping his large hand over the top of the gun and pushing it down toward the floor.

He was stronger than I was, and trying to get into an arm-wrestling match was going to end badly for me. I moved my finger from the trigger automatically, unwilling to shoot my downstairs neighbor by accident.

His body was a hot line against mine, and I realized the towel had dropped during the scuffle. Dagger realized it too, our eyes meeting for a brief second. I saw the hunger burning in his gaze, and I hoped like hell he didn't see it mirrored in mine.

I dropped the gun to the dove gray rug, hoping he'd let go of my hand.

His green eyes bounced around my face, taking in my wet hair before going lower. He took a step back. "Fuck," he barked, staring back at me. "Go shower."

My eyes darted to my sidearm. I couldn't leave it in the middle of the floor. Stooping, I picked it up, holding it against my thigh, along with my towel. Awkwardly, I wrapped the terry cloth around my breasts while still juggling the gun, then walked back to the bathroom. I shut the door. Locked it. Waited to see whether Dagger would try to bust in here. When he didn't, I turned on the shower and finished washing my hair then took my time drying it.

I didn't usually get dressed in the bathroom, so I wrapped a dry towel around me and walked to my bedroom. Dagger was waiting on my bed. Although my heart was trying to climb out of my throat, there was a part of me that was thrilled by him being in my apartment. There was something about the bad boy that I liked, apparently. It hadn't served me well in the past though, and I doubted it would serve me well now.

"Get out," I told him.

He shook his head and shifted in his seat. I realized then that he was hard—obscenely so. Over his broad shoulders was a black leather holster, the butt of what looked like a Browning Hi-Power sticking out from under his arm. He was here to fuck me, but he wouldn't go without his gun. I found that odd…

"Take off the towel."

"Why?"

"Because that's how blackmail works. I make demands. You comply. Otherwise, I'll make sure your boss knows exactly how you're gathering information. Now…" he slipped the holster from his shoulders, "… drop the fucking towel."

Straightening my spine, I pulled at the corner I'd tucked in under my arm, and the towel fell away. My nipples immediately puckered in the kiss of cool air. Dagger was staring at them, and that same hunger as before blazed back to life.

"Sit on the bed."

"Why?"

"Sit on the bed. Legs wide."

Keeping my chin high, I walked past him and sat on the edge of the bed. Placing my hands on my knees, I spread them apart.

He came to stand in front of me. "Wider."

I inched them apart a little more.

"Wider," he said again, his voice a little hoarse this time. He was acting like he'd never seen a pussy before. Hard to believe if he worked at the Dollhouse. I had no doubt women threw themselves at him. I had to be blind not to see how fucking attractive he was.

I wasn't blind.

I saw it.

His hands bunched into fists. "Wider."

I opened my legs to the limits of my flexibility, feeling vulnerable. But I wouldn't let him see that on my face. "Now what?" I asked, trying to ignore the breathy quality to my voice.

He lowered himself to his knees so we were face-to-face. He placed his hands on my thighs, his thick fingers digging into my flesh until it dimpled. I didn't make a sound. I didn't want to give him the satisfaction.

"This is mine," he said, jerking his chin to what was between my legs. "All of this. Mine. Do you understand me?"

"I understand that you're a fucking possessive bastard."

He glowered at me. "While we're fucking, this is mine and only mine."

I stared at him, putting all my hatred into my eyes. "Is this a one-way street? Do I get to make the same demand of you?"

He shook his head. "I can fuck whoever I want. Will I? Well, that's something else entirely." His hungry eyes settled on my cunt again, and I felt it with an invisible weight. "Say that it's mine."

Stubbornly, I shook my head.

He got back onto his feet and gestured for me to stand. I did, teetering—drunk on his dominance. Stepping into the line of my body, he shoved his hand between my thighs and stroked through my folds. He gave a soft, guttural growl as he brought his fingers up between us.

"Open your mouth."

I did, and he shoved the digits in. I tasted myself and even though it disgusted me to be in this position, there was something heady about how dominating he was being. He slipped the now soaked fingers back between my legs, thrusting one, then a second, digit into my wet heat. I cried out at the invasion, but clamped my lips shut before the sound could escape. I didn't want to give him the pleasure of knowing he was getting me off.

He smirked. "You like it rough." Drawing his fingers away, he circled my clit with his thumb then thrust back inside. Again and again, he did this, making me wetter and wetter. I felt it slip down the inside of my thigh and into his waiting palm.

"Say it's mine." He bit out the words, the strain beginning to show in the tightness of his jaw.

Pressing my lips together, I shook my head. If I opened my mouth, I would scream my pleasure. Pressure was building inside me like a storm on the horizon threatening to break. With each thrust, he brought me closer to an orgasm I didn't want to give him. He started to scissor his fingers, stretching me further and further until his fingers were so deep inside me that the palm of his hand was pounding against my clit.

I stared at him with wild eyes, but his expression was carefully blank. He'd released his cock and was stroking it as he finger-fucked me into oblivion. He was getting off on this. Even though it was a sick fucking situation, that knowledge pushed me over the edge, and I came on his fingers. Hard. Overwhelmed with sensations, I gripped his wrist with one hand to stop the relentless pace, and the other went to his shoulder. I dug my fingers in, the digits spasming with each shudder and rock of my release.

When the last of the tremors ebbed away, he eased his slick fingers from my body and brought them to his mouth, licking them clean.

I watched, transfixed, as he tasted me completely, a rumble of satisfaction vibrating in his chest. With his eyes still on me, he herded me closer to the bed until I was forced to sit down.

This new position left my face at hip height so there was no way to avoid looking at his cock. The shaft was long and broad, thick with veins. The head was blush pink, and a bead of precum glistened on the tip. He ran his palm up the length, making it kick in his grip.

"Open your mouth," he commanded.

"No."

"Open your mouth." He bit out the words this time. When I refused again, he dug his fingers into my jaw. "When I tell you to do something, you do it."

I pressed my lips more tightly together.

He obviously saw the 'fuck you' in my eyes because he laughed. It was a dark sound that spilled heat into his green irises and touched my throbbing pussy with invisible fingers.

Anticipation made his voice lower. "Fight me all you want. Your complete submission, when I get it, will be a fucking high like no other."

My nostrils flared with my hard breathing, an odd combination of anger and *longing* burning through my defenses. I couldn't keep refusing him like this. I couldn't keep pushing him. I was startled to find that I also didn't *want* to keep refusing him. I wanted him.

"I'm going to fight you the whole time," I told him. "I'll give you my body, but you won't take my heart and soul."

The light in his eyes dimmed. "I know, *cara*. Now, suck my dick until I tell you to stop."

I gave in.

I gave him what he wanted—what I wanted too.

I couldn't fight it anymore.

I opened my mouth, and he slammed himself home, hitting the back of my throat. It drew a low groan from his mouth, as well as—embarrassingly—mine. It was fucking sick that his dominating personality was getting me off. I usually liked submissive men who did as I asked, but Dagger was anything but submissive.

Drawing back his hips, he shoved into my mouth once more. I sucked hard, creating a vacuum, hollowing my cheeks. I was so turned on that my arousal was sliding down the inside of my thighs. Reaching down, I skimmed my fingers through the wet heat between my legs, rubbing at my thrumming clit.

He was panting hard when he gripped my hair and pulled my head away.

With his free hand, he ran his fingertips across my bottom lip. "I like seeing my cock in your mouth." His gaze skated down to where I was frantically rubbing myself closer to orgasm. "It seems you do too."

He shoved in again, and I took every inch of him. Holding my head still, he fucked my mouth until saliva dripped from the corners of my lips, landing in steady streams on my bared breasts.

Dagger suddenly barked a loud, "Fuck!" then he was coming in my mouth, jetting into the back of my throat. I orgasmed at the same time he did, my whole body lighting up like a live wire. He groaned as he pumped a few more times, my moans vibrating through his shaft and prolonging his pleasure.

"Don't swallow yet," he hissed in a strained voice, still coming on my tongue. With one final groan, he stepped back and barked, "Open your mouth. I want to see my cum in the back of your throat."

Opening my mouth wider, I showed him.

He growled in pleasure. "Swallow it. All of it."

A shudder moved through my body. Closing my mouth, I swallowed him down.

"Now, lick me clean."

Wrapping my lips around his still-hard dick, I sucked him back into my mouth, swirling my tongue around the crown. His hips thrust forward, and he gripped a handful of my hair.

When he released me, he commanded, "Stand up."

I pushed to my feet, my pulse pounding, my breathing rushing through my lungs and out of my mouth. It was as if I'd run a marathon, when all I'd done was let this man—my *blackmailer*—use my mouth until he spilled inside of it. I should've felt something. Anger, maybe. Embarrassment. The anger was there, but it was being tempered by something else. Something that I never thought I'd feel.

Lust.

The silence of the room was broken when his cell started to ring in his pocket. He pulled it out, looked at the number and said, "I have to take this." His eyes traveled slowly down my body before returning to my face.

Regret shimmered in his cold eyes.

Then he turned and left.

9

Dagger

FUCK, MY COCK WAS READY FOR ROUND TWO AS I shut Cox's apartment door behind me, but I had more pressing things to attend to, so I answered the call, "Yeah?"

"Dagger? It's Caesar."

"What have you got for me, kid?"

Caesar was a local kid who kept his eyes and ears open for me. In exchange, I sent his mother money anonymously every month since Caesar's father was a piece of shit who left them when the kid was only three and refused to pay child support.

"I heard shots coming from Remi's place."

"Santiago's?" I demanded, my free hand curling into a fist. "When did this happen?"

"In the last five minutes."

"Jesus Christ." I had to get over there. "I'll be there as soon as I can."

Hauling ass out to my car, I popped open the glove

compartment and pulled out a pair of black leather driving gloves. Slipping them onto my hands, I drove as fast as I could without drawing any unwanted attention. Remi Santiago was one of Bane's dealers—or at least he was—if those gunshots were an indication of anything.

When I got to the apartment building, I parked where no one would notice me, grabbed my suit jacket to cover the gun, then ran into the building, taking the stairs two, sometimes three at a time. Nobody was out in the hallway wondering whether they'd heard gunshots. Wondering if someone needed an ambulance. They fucking knew the sound. They fucking knew the only thing that was coming was the coroner's van.

On the fourth floor, I found Remi's apartment door ajar, light from inside spilling out into the hallway. Pulling the Browning Hi-Power from under my arm, I brought it up in a single-handed grip and moved to the edge of the doorway. I couldn't hear anything except for the low-level whirr from a pedestal fan inside the apartment. I kicked open the door, waiting to see if anyone was going to shoot at me. When it remained as quiet as the grave, I stepped inside, easing the door shut behind me.

Remi was lying in the middle of the rug in the living room. His eyes were still open, staring sightlessly up at the ceiling. There were two bullet holes in his chest and another in the center of his forehead. Blood had flowed from the chest wounds, but the one on his head had only a trickle. The first two had killed him. The final bullet was a message.

I scanned the area, looking for the stash of drugs I knew were going to be there. Unlike Malachiah, Remi was a little smarter about concealing what he did. He would have hidden his supply somewhere out of sight, but it wasn't like I had all night to look for it. Someone would've called the cops by now.

I yanked open every single drawer and cupboard in the cramped kitchen, tore the cushions from the couch and cleared out the wardrobe in the single bedroom.

"Fuck!"

As I walked past the bed, one of the floorboards squeaked. Shifting my weight, I heard the squeak again. There was a loose board under the bed. Outside the grimy glass of the window, I heard the faint wail of sirens, and I knew I was running out of time. Putting up my gun, I lowered to my knees and leaned my palms against the wood, pressing my lower body down until I could see under the bed. One of the boards was lower than the rest, and when I reached out to test it, it moved.

The sirens were getting closer.

Pulling a knife from my hip sheath, I hooked the tip into a space between the wood and leveraged it up. Reaching inside the cavity, I pulled out two bricks of Bane's coke and carefully replaced the board.

Finding a backpack in the closet, I stashed the drugs inside, threw it over my shoulder, then walked toward the door only to stop when I heard footsteps out in the hall. I was out of time.

Glancing over my shoulder, I saw the open window in the living room. Once I was out on the metal landing, I went down the fire escape, finding myself outside the window of the apartment below. Running my fingers along the lip, I tried the sash and found it unlocked. Sliding the glass upward, I stepped into the room, glancing up at the last minute to see a cop sticking his head out of the window I'd just come through from Caesar's apartment.

I turned around, looking at where I'd found myself. There was an older couple sitting at a two-seater square table, a game of cards between them. The man said something, anger shading his words. I rifled through my memories and ID'd the language as Armenian.

"Knerek' yndhatman hamar," I said as I passed, yanking open their front door and stepping into the hall. His curses continued behind me.

"Stop where you are!" someone shouted at me.

I turned and found a uniformed cop. Behind him, more cops streamed past him up to the next level. The uniformed had his gun naked in his hand, and I put my hands up, careful not to reveal my Browning tucked safe and sound under my arm or the two bricks of coke in the backpack over my shoulder.

"Sir, what are you doing here?"

"Visiting my cousin," I lied.

The cop's gaze darted to the apartment doors flowing out behind me.

"Which apartment?"

"320."

He seemed to think about that for a moment, wondering whether I was telling the truth or not.

"I'd advise you to wait outside, sir. It's not safe in here right now."

"Of course, officer," I replied, even flashing him a smile. He stared at me for a long minute before nodding and knocking on the next apartment door.

I started down the stairs, keeping out of the way of the good old boys and girls in blue. When I reached the lobby, I pushed out the building, making sure to keep my hands visible. The cops who were there ushered me out of the way, and I ducked under the tape.

"What are you doing here?"

I turned at the question. Cox was standing there in one of her pantsuits, her slick hair still wet from the shower she'd taken. Arms folded across her breasts, she waited for my reply.

"I prefer you in the towel," I said.

Her eyes widened, and she grabbed my arm, dragging me away from the other responding officers. Under her breath and in a hiss, she said, "Keep your goddamn voice down."

"Afraid your colleagues will find out about us?"

"There is no *us*. You're blackmailing me."

I let her see the amusement in my eyes. "That's right. I'm your blackmailer, and you'll do whatever I say because you can't let anyone know how far you'll go to solve the case."

She ignored my jab, instead asking her own question. "What are you doing here? Did that phone call have anything to do with it?"

"I was driving past and saw the cops show up. I was just enjoying the show."

Her gray eyes narrowed on my face. "You're lying."

I leaned in a little, crowding her, getting in her personal space. "Prove it." Her mouth was less than an inch from my own, and like she was thinking about that fact too, she swiped her tongue over her bottom lip.

"Do you know something about what happened here?"

"No."

"I don't believe you."

"Not my problem," I said, easing back to give her some breathing room. "Goodbye, Detective."

I walked away from the apartment building, cutting down the

next block to where I'd parked my car. Popping the trunk, I removed the custom panel on the inside and stashed the drugs in there. The compartment was smooth against the existing interior, so unless you knew it was there, you wouldn't notice it.

I'd just shut the trunk when the skin between my shoulder blades tightened. I drew my gun without thinking, flicking off the safety and turning around to aim it at the chest of the person who had snuck up behind me.

"Jesus *fucking* Christ, kid." I put up the gun, pointing it up to the sky. "Don't sneak up on me. I was going to put a bullet in your skull."

"I'm sorry," Caesar replied, lowering his arms slowly like he didn't want to startle me. "Did you see him? Was Remi dead?"

"Yeah. He was. Did you see anything suspicious? See anyone leave the building? Anyone who doesn't belong in this neighborhood?"

He shook his head. "Nothing."

I nodded and reached into my pocket, drawing out a couple of hundred-dollar bills. "Make sure your mother gets that." I gestured to the cash with my chin. "Now, go on home. It's too fucking late for you to be out. Your mom must be wondering where you are."

"She's working the late shift," he replied, looking every bit like the sixteen-year-old kid he was.

"She'll want to know you're home, though. Go on."

Holding his fist out to me, I returned the gesture. "See you, Dagger."

"See you, kid." I watched him go into the neighboring apartment building, safe once more.

By the time I got back on the road, it was close to dawn. I

drove home to Brentwood Park, pulling into the driveway of the single-level, ranch-style house I'd grown up in. I waited until the garage door was all the way down before I got out of the car, then retrieved the drugs and went inside.

Not bothering to turn on the lights, I walked to my bedroom, stripping off my weapons as I went. The Browning went on my nightstand, one blade under the pillow and the others stayed in their sheaths and deposited on the top of the armoire. Grabbing the neck of my shirt, I pulled the fabric over my head and let it go. It dropped to the floor, sitting shotgun next to the boots which I pulled off next.

I hesitated when the doorbell rang. Grabbing a blade, I walked through the house to the front door. Peering through the curtains covering the glass window in the door, I cursed when I saw who it was.

10

Cox

DAGGER OPENED THE DOOR NAKED FROM THE WAIST
up. My gaze went straight to the scars on his chest—long,
linear scars that were thick and shiny. Some part of me knew
they weren't new scars but old ones that had been caused by
something so violent that his skin and muscle hadn't been able
to heal properly.

I had those same scars too, except mine weren't visible.

"What—"

My demand to know why the hell he was at the scene of a
crime was snatched away when Dagger grabbed the front of
my jacket and yanked me inside. Slamming the door shut, he
threw me up against it, wrapping his palm around my throat
and his arm against my chest. I could feel the strength in his
fingers, but he wasn't applying pressure.

He wasn't trying to harm me.

Scare me? Definitely. But not harm.

At least, not yet.

A small sound escaped me when he leaned his face closer to mine, and he pressed his groin against me. The twin pressures—one against my throat, the other in the cradle of my hips—made a part of me loosen. Soften. Dagger was dominating my senses, and even though I should've hated him for it, I pressed my lower body a little closer to his.

He searched my eyes for something, although what it was, I didn't know. We were locked in a great tug-of-war that ended when he eased the weight off his arm and the pressure off my throat.

I drew in a deep breath through my mouth. It shuddered through me but caught when he put his mouth to my ear and whispered, "I'm going to fuck you now."

Heat thrilled through me, but I shook my head.

"You don't get to deny me your body. It's mine, remember?"

I gasped when he pulled a blade as long as my forearm from somewhere behind him. Dammit, I'd been too distracted by him that I hadn't noticed he was armed. I stared at the nearly-foot-long length of steel as it was held in his capable hands. "What are you going to do with that?"

"You'll find out."

He trailed his free hand from around my throat down between my breasts and onto my stomach. My breathing quickened with every inch of my body he touched. By the time he reached the bottom of my blouse, I was panting. In that moment, I hated how my body reacted to him. I should be disgusted by this dominating, *He-Man* bullshit, but with Dagger, I felt like I needed his next touch more than I needed my next breath.

Which was ridiculous.

He was a fucking criminal.

I was torn from my thoughts when he slid the tip of the dagger against the final button holding my blouse together. Glancing up, I saw his gaze was intense—hyper-focused, even. Not wanting to give him the satisfaction of scaring me, I stared right back, daring him to remove the button.

Whatever he saw in my eyes must've been enough because with the practiced flick of his wrist, he sliced through the cotton thread that held button to shirt. The plastic disc fell to the hardwood floor with an audible *tap, tap, tap.*

Dagger placed the tip of the knife to the next button, and the next, slicing through the fragile thread and exposing more of my torso. He watched my face when he removed the last button, his expression unreadable. All except for his eyes. They were blazing with heat—with desire.

I swallowed, his gaze darting to the column of my throat. I felt like I was in the presence of a predator. He ran his hand up the center of my body—the reverse of what he'd done before—with his palm coming to rest around my throat. He dropped his eyes to my breasts, the side of his mouth twitching like he was laughing at some private joke.

When all he did was stare, I tried to push off the wall. That slight movement brought his serious eyes back to my face.

Slowly, he shook his head, and I froze. Bringing the knife up between us, he showed me the sharp tip, turning it from side to side so the light caught the sharp surfaces. I watched—breathless—as he drew the tip slowly down to the front of my white lace bra and slid it between the lace and my body.

"Don't move," he breathed out, his green eyes staring almost unfocused down at where steel met flesh.

My heart gave a painful pound in my chest, instinct screaming at me to run away, that this was dangerous, that he could seriously hurt me, but underneath all that fear, all that worry, all that anxiety was a knowledge that Dagger was in control.

I could see that in the way his hand was steady.

His breathing was steady.

The blade cut through the lace in a single stroke. The two cups slid to the side, exposing my breasts to him. The straps dangled from my shoulders, and I left them there. I wouldn't show him how much I wanted to cover up, to hide myself from him. He wanted me to be afraid, but I wouldn't give him the satisfaction to see just how scared I was.

Slowly, as if remembering how to use his hand, he unwrapped the fingers from around my throat and cupped one of my breasts. His hand was warm and calloused against my skin, and my eyes shuddered shut when he flicked his thumb across my hard nipple. I moaned, my back arching involuntarily. It had been an expectionally long time since a man had touched me like this.

It had been even longer since I'd *wanted* a man to touch me like this.

A surprised look passed over his face briefly before he settled his expression back into cold indifference. He released my breast suddenly, and I almost cried out, almost told him to put his hand on me again, but I quickly realized that what was to come was going to be oh so much better.

He looked down at the waist of my pants, dipping the tip of the knife into the band. A small, abrupt exhale left my lips, but otherwise I remained motionless as he brought the sharp tip of steel to the button that fastened them together. He slid it through the cotton, neatly severing the button from my pants. With his free hand, he drew the zipper down and took a step backward. The dagger was held loosely in his right hand, his left hand, clenching and unclenching into a tight fist with each exhalation he took.

"Take them off." His rough command tightened things down low in my belly. When I made no move to do as he demanded, he added, "Now."

Sliding my thumbs into the loose waistband, I eased the fabric down my legs but paused when I got to my feet. I was still wearing stilettos.

Dagger said, "Leave the heels."

Letting out a long breath, I stepped from the legs of my pants, feeling the sway of my breasts from the bent position. When I straightened, his eyes were on my breasts. The bra was still clinging to my shoulders, and he approached me with the knife raised. Like before, he carefully slid the tip of the dagger under the straps and pushed them off my shoulders.

The blade was cold against my bare skin, but I felt a thrill thinking about having something that dangerous close to my body. My blood hummed and pulsed in anticipation. I was momentarily stunned by the reaction. I shouldn't like this. I despised women who gave themselves over to domineering men because they thought there was no other choice, and right now—in this moment—I hated myself for craving his touch.

I let out a gasp when he dragged the tip of the blade down my left shoulder and over my left breast, where he circled the point around my areola. I looked down, expecting to see a well of blood, but I noticed that the blade wasn't angled to cut. He held it so that the pressure was there but the cutting edge wasn't.

My head jerked up as I stared into his green eyes. They'd gone a little darker—with lust, with the desire to scare me.

Dagger said, "Edge play is a different way to purge your sins. Make you forget."

I wasn't sure if he was talking to me, or to himself, but as the blade skimmed along my waist, to my hip, then down the front of my panties, I didn't give a fuck. Gently, he rubbed the steel back and forth across me, moving lower by fractions of an inch until he reached my labia. He shifted the angle, making the blade less flat and more vertical, then continued stroking.

He slid the dull spine into my pussy, using the lace of my panties and my lips as a guide. I felt it push against my clit, and I gripped his wrist, stopping him. I stared into his face, trying to see what he was thinking. He was closed to me, but there was that flicker again—the one in his eyes that betrayed how he was feeling. Desire burned through him, and when I looked down his body, his erection was straining against his slacks.

"This is mine," he reminded me in dark voice that held a promise of pleasure.

Uncurling my fingers, I released my hold on him, feeling my breathing pick up. I was turned on, yes, but that hint of danger had more weight to it than it did before.

"Palms against the door behind you."

Taking in a deep breath, I did as he asked. Dagger slid the spine up and down—slowly—against my clit until I was panting and moaning, mewling and groaning, feeling an orgasm form like an atomic bomb detonating through my body.

The pleasure crested like a ravening wave, crashing over me, taking me down into the undertow. I came so hard that my vision turned spotty and my knees went weak. I remembered falling, but being caught in Dagger's strong arms. I blinked open my eyes to see him there, holding me, a look of astonishment on his usually unreadable face.

Wordlessly, he helped me up, gently corralling me back against the door then turning me around. I stood with my face pressed into the wood, my breasts and stomach too, while he pulled my hips away.

The cold bite of a blade was at my waist for a moment before he withdrew it—and my panties—away. I was standing there, completely naked, still riding the high of an orgasm I'd gotten from a fucking knife.

There was a *clang,* and I looked down to the find the dagger he'd been using on me on a small hall table not more than three feet away from us. I could reach for it if I wanted to, which meant Dagger knew this as well.

He wrapped his large hands around my hips, caressing the skin on my ass and lower back. His fingers were strong and sure. He knew how to touch a woman. He lifted one hand briefly, then I heard a zipper being lowered and the tell-tale rip of a foil packet. We were doing this. *I* was doing this. I was going to let this man have me in order to keep his silence.

All thoughts that this was wrong fled me when he stroked my ass then spanked me once on each cheek. Each strike was the perfect amount of pressure, and as he eased away the sting, I knew that even if there wasn't blackmail involved, I would've fallen into this man's bed in the end. For whatever reason, I was drawn to him.

"Bite down on this."

I blinked and refocused on the room. Dagger was holding out his leather belt, the length of it folded in on itself about three times until it was half a foot long and thick enough for me to sink my teeth into.

"What for?" And yes, my breath sounded that wanton.

"This neighborhood doesn't hear screaming very often." He stroked a hand down the length of my spine, like he was picturing it was something else. "And with the way I fuck, you'll be screaming out in pleasure *a lot.*"

Somehow, I didn't doubt him.

I opened my mouth, slid the belt in between my lips, and bit down.

11

Dagger

FOR NOT THE FIRST TIME TONIGHT, I MARVELED AT the woman in front of me. I'd brought her to orgasm with a knife and nothing else. She responded to my touch, to my cues. She was just as turned on by danger as I was. I guess you don't become a cop by being squeamish around dangerous situations, just like you didn't join the Marines if you had a sense of self-preservation.

It made me wonder what had happened in Chantelle Cox's life that had molded her to be that way. Whatever it was, the fact that she'd gotten off on knife play had been a surprise to her.

I watched as she bit down on the leather belt in between her teeth, feeling my dick getting harder and harder. This beautiful creature didn't submit to just anyone, but she was submitting to me.

Was I an asshole for forcing her into this? Maybe. Yeah.

Did I give a fuck?

Zero.

Fucks.

Given.

Stepping back so I was behind her once more, I stared at the curve of her ass, the gentle slope of her back. She worked out so her muscles were firm beneath her skin. Strong. As I ran my fingers up and down her back, all I could think of was marking it—marking her.

I spanked her ass once, and she moaned. She writhed. She rocked her hips backward and forward like she could already feel my dick between her thighs. Forcing her legs open a little wider, I prepared to give her what she needed. Fisting my cock, I lined myself up and pushed into her tight, wet sheath. She felt fucking phenomenal—so phenomenal that I was forced to chew the inside of my cheek to stop myself from telling her every illicit thought cycling through my mind. She gloved my cock perfectly, her inner walls clamping down in an almost bruising grip. Wrapping her hair around my fist, I pushed into her lower back, exaggerating the bow in her spine.

Jerking my hips back, I slammed into her again, driving myself so deep that I knew she would be feeling it tomorrow morning. She grasped desperately at my arm, digging her fingers in—not to pull me away. To hold me more tightly. I was getting off on knowing she was drowning in the pleasure of my cock inside her.

I pounded into her pussy, feeling my balls tighten as my release fought its way to the front too fucking quickly.

"Oh, fuck, I'm—" Chantelle started to say but stopped herself.

"You're what?" I demanded, the question coming out between clenched teeth because pleasure was barreling through my body and making black stars bloom in front of my eyes.

"I'm going to come."

"You come when I tell you to come. Understood?"

She whimpered.

I pulled her hair a little more tightly. "*Understood?* Talk to me, *cara*."

"Fuck you. Yes, I understand," she whispered, rolling her hips to take more of me.

With a dark chuckle, I tightened my grip on her hair and pounded even harder, slamming my pelvis against her ass. The fleshy slap of dirty, violent sex filled the air, the constant *slap, slap, slap* driving my hips faster. I had a brief thought that I wanted to pull out, snatch the condom away and slam back inside her so I could mark her—inside and out.

A low moan escaped her throat right before her inner walls clamped down on my cock.

"Not yet," I hissed in warning, swatting her on the ass. An accompanying moan was torn from her throat, and I knew she couldn't wait much longer. Being the sick fuck I was, I wanted to see how far I could push her. I wanted to hear her beg for it.

This time it was a mewl of pain that I echoed in a harsh bark. She dug her nails into my arm, drawing blood. When her desperation was clawing at her, I bit out, "Beg me. Beg me to let you come."

"Please," she whimpered. "Please, Dagger, please."

A thrill of power went through me. "Come, *cara*. Come."

She came cursing my name, drawing more blood on my arm. I didn't give a shit about the scratches. As far as I was concerned, she could bleed me as much as she liked when we fucked.

I waited until the contractions eased, then slowed my thrusts until just the head of my dick entered her. She was panting hard as she looked at me over her shoulder. Her gray eyes were accusatory. Nope, there was no post-coital glow for Detective Chantelle Cox. Slowly, like I was retreating from a skittish animal, I released my hold on her hair. She straightened and spun around to face me in one swift movement, her back plastered to the door.

Harsh breaths barreled from her, her breasts rising and falling quickly. Her skin was flushed with sweat, and my attention was drawn to her mouth as she sucked in her bottom lip.

Unrolling the condom from my still hard cock, I threw it to the ground. Her slate-gray eyes dropped to my groin and I crooked my finger at her. She came, stopping a foot in front of me.

I pressed down on the top of her shoulders, urging her to her knees.

Looking up at me, she asked, "Why were you at the scene of the crime?"

Ignoring her question, I touched her pretty mouth, pulling the plump flesh of her bottom lip down with my thumb. "I want to be bare when I release inside you. Whether it's your mouth or your cunt, I don't care, but I have a feeling you do."

"Why were you at the scene of the crime?" she repeated, undeterred.

Growling, I said, "I want to come in your throat. I want to watch you getting off on that and all you want to know is where I was tonight? You can't let shit go, can you?"

She shook her head. "You're distracting me on purpose, but I *will* get your answer."

Before I could tell her to drop it, her fuckable lips were wrapped around my shaft, and she swallowed down more than half my length. I groaned, grabbing a handful of her hair and closing my fist around it. She drew back then took me again, covering more of me this time. Through slitted eyes, I watched her swallow inch after inch of my cock until her lips were pressed to my body. Her tongue swirled around my shaft, teasing me. She licked up the length, running the tip of her tongue over the head of my cock and massaging the glans.

"Fuuuck." It sounded like a multi-syllabic word, pleasure drawing the sound out of my throat. With my hand still wrapped in her hair, I took her jaw in the other hand and held her immobile. I wanted complete control when I came.

Flexing my hips forward, I slammed into the wet recess of her mouth, her teeth scraping lightly over the top of my dick and making me groan. I withdrew slowly before slamming in once more. This time she choked, her convulsing throat adding another layer to my already overflowing cup of sensations. Movement caught my eye, and I saw that she had slid her hand down between her thighs. Like before, she was masturbating while I fucked her mouth, and just like that, I knew my battle was over.

My balls bunched up tight, and I drew back a little to see the crown of my cock and the cum that spilled from it. It hit the back of her throat and tongue, as I came in her mouth. She swallowed me back inside, taking me to the back of her throat as she came too. Her groans turned to vibrations though, as she found her release and the feeling of it made me shudder.

I stepped back from her, feeling like my legs maybe wouldn't hold me up. When I was sure I wouldn't collapse, I stared down at her. She ran her fingertip under her mouth, tasting me all over again.

"Fuck," I breathed.

She got to her feet in one elegant motion. "Tell me why you were at the scene of a crime tonight."

I barked a humorless laugh. "You're like a fucking dog with a bone."

"I'm persistent. It's what makes me a good cop."

Shaking my head, I wondered how long I could drag this out. I couldn't tell her the truth, but I could tell her a version of the truth—one that didn't incriminate Bane or me.

"I had a friend in that building."

"*Had* a friend? Past tense." She narrowed her gray eyes, and the effect of them would've been much more intimidating if she weren't buck naked, her skin flushed from the orgasms I'd given her.

"I'm going to take a shower," I told her, leaving the option open to her if she wanted to follow or if she wanted to stay. I smirked when I heard her trail behind me. She hesitated at the doorway to the bathroom, like she just realized what she was doing. Ignoring her, I leaned into the shower and turned on the hot water. I stripped out of my pants and left them pooled on the bathroom floor. Stepping into the shower, I glanced over at Chantelle and caught her staring.

I crooked my finger.

She came. Her steps were hesitant at first, but when her eyes drifted down to my naked body and my already semi-hard dick, I knew she wanted more of what I could give her.

Placing myself directly under the spray, I cupped her breasts, feeling her nipples harden. She arched into my touch, filling my hands more completely. Leaning down, I kept my eyes on her face. This woman was still my enemy, despite the position she currently found herself in. I sucked on one nipple. A gasp. A shudder. Fucking surrender under my mouth, lips, and tongue. I rolled her sensitive flesh around, biting down gently, learning what she liked. Switching to her other nipple, I gave it the same treatment until her hands fisted in my hair—the tension of her grip sharp and painful.

Kissing my way up her chest, I licked along her collarbone, up her neck, across her jaw.

I hovered my lips over her mouth when she jerked back and hissed, "No kissing. It's too intimate."

I smiled, and there was nothing friendly about it. She trusted me enough for edge play but not enough to put my mouth to hers?

When my words came out, they were far more emotionally charged than I'd intended. "I can shove my dick in your mouth and come all over your tongue, but I can't kiss you?"

She gaped at me, as if the reminder of what she'd done no less than five minutes ago was somehow forgotten. "This is blackmail. Treat it like it is."

"As you wish, Detective." Reaching down between her legs, I slid two fingers into her wet sheath. She gasped, her fists closing more tightly around my hair. I pumped my fingers in and out.

In.

Out.

In.

Out.

Until she mewled softly. Her slickness covered my fingers, and if I hadn't known any better, I would've said she enjoyed the way I took control. Chantelle hooked one thigh around my hip, her own hips moving in that subtle wave that women had when they were turned the fuck on and wanted a hard cock to fill them.

I pulled my fingers out and grabbed my length. It kicked in my hand. I lined myself up, the head brushing past her full, wet cunt. I had to bite back the groan when I swept through her soft folds, knowing that just a little push and I'd be inside her. Fuck, I wanted to be inside her bare.

She'd stiffened in my arms, obviously aware of what I'd been thinking.

"Tell me to stop," I said. "Tell me to stop, and I will."

She was quiet for a moment, the sound of the water pounding down on naked flesh the only thing to take away from the tension. She let out a shuddered breath and unhooked her leg, taking an unsteady step away from me. Looking up at me with her slate gray eyes, I tried to decipher whatever it was that she was seeing. It was beyond me, beyond this shower, my house. It was far away from this place, and I wasn't even sure it was this time. She had that haunted look of someone reliving something terrible from their past.

Chantelle took another step back, tripping over her feet. I reached for her, but she caught herself on the glass door before I could get to her, righting herself. Water was beading down her skin, dripping from the ends of her blonde hair. I watched her impassively as she stepped from the shower stall and left the bathroom.

Seeing her walking away from me hurt, but I wasn't sure why that was. She was nothing to me. A means to an end. She was my guarantee of protection for Bane, but that didn't seem to matter. Something had broken inside her just then, and I wanted to find out what it was, *who* it was, then put a fucking bullet in that person's skull.

The feeling was so foreign, so unexpected that I couldn't move for a full minute. I only snapped out of my reverie when I heard the front door slam shut.

12

Cox

IT WAS TOO BRIGHT TO BE OUTSIDE THIS EARLY WITH so little sleep under my belt. Sliding on a pair of shades, I put my car in park and stared out at the usually quiet suburban street. I was in Burbank, as white-collar, family-centered and close-knit as you could get in California. Usually, any crimes that were committed here ran along the line of burglary rather than murder.

Today was a day that bucked against the norm.

Today was the day that would stain everyone's memories.

There were at least a dozen police cars lining the street, along with two ambulances, one fire truck, and about twenty-five concerned citizens and neighbors huddling around the yellow police tape, trying to get a look at a corpse.

I opened the door to my unmarked and stepped out, making my way across the road to the house that looked like it should've been on the cover of *Home Beautiful*. One of the uniformed cops lifted the tape before I could get there, waving me through. Ducking under the tape, I stepped on the footpath that wound toward the front door, being careful not to stand too close to the edge and have my stiletto heels sink into the lawn.

Despite the water restrictions currently in place for the state, this lawn was lush and vibrant green—the kind of color that could only come from regular watering and tending. Given the neighborhood, I wasn't surprised.

I walked to the front of the property, my heels clicking angrily against the asphalt as if my rage was channeling through my body and down to my feet. There was a small table set up on the porch. Forensic gloves. Hand sanitizer. Booties for shoes. Extra trash bags. Snapping two gloves from the box, I slid them on and entered the house.

To my left was a man with his arm wrapped around the shoulders of a woman, who was sobbing into her hands. He looked up as I entered, the pain in his eyes unmistakable. I looked away, focusing on my task instead.

"The body is upstairs."

I turned to look at the uniformed officer who'd spoken. "Thanks, Franklins."

His eyes flared like he couldn't believe I'd remembered who he was, but he quickly settled his expression back into his good, empty cop face. I took the stairs to the second level, already feeling like something was off about this crime. The carpets on the landing were a pale honey color that stretched out and beyond into the four bedrooms I could see from my vantage point. To my left was another door where a marble lip across the bottom told me it was the bathroom.

Outside the room directly ahead of me, a trash bag sagged

on the floor, and the sound of a camera clicking and the soft murmurs of investigators could be heard. I stepped into the room, my eyes landing on the body slumped in the king-size bed. It took my brain a moment to piece together what it was seeing. The vic was male. Blond hair. Shirtless, but not naked, so I could see he had a swimmer's body. He couldn't have been any older than eighteen.

I scanned the rest of the room, learning what I could about him before his life was snuffed out. There was a football helmet on one of the shelves, along with a bunch of trophies. Some looked old—peewee league, perhaps—while others were from the last few years. Scattered through the trophies were framed photos of the kid with his parents. There were also quite a few with the vic and a young brunette woman. Some of the images were candid shots of her, while others were more formal like the ones of them at junior prom. Jesus, I didn't need a reminder that the kid was young.

I looked over at the body on the bed. "Why is there so much blood on the chin?" I asked out loud.

Ella Murdoch was already there, and she waved me over. "His tongue was cut out." She opened up the boy's mouth, and I got a look inside.

"Cut out? Are they sending a message?"

Ella shrugged her slender shoulders. "Maybe?"

"What killed him?"

"GSW to the stomach. My guess is they had a suppressor on the gun to dampen the noise. That would explain why the parents didn't wake. The kid bled out in his own bed while his parents were asleep in the other room."

That was a messed-up way to go—not that I'd ever say that out loud. "Who is he?" Maybe knowing that would give me a lead on why he was killed so violently and cruelly.

"His name is Troy Anwa."

"Anwa like Denis Anwa of Energize?" Energize were the biggest producer of wind turbines in the USA and was one of Forbes Fortune 500 companies.

"That was the man downstairs. He was the one who found his son."

Jesus. Having a high-profile case like this was going to be hard to keep out of the media. "Why the hell was I called in? This seems like a straightforward homicide."

Ella's gaze darted to the closet. "Take a look in there."

I frowned then did as she asked, pulling open the closet door. It looked like an ordinary closet until my eyes shifted up to the shelf above all the clothes. There were five bricks of cocaine sitting there, metaphorically flapping in the wind.

"What the hell?" I turned back to Ella. "Is that what I think it is?"

She nodded, her long brown ponytail streaked with gray sliding against her shoulder. "It sure is."

"Fuck." I pulled down one of the bricks and turned it over in my hands. The packaging was clean, so we weren't dealing with the same supplier as the other two murders. I turned back to the body—that's what it was now. Not Troy Anwa. Not Denis Anwa's son. The body. This murder couldn't have been done by the same killer as the other two dealers. For one, they were too messy. The other shots were to the chest or head—not the stomach. Secondly, this kill seemed too intimate. Anything more than a bullet to the heart, and you were starting to talk about the perp being someone who knew their victim.

"This kill was personal."

I looked over at Mayberry. The question now was just how personal was it? "Yeah, it was."

Harper's words were suddenly echoing through my mind. Was this the hit her John told her about? And if it was, what was the motive?

"Detective?"

Blinking rapidly, I cleared my throat and said, "Do you have an estimated time of death?"

"Rigor has set in so somewhere between three and eight hours."

I glanced at my watch. It was a little after eight in the morning. "All right. Bag everything up for evidence. I'm going to go speak to his parents."

I snapped off the gloves and shoved them into the trash bag just outside the door. Downstairs, I found the boy's parents in the same room, in the same huddled position.

"Denis Anwa?" I asked. At his shaky nod, I said, "I'm Detective Cox, and I'm going to find out who did this to Troy."

As soon as I said their son's name, his wife moaned, like the very sound of her baby boy's name caused her pain. I shut my eyes for a moment, took in a deep breath, then let it out. I knew that pain, but it wouldn't be helping me on this case.

"I know this is difficult, but were you aware of your son's involvement in distributing drugs?"

Denis startled like I'd just pulled a gun on him. "What do you mean *drugs*?"

"I mean there were at least five keys of coke in his closet. That much isn't for personal use. He was either dealing or holding it for someone else."

"Troy was a good boy," his mother said in a shaky voice. "He would never do anything like that."

"Mrs. Anwa, ma'am, I'm sorry, but evidence doesn't lie. What I can do is promise you I *will* find his killer. I just need to know who his friends were. That might help me find out where he got the drugs."

"He would never deal drugs," his mother hissed. There was fire in her words—her rage had finally caught up with her grief.

"Maybe not, ma'am, but it doesn't change the fact that there were drugs in his bedroom. I have to approach this case as if he was."

"He would never…" she whispered, burying her head back into her husband's shoulder.

"He was a popular kid at school," Denis said quickly, trying to smooth things over. He needn't have bothered for my sake. "I don't recall the names of his friends. He never brought them here because he didn't want to be judged because of my wealth."

This kid sounded too smart—too sensitive. He didn't sound like a drug dealer. But if he wasn't a drug dealer, who the hell was he, and why had he drawn enough attention to get himself killed?

"What time did he go to bed?"

He glanced at his wife for confirmation before he said, "Around ten, maybe? No later than eleven."

"Did either of you check on him before you went to bed?"

"He's an eighteen-year-old kid. He wouldn't appreciate that," Denis replied.

"So, he could've snuck someone in through the window after you both went to bed?"

His face screwed up like the idea was distasteful. Hell, maybe it was for him. He had his life ordered. Trophy wife. Jock son. Money lining his pockets.

"And neither of you heard anything?"

Denis shook his head slowly, processing what I'd just told him. "Nothing."

I had to look at this from a different angle. "What were you doing yesterday afternoon?"

He rubbed his wife's shoulders—absently, like he didn't realize he was doing it. "Troy came with me to an art gallery in Brookside. We were looking for a new piece for his room."

From the inside pocket of my jacket, I pulled out a notepad and pen. "Which gallery was this?"

"Sanderson's."

I paused. Looked up. "*Peter* Sanderson?"

"Yes, that's the one. He had a new artist's work displayed, and Troy wanted to see it."

"Did you purchase a piece?"

"Yes. I filled out the order form before we left. It's due to be delivered later in the week." His words slowly dropped off as he spoke, like he was finally realizing his son wouldn't be able to enjoy his new artwork like he'd planned.

I didn't believe in coincidences, and this was too big to ignore.

"Thank you, Mr. Anwa. If you think of anything, don't hesitate to reach out."

I left them with my card and drove out to Brookside.

PETER SANDERSON'S TIE WAS BRIGHT ORANGE—GARISH against his dark plum suit. He greeted me with a smile and a firm handshake.

"Detective, it's a pleasure to see you again."

"I'm working a case, Sanderson. A case where your name has

come up twice now."

He looked startled, holding a hand to his chest like he couldn't believe it. "Whatever do you mean?"

Not buying the whole innocent act, I asked, "Can you confirm Mr. Denis Anwa and his son, Troy, were here yesterday afternoon?"

"Yes, they were. They purchased a piece from me."

"Which one?"

"'Rage.'"

My eyes darted to the piece with the torn canvas. "When is it due for delivery?"

"Later this week."

I took another look through the gallery, wondering what I was missing. Harper had said this guy's territory and Bane's ran up against each other's. Bane's dealers were getting hit. And now this kid had been found with drugs in his closet. Were the two cases linked? And if they were, what was the connection? My gaze shifted back to Sanderson who was staring at me with cold, dead eyes once more.

He seemed to do that—slip between his good-old-boy persona and this one. This one gave me the same feeling as if I was looking at an adder dead in the eyes. "Is there anything else I can help you with, Detective?"

"No."

"Can I offer you some advice then?"

"If you feel you have to."

He smiled, but it didn't reach his dead eyes. "Speak with Mr. Rivera. If you're looking to cut the head off the snake, that is where you should start."

I frowned. "Why do you have such a hard-on for Rivera?"

His responding laugh was deprecating. "I don't like scum like him ruining our fair city."

Narrowing my eyes at him, I said, "Scum or competition to your drug empire?"

I watched him carefully, waiting for a change in his expression, but he remained immobile. "Why would you think that I deal drugs?"

"I didn't say you dealt drugs. I'm saying you're the head of a drug empire."

"And who is your source of this information?"

"Nobody you're acquainted with, I can assure you."

He pulled at the cuff of his shirt, tugging it down. *A nervous tell?* "Is that what Rivera told you?"

"Why would you think that?" I replied. He hadn't denied it yet, but I also had no proof. "I'll be in touch with you soon, Mr. Sanderson."

Turning on my heel, I left the gallery. It was barely ten in the morning, but the heat of the day was oppressive. As if my bare acknowledgment of the weather was enough, sweat started to bead on my brow and trickled down between my breasts. I walked back in the direction of my car, which I'd parked in the lot at the rear.

Pulling out my phone, I hit redial on the number Harper called me on.

She answered on the third ring. "Paris here."

"Harper? Cox."

There was an audible sigh on the other end of the line. "I've told you everything I know."

"I know, but I have one more question."

The sound of sheets slithering over skin. The soft murmur of a man's voice. Then there was a click like a door shutting. "If I can answer it for you, I will."

"Did your John tell you *where* he was going to be when he canceled your date last night?"

She stayed quiet for too long.

"Harper?"

"He's in the bed right now." Her voice was low—whispery. "He called early this morning. Asked if we could meet up."

"What time did he call?"

"A little after four."

Four in the morning was the middle of the death range. "What's his name, Harper?"

"I can't tell you that."

"He killed a boy last night. An eighteen-year-old kid is dead because your John's boss told him to make the hit."

There was a long, shuddering breath then, "He had blood on his clothes when he came to me. I asked him how it had gotten there, he refused to tell me, but he did let it slip that he killed *them*."

Them.

More than one person.

Another call came through.

"I have to go. Harper, get out of there. Now."

I hung up and answered the waiting call.

Captain Holt was on the other end. "Get down to South Breed and 7th Street. There's been a double homicide."

13

Dagger

I COULDN'T GET MY MIND OFF COX—HOW SHE'D LEFT my place after I'd brought her to orgasm, how she'd looked at me. I hadn't seen her for nearly twenty-four hours, and although I could've shown up at her place, I felt that she needed some space. I frowned at the thought. Since when had I ever done something differently on account of someone's feelings?

Fuck, this woman was getting under my skin.

"Hey, Dagger."

I turned my head toward the end of the bar to find Chastity. She held open the door that led into the staff area, ushering through Sierra Storm. Dressed in clean jeans and an oversized vintage rock T-shirt that swamped her small body, her face was clean of grime, and I realized she was going to be a fucking looker when she was older.

Her wide-eyed gaze darted around the Dollhouse, taking it

all in. Chas watched her just as carefully as I did, wondering what her next reaction was going to be. When Sierra looked back at me, a glint of excitement lit up her face.

"What do you think, kid?"

"This is amazing."

I glanced around, trying to see what she saw. Bane had created this place to be exclusive, to demand a six-figure membership fee to attend. The décor was rich reds and glittering golds. The walls were black, the poles and stages where the Dolls danced were polished to within an inch of perfection. Plush red velvet couches and dark brown leather chesterfield armchairs were scattered around, all oriented to get the best view of the Dolls while they worked.

She turned to Chas. "Do you really work here?"

The other woman nodded.

"Chas is one of the best," I said. "Want to see where you'll be spending most of your time?"

Sierra nibbled on her bottom lip. "Sure."

I led the way to the five private rooms. "Room one is the exhibitionist room." I opened the door and showed her inside. There was a single black leather couch in the center of the room facing a curtained window and a bed against the wall behind it.

"Why are there drapes in here?" Sierra asked.

I jerked my chin at Chas and she stepped out of the room. A moment later, the drapes parted and we saw Chastity on the other side of the glass. She took a seat on the bench facing the window and waved.

"Consenting voyeurs sit out there and watch the patrons who enjoy exhibitionism." I walked across the room to the concealed door in the rear of the room. Sierra made a small surprised noise, and I turned to look at her. "This is how you'll get in and out of the room. There's a hallway behind all of the private rooms. There's also a supply cupboard with the cleaning products you'll need. There's a bathroom, as well as a kitchenette where you can make yourself something to eat between cleans."

I walked out of the exhibitionist room and into the private hallway, crooking my finger at Sierra to follow. The walls were black with small dim lights running in a track along them. It was enough light to see with, but not bright enough to be intrusive under the doors of the rooms.

Along the longest wall of the hall were the four remaining doors to the other rooms. I pointed them out to her, then to the one directly behind us. "That's your private entry. You can get there through the staff wing of the club."

She bit her bottom lip again, and I realized she did it when she was nervous. "How will I know when they're done?"

"When the Dolls leave, they push a button beside the door." I pointed up at the ceiling. "A red light will come on when they leave. The door will lock behind them so you won't ever have someone walk in on you while you're cleaning."

Once more, she worried her bottom lip with her teeth. Shit.

"Sierra, if you feel like you can't do this, it's okay. I can get someone else."

"No, no, I can do it. It's just…" She hugged her arms around her torso like she was holding herself together. "I don't have to actually… you know…" She let her sentence drift off, and I whispered a curse.

"Fuck, no, Sierra. You're just a kid. You're under my protection, but I can assure you nobody will even know you're here. You can stay back here the whole night, and nobody will bother you.

There's one other girl who cleans for us too. Her name's Velvet. You can shadow her… work together on the rooms." Reaching out, I patted her shoulder. "You're safe here, kid."

She stared up into my face, and a slow smile spread across her lips. "Okay."

Jesus, such trust in me already. I didn't know whether that was a good thing or a bad thing. Gruffly, I said, "Come on, I'll show you the other rooms so you know what to expect when you go in to clean them."

Opening up the door marked with a '2,' I showed her into the cuckholding room. "This room is for men who want to explore cuckholding."

Sierra's nose wrinkled. "What's that? It sounds painful."

"The cuck, the husband in this instance, brings his wife here to have sex with another man or woman. Everyone is consenting, but the idea behind the humiliation is a power-play dynamic."

"Men actually *like* that?"

"Some do."

"Do you?" she asked in a whisper.

The idea of Cox with another man made me want to commit murder.

Sierra licked her lips nervously. "Forget I asked. Sorry," she said in a rush.

When I was sure my temper was under control, I said, "It's forgotten. Want to see the next one?"

She nodded.

Room three was the most traditional-looking setting among all the rooms. A king-size bed was against one wall, complete with side tables filled with lube and condoms. Black armoires were pressed against one wall, each of them containing male and female costumes of varying sizes along with props.

Sierra walked over to one and opened it, looking inside. "Costumes?" she asked, puzzled.

I leaned against the jamb and folded my arms. "This is the role play room. Anything the patron wants, he can find. Once the costumes have been used, you'll be responsible for collecting them and ensuring they're cleaned and sanitized."

She nodded. "What's next?"

"Room four. The Shibari/bondage room." I showed her in and stepped back, letting her explore. There was a leather armchair in the center of the room along with a cupboard on the wall. Sierra opened it and touched the supply of shibari ropes, cuffs, scarves, and other toys. "A few of our Dolls are Riggers." At her raised brows, I added, "They do the tying. Generally, the men who use this room are Bottoms. We can't allow them to be Tops since it becomes a security issue."

Pushing off the frame, I walked back into the cleaning hallway and waited for Sierra to follow me out. I walked to the final door and opened it. The kid actually hesitated before stepping inside. Her blue eyes were wide as she took in the room. There was a Saint Andrews Cross against the wall, a spanking bench, a queening chair, bars and stocks suspended from the ceilings, a sex swing, and an array of whips, chains, paddles, and cuffs. The main attraction, though, was a giant four-poster bed with anchor points all over it.

"The BDSM room. Hardcore. This room has a bathroom attached for aftercare purposes. That will need to be cleaned regularly too."

"Got it."

We exited through the main door to the room and found

Chastity waiting for us.

She wrapped Sierra in a hug. "What do you think? Think you could work here?"

Sierra glanced over her shoulder at me. "Yeah, I think so."

"Amazing. I can't wait to see you here every night." Chas grinned at me. "Is there anything else she needs to know?"

"Just show her the staff room and showers. Get her a locker, and I'll do everything else."

Releasing Sierra, Chastity came over and kissed me on the cheek chastely. "Thank you. She's a good kid."

"Get out of here, you two," I replied gruffly.

My phone rang in my pocket as I watched them leave. Pulling the device out, I looked at the screen and answered the call.

"Caesar?"

"There've been two more hits. Boyle Heights."

"Rabbit and Red," I bit out. "When?"

"Don't know. I just got here, and the cops have already removed the bodies."

Shit. "Thanks, kid." I hung up and shoved the phone back into my pocket. Rabbit and Red were tight—shared a place together and all. This shit was getting out of control. Walking briskly, I went up the stairs to his office and stepped into the room.

After getting a look at my face, Bane hissed, "No," then slammed back a shot of whisky.

"Two more hits. Simultaneous."

He curled his free hand into a fist. "Who this time?"

"Rabbit and Red."

"Fuck."

"We need to retaliate, boss. Sitting here with our hands on our dicks is sending the wrong message."

Bane was out of his seat and around the other side of his desk, moving quickly. I tensed right before he slammed me against the wall, his thick forearm against my throat. Putting his face close to mine, he hissed, "You think I don't know that? You think I like sitting here waiting for the next dealer to go down?"

I gave him my blank face and said nothing. There was nothing I could say.

"Goddammit!" He wrenched himself away from me and began to pace in a tight line in front of the desk. He raked his hands through his hair, his fingers cranked into claws.

In a careful voice, I said, "I have a guy we can use. He'll find out what's going on, then dispose of the culprits discreetly if needed."

"Fucking do it."

I left his office and went down to mine. Shoving into my bathroom, I washed my face then pulled out my phone.

"Master Guns," Devil said. "If I didn't know any better, I'd have said you were missing me."

Fucking comedian. "I need your services."

"What do you need?" His whole tone of voice changed in a heartbeat—it was the instant switch from civilian to military trained.

"My boss is losing men. We need to know who it is then have them disposed of discreetly."

"Come to the office tomorrow morning. We can discuss details."

"Sure."

There was a beat of silence, then he added, "You still want to keep tabs on that vice cop?"

I ground my molars together. "Yeah."

"Hex put a tracker on her. I'll have him send you locations in real-time."

I shook my head. Knowing where she was at any given moment of the day was a fucking bad idea. Instead of saying as much, I said, "Fine."

"Done. I'll be in touch soon."

I hung up and stared at my reflection in the mirror. Fuck, I was wired, and I needed to let that frustration out somehow.

My phone *pinged* with a message.

It was from Hex.

"Damn, that boy works fast," I said to myself. Clicking into the message, I scanned what was written there and smiled.

I suddenly knew how to dull the edge of my need.

14

Cox

I COULDN'T BELIEVE I WAS MEETING THIS GUY. Marjory's nephew, Charlie, had called to confirm the time and location, claiming he was looking forward to meeting me. I should've called the whole thing off then, but I'd stopped myself. Maybe Marjory was right, and I needed to find the right kind of man instead of going after the bad boys.

Dagger was definitely one of the bad boys. Fuck, why the hell was I thinking about him now? Probably because his boss's drug dealers were getting hit. I'd finally been able to confirm that the crown was Bane Rivera's stamp on his drugs. I'd also searched the databases and found the names of at least another three known dealers who worked for him.

I was closing in on the bastard.

In the bathroom, I applied a little bit of makeup, keeping my face generally clear of anything too heavy, and fixed my hair. I tied it back into a twist, keeping that shit out of my face. Back in the bedroom, I'd laid out two outfits. One was a black pantsuit not dissimilar to what I wore every day for work. The other was a shift dress in dove gray. It brought out my eyes and fell just below my knees. I'd paired that outfit with glossy black pumps.

Trying on the gray dress, I slipped on the shoes, then looked in the mirror. I didn't look like myself. The color had softened my appearance. Made me vulnerable in some small way I couldn't put my finger on.

"Fucking ridiculous," I muttered to myself and reached behind me to unzip the dress. I froze when the doorbell rang, and I wondered whether I'd asked Charlie to pick me up instead of meeting him at the restaurant. Shit.

The bell rang again, right before someone began hammering against the wood.

I picked up my gun and held it down by my side as I walked to the door. Peering through the peephole for a second, I stepped back, trying to ignore the way heat rushed through my body. Fuck, it was like a Pavlovian response to stimuli, except Dagger was my stimuli, and my body knew exactly what he could do to it.

Sliding the chain across the door, I opened it the few inches it allowed. Dagger was dressed in a black button-down shirt tucked into a pair of black slacks. His green eyes slid down to the brass chain cutting a line across my chest, then returned to my face.

"Let me in, *cara*."

"What do you want?" I asked, not budging an inch. I wouldn't let this man control more of my life. My body, he seemed to already have. My thoughts were quickly joining it, but I could control whether I let him into my personal space or not.

"Let me in, and I'll tell you."

"No." I tried to shut the door, but he shoved against it, snapping the chain in the slide. I backed away from the door—not from fear—but from a terrible desire to run to him. His hungry gaze tracked down my body, taking in the dress and the heels. When his eyes returned to my face, his mouth was parted.

"Where are you going?"

"On a date... not that it's any of your business."

"It is my business, *cara*. I told you I don't share."

"Fuck you, Dagger. You can't control who I choose to date."

He stepped forward menacingly, his hands curling into loose fists at his sides. "Where are you going?"

"I'm not telling you a thing so you might as well leave."

He was suddenly in front of me, and out of instinct, I brought my gun up between us. Given how closely we were standing, it was angled up under his ribs—a kill shot. Whether he realized this or not, he didn't seem to care. Did he think I wouldn't do it?

He looked down between our bodies and smirked. "You like danger when you fuck."

"You make me nervous," I admitted and wished I hadn't. Men like him didn't need extra encouragement.

"This is how you treat something that makes you nervous?" He cocked his head to the side, watching me.

"What the fuck do you want?"

"You. On your knees. Now."

Heat shot through me, but I shook my head. I wasn't going to suck his cock when I was getting ready for a date with another man. "You don't get the right to mark your fucking territory with me."

He wrapped a large palm around the front of my throat, applying just enough pressure to be pleasurable. His thumb stroked across my pulse, teasing my body, driving my need higher with nothing more than a little restraint. "Call him. Tell him the date's off."

I frowned. Even though that's what I'd been thinking about not more than ten minutes ago, I wasn't going to do it. "No."

His free hand landed on my hip. My gun was still pressed against his ribs, but he hardly took notice of it. He slid his palm down my thigh then under the hem of my dress. My eyes shuddered closed as he touched my inner thigh, moving higher until he stroked my pussy through the fabric of my panties. It felt good, so I dug the gun in a little harder.

He sucked in a hiss even as he shoved the scrap of silk aside and stroked into me. My fingers tightened on the butt of my gun, and I had a choice. I could either hold my position and potentially shoot him by accident, or I could drop the weapon. I released my fingers, letting the gun clatter to the floor.

Dagger smirked and leaned down, catching my mouth in a fierce, possessive kiss. His tongue plunged inside me. I kissed him back, unable to stop myself. Fighting with the man was a fucking aphrodisiac I never knew I liked. Another finger slid into my pussy, and he pumped them in and out—slowly—like he knew he was torturing me with his touch. My hips writhed as I tried to take more of him into my body. I hated this man, but as soon as he touched me, all I wanted was him.

His thumb circled my clit, applying pressure to the tiny knot of flesh that could give me such pleasure.

"Come for me, *cara*," he breathed into my ear, biting down on my earlobe. "Come so hard I have to catch you."

I screamed out my release, feeling my knees go weak as I did. Waves of pleasure washed over me, dragging me to a place where I was sure I'd forgotten to breathe. My eyes fluttered open. He was staring at me with something akin to wonder in his eyes. I moaned when his fingers slid free of my body. He brought two digits to his mouth and sucked them clean, his forest green gaze on me the entire time.

I trembled. "Get out." The words came out as a whisper. Clearing my throat, I tried again. "Get out, you motherfucking *bastard.*"

He released me abruptly, making me stumble back a step, and walked to the door. His expression shifted as he stepped from my apartment—the look was a dark promise to come back and finish what he started. I shut the door behind him, flipping the only other functional lock into place. My chest was rising and falling too quickly, forcing me to collapse onto my couch and lower my head between my knees. I jerked upward again when I touched the edge of my panic, touched that place where I never wanted to be afraid of any man ever again.

But I wasn't afraid of Dagger.

I was afraid of what he could make me feel.

I was terrified that he'd be able to breach my walls of self-control and self-denial. I didn't deserve to be happy. I didn't deserve anything. So why was I going on this date?

Standing, I stalked back into my bedroom and snatched up my phone, bringing up the messaging app. I typed out a quick 'Sorry, I won't be able to make it,' but paused when it came to sending it. Going on this date would enrage Dagger, and the spiteful part of me wanted him to suffer.

I deleted the message and finished getting ready.

CHARLIE HARTNETT WAS TALL AND HAD DARK HAIR AND

brown eyes the same shade as milk chocolate. He was waiting for me outside the restaurant, Rivera, with a bunch of flowers and a gentle smile. I studied his face as I approached and automatically put him into the 'too soft' category, which startled me. I usually went for non-threatening men, men who didn't physically intimidate me. So, why the sudden change of heart?

I shook my head, and Charlie's smile faltered. "Are the flowers too much?" he asked, lowering his arm. "Aunt Marjory said you might like them."

"Marjory is a sweetheart, but I'm not a flowers and candy girl."

He stood there, unsure what to do with the gift until I reached out and gently took them from him.

"Thank you in any case."

His smile made another appearance, but it was just a smile. There was no conceited arrogance. No dirty comment to accompany it.

"Shall we?" He gestured to the restaurant door, and I nodded.

I walked forward, and he rushed the grab the door. He pulled it wide and ushered me inside.

I had never been to Rivera before. The interior matched the exterior—sleek and industrial—with steel and glass for almost every surface.

"May I help you?" a man with a British accent asked a few steps in.

"I have a reservation for two. Under Hartnett," Charlie answered.

The man looked down at his tablet, scrolling through the digital page with his finger. He stopped, tapped, then looked back up.

"Of course. Your table is ready." With one arm out wide, he ushered us into the restaurant where nearly three dozen copper trimmed tables glistened in the ambient lights. At the back of the room was, what I assumed, a private dining room with reflective glass on all sides. The man stopped at a table, and I took the seat that faced the door, leaving my purse and the small bunch of roses on the floor by my feet.

What could I say? Old habits died hard.

Charlie sat opposite, looking around at the other diners. "I've wanted to try this place for a while," he said, sitting back in his seat as a server magically appeared and settled a napkin on his lap. The man turned to me, but I shook my head. I could shake out my own damn napkin.

"So, Aunt Marjory says you're a detective with vice?"

"Yes."

"Wow. That sounds like it could be exciting."

I raised a brow at him and took a sip from my water glass. "It's dangerous. Dirty. You see the worst in people."

Charlie blinked at me—long and slow—like he wasn't sure what he could possibly say to that.

Jesus-fucking-Christ. "I'm sorry. I'm really out of practice with this whole dating thing."

He grinned, making him look younger than I'd originally thought he was. "Me too."

"How old are you?"

He startled, then recovered with a sip of water. "Twenty-six."

"I'm a whole decade older than you."

That grin was back. "I don't mind."

Jesus. We were in Cougar Country. I took another sip of water and looked around for the waiter needing something stronger to get through this night. As I scanned the restaurant, I felt like someone was staring at me. I was starting my second pass of the room when my gaze snagged on Dagger. He was sitting a few tables away. His dark green eyes skated in Charlie's direction first before returning to my face.

Fuck. How in the hell did he know I was going to be here? Had he followed me?

"—would you like? Chantelle?"

"What?" I snapped, refocusing on Charlie.

He gestured to the waitress standing by our table. "I was just asking whether you wanted red or white with dinner?"

"Vodka tonic, please," I replied, my eyes straying to Dagger.

Charlie looked over his shoulder then asked, "Is everything okay? You look like you've seen a ghost."

"Fine," I replied. "Just thought I saw someone I knew, that's all."

He nodded and picked up his menu, looking through the options. He was talking about something, but I couldn't focus on a word he was saying because Dagger had brought a knife onto his thigh, and he was stroking it under the table. He knew I could see it there, and the look on his face said he wanted me to.

"Will you excuse me?" I said abruptly, cutting Charlie off. I rose from my seat, balling up the napkin and leaving it beside my water glass.

"Sure," Charlie replied even as I left the table and made my way to the restrooms. I needed to get a grip on myself. The restrooms were down a long hallway with multiple doors coming off of it. I looked for the universal sign for the ladies' room and was about to open the door when I felt someone grab my wrist. It was Dagger. His eyes were burning with heat, and I didn't need to know what he was thinking. Every single thought was on his face to see. He stabbed on the bar to the emergency exit door with a sharp jerk of his hand, dragging me out into the alley beside the restaurant.

I wrenched my arm from his grip, twisting my wrist toward his thumb at the same time as I pulled away. Stepping back, I was brought to an abrupt stop when the brick wall came to meet me. My chest rose and fell with my harsh breathing, the adrenaline from his abrupt appearance still working through my body.

With a fluid grace, he stalked closer. "I told you... I. Don't. Share." His voice was a low, crawling growl that instantly turned me on.

Licking my lips, I said, "And I told *you*... you can't tell me what to do or who to date."

With a too-fast movement, he wrapped his large hand around the back of my neck and pulled me against his body. His chest was hard—unyielding against the softness of my breasts. His other hand tore the pins from my hair, sending it unfurling over my shoulder. It didn't stay loose for long. Grabbing the end of my hair, he twisted it around his wrist until I couldn't move.

Pinned between the wall and him with one hand controlling my head and the other on my neck made my brain and body disconnect. He was completely dominating me—physically. Mentally. And I wanted him to. My hips rolled forward against his groin in the hopes that I could feel how turned on he was.

A whimper escaped my mouth as the hardness of him rubbed against my aching center.

"Jesus *Christ*," he whispered harshly. Releasing the control on my neck, he reached between our bodies and pulled up the hem of my dress, bunching it at my waist. There was a tearing sound, and I knew that my panties were fluttering to the ground.

"I'm going to fuck you, *cara*." Dagger's voice was still that dirty, rough sound that I was growing to respond to. "If you don't want that to happen, now's the time to say so."

I arched my back, making the tension on my hair more intense.

Dagger yanked my head back to face his, his eyes wild. "I need you to say the words, *cara.*"

I stopped fighting him and gave in. "Fuck me," I mewled, my eyes closing. "Fuck me, fuck me, fuck me. *Please.*" My body was still primed from when he came to my apartment. It knew what it wanted.

Dagger ate at my mouth as he drew down the zipper on his slacks. His tongue was a harsh demand, and I met him thrust for thrust, until losing the rhythm when I felt the blunt head of his cock pushing against my bared entrance.

"You're wet," he ground out.

"Fuck me," I whispered again, my eyes opening to slits to watch the look of concentration on his face.

He pushed in an inch and cursed again.

"You're tight, *cara,* so damn tight."

My body writhed like a wave, inviting him in. He slid in another half an inch, stretching me, filling me like only a man can. He cursed again, and I felt empowered by it. Here was a man who was known for his control, and he was losing it with me. With a grunt, he sheathed himself completely, making my hands curl and my nails dig into his back.

Hooking a hand under my thigh, he lifted it and wrapped it around his waist. I brought my other leg up so he was holding my weight and could control how deep each thrust was. And they were deep. So deliciously deep. I felt him bump the very end of me, the sensation dancing between pleasure and pain.

He released his grip on my hair, planting his hand on the wall beside my head. Our faces were so close I could see the flecks of brown in his green eyes. Before it could become too intimate, he slammed his mouth to mine, stealing my breath and my mind.

All I knew was Dagger's body moving in and out of mine, the feel of him between my thighs. His pace increased, his thrusts beginning to lose their rhythm. He was close to coming, and that thought brought my own orgasm forward, barreling through me like a freight train.

"Oh, fuck," I whispered before I was coming hard on his cock.

Dagger swore under his breath before unloading into me, pumping into me as I rode my orgasm to completion. His harsh breaths ruffled my unbound hair, and as the heat of our lust cooled, other things came back online too.

We were outside.

We'd fucked in public.

And I'd been too absorbed by the man to care.

I squirmed to get out of his grip, and as my feet touched the asphalt, I had another realization.

He'd fucked me bare.

"You bastard," I hissed.

Reaching between my thighs, he ran his fingers through my pussy, rubbing against my too-sensitive clit. My body convulsed, the aftershocks doing nothing to dampen the fact that we'd had unprotected sex. "I want you to sit there on your date with my cum running down the inside of your thigh. I want you to remember that I'm the only one who can make you scream like that."

"You *bastard!*" With sharp movements, I yanked my dress back into place then looked down to find my panties. They were nothing but a scrap of tattered black silk. I threw them into Dagger's face then turned for the door. I escaped into the restroom, cleaning up before I returned to my date. In the mirror, I discovered my makeup had smeared from Dagger's rough treatment. Fixing it the best I could, I took in a deep breath and gave myself a pep talk.

"You've got an IUD. You can't get pregnant from this." A disease, however, was another story completely. I didn't know Dagger well enough to know whether or not he'd do that to me on purpose.

When I felt as calm as I could, I pulled open the restroom door and stepped out into the hall. I was brought to an abrupt stop when I found Charlie standing there. He looked embarrassed, ducking his head like he'd been caught doing something he shouldn't have.

"Charlie," I said.

He glanced back at me. "Sorry. You were gone such a long time. I wanted to make sure you were okay."

"Fine." I brushed past him. "I saw someone I haven't seen in years. We got busy talking. I'm sorry."

He followed me back to the table, rushing ahead to pull out my chair for me. I would've waved him off, but I was the one who'd fucked up. I sat down, scanning the restaurant for Dagger.

He was gone.

"I ordered you a salad," Charlie said. "I wasn't sure what you wanted and that seemed like a safe choice."

My eyes darted back to his face. "Thanks." I reached for my vodka tonic and slammed the whole thing back.

Charlie's eyes widened, but he didn't say anything.

Smart man.

15

Dagger

I WALKED INTO THE OFFICES OF PHANTOM SECURITY on Tuesday morning, stopping at the reception desk where a young woman was finishing up a call. She looked like she was in her early twenties, her sky-blue eyes standing out against her strawberry-blonde hair and pale complexion.

"Welcome to Phantom Security. Do you have an appointment?"

"I'm here to see Fox Wolverton," I said. "Name's Dagger."

She didn't bat an eyelid at the name—just dropped her gaze to the computer screen and started typing. "Mr. Wolverton is running a little behind this morning. Please take a seat." She gestured to the small sitting area of black leather armchairs. They matched the whole aesthetic of the glass and steel office. I sat, crossing an ankle at my knee.

A minute later, Fox walked through the glass doors behind the reception area. His eyes were on the receptionist.

"Hey, Jen, I'm expecting—"

She pointed in my direction. "He's here."

Fox shifted his gaze to me, a smile turning up the corner of his mouth. The motherfucker was tall—nearly seven feet, his frame stacked with muscle that came from serious weightlifting. His suit was tailored to fit his broad shoulders, but it did nothing to camouflage that this guy was a force to be reckoned with. His hair was just as dark as his eyes, and when he looked at you, you knew it.

He held out his hand to me as he approached, and I rose from my chair, meeting him by clasping him by the forearm and pulling him into a quick hug. He turned back the way he'd come.

"Come and meet the rest of the team," he said, then to Jen he added, "Hold all my calls."

Inside the glass wall, we stepped into a large, mostly open space—aside from the glass conference room in the center. Devil led me around to the left where private offices lined the perimeter.

"King's office," Devil said, gesturing to the first office. "Shit's hit the fan at home. His wife upped and left, leaving him with their one-year-old daughter. He's on leave until he can sort that shit out."

Continuing on, he gestured to the offices along the hall. "Ace's office. Joker's. Deuce's." Pointing farther down the hall, he added, "Hex." He rolled to a stop in front of the corner office. "This is me."

He opened the glass door and waved me in. I took a seat on the black leather couch while Devil parked it behind the desk. "Tell me what's going on, Master Guns."

I licked my lips. "My boss is losing men."

"What kind of men?"

"Coke dealers. Low-level shit, but they're ours, and we don't take too kindly to people killing our guys."

"Who's your boss?"

I hesitated. Telling anyone about Bane's business was an automatic fuck no, but Devil and I had served together. The tie that bound us together was unbreakable. "Bane Rivera."

He nodded, getting right down to business. "I heard he had a side business. How many guys have you lost?"

"So far? Five."

"Enough to make you pay attention," Devil surmised.

"Exactly."

"How are they getting popped?"

I sat forward in my seat, resting my forearms on the top of my thighs. "Shot point-blank in the chest. They're getting hit in their homes."

"Which would indicate whoever is giving the orders has been watching them."

I gave him a tight nod. The fact that someone had been paying attention to our operation for more than a month made me twitchy.

"Anything else I need to know about how they're getting taken out?"

"Every scene has had drugs left behind... drugs that could lead to my boss if anyone decided to talk about whose mark is a crown."

Devil cocked his head to the side. "Why?"

"Fucked if I know. I've managed to clear one scene, but the cops have put the other bricks into evidence."

He steepled his fingers in front of his mouth, thinking. "Does your boss have any enemies?'"

"He's the fucking head of a drug operation, who's encroached on two rival boss's turf, so yeah, he has enemies."

"Manzetti and Sanderson, right?" Devil sat back in his office chair, making the leather creak with the movement. "You looked into them yet?"

"I can't get close enough." I met his dark gaze. "But you and your team can."

He conceded my statement with a shallow nod and said, "Yeah, we can, but what do you want done after we get close enough?"

"Put a bullet into the head of the guilty party. I assume you still do the wet work when needed?"

For a moment, he got a haunted look in his eyes, and it reminded me too damn much of how Cox had looked when we'd almost fucked in the shower. Some hard truth lurked behind his eyes, something that ate at his soul. Whatever thought had passed through his head was suddenly gone, and he blinked at me. "I do. When necessary."

"It might not come to that, but I like to have a contingency in place." I rose from my chair and approached his desk. "I appreciate you taking the time to meet this morning."

"Anything for you, Master Guns." He stood, offering me his hand. "Can I offer you some advice?"

"Shoot."

"Talk to the dealers still breathing. Maybe they can tell you something about being approached by one of Sanderson's or Manzetti's men, or noticed someone hanging around."

I nodded. "Will do."

I TOOK DEVIL'S ADVICE AND WENT TO SEE HUGO Ramirez. The kid was at the ball courts on East 6th and Gladys, hanging with Dolla. I wasn't in the mood for Dolla's shit though, so I took Ramirez off to one side of the court.

Shoving his long hair out of his face, he asked, "What's up, Dagger? Does the boss have more product for us?"

"I'm going to ask you some questions, and I need you to be real fucking honest with me."

The kid straightened, the tone of my voice letting him know I wasn't fucking around anymore. "Of course."

"Has anyone approached you recently, asking questions about Bane, how he runs his operation, where you do your pick-ups? Anything?

"No, Dagger. Nobody."

Out of instinct, I glanced around the court at the ballers, at the people watching the game. Knowing that Manzetti or Sanderson's men could be watching us right now make me want to fucking scream. I returned my gaze to Hugo, and he flinched.

"Have you noticed anyone following you?"

"No. Nobody. Why? What's going on?"

I clenched my jaw shut tight. "Are you still strapped?"

He lifted his black overshirt away from his body to reveal a Sig Sauer tucked into the front of his jeans. "I wouldn't leave home without it."

"Keep it on you at all times and don't trust a fucking soul."

"What's going on?" he asked again, but this time fear tainted his words. Good. I wanted him to be afraid.

"I'll be in touch."

I left the park, waving off the people behind the charity table trying to offer me a meal. Turning left, I walked the block back to my car, the back of my neck prickling the entire fucking time.

I was being followed.

Walking straight past my car, I turned down the next street and waited—pressed tight to the wall. Reaching down, I slid a dagger free from its sheath and held it against my thigh.

The sound of grit crunching under someone's shoe was my signal. As soon as they rounded the corner, I grabbed the front of their jacket and shoved them against the wall, pressing the tip of the knife to their throat. A small, surprised exhalation let me know it was a female, but it took me a second for my eyes to fix on her face. When I saw who it was, a smile curved the corner of my mouth.

I eased back but kept the knife exactly where it was.

"Let me go," Cox hissed, her gray eyes igniting. *Was it fear or lust?* I wasn't sure. Whatever it was, I was fucking into it.

"Not until you tell me why you're following me," I drawled, keeping my face close to hers. Burying my nose behind her ear, I drew in her scent.

My little rabbit froze.

"Don't." It was one word, but it was strangled like she was pained. I eased back an inch to find her breathing erratic, her nipples hard and pressing through the silk of her shirt. She was fucking turned on by me, by the fact that I had her pinned to the wall with a blade to her throat.

"Or what?"

She swallowed, the motion making the tip of the dagger undulate. I sucked in a hiss when she jammed the muzzle of her gun into my ribs. "Or I blow you away."

I laughed, the sound startling her and making her lose her grip on the gun. She tightened her hand and shoved the gun in harder.

In a low voice, I said, "I can give you something to blow."

Her mouth parted on a gasp, but her lips pressed together a moment later, grim determination shining in her gray eyes. "You disgust me."

"No, I don't. You want me to fuck you again." I leaned a little closer to her ear, running my lips along the shell. "You want me to fuck you after I bring you to orgasm with a knife."

A shudder seemed to work its way down her body, terror filling her eyes because she knew it was true. She loved edge play and that made her a perfect fuck for me.

"No," she whispered.

"You can't lie to me, Cox. To yourself? Sure. But not to me." I popped the button free on her slacks and dipped my fingers into her panties. Her cunt was wet and wanting. "I know you want to have me between your thighs again."

"So what if I do?" she replied, heat beginning to trickle into her voice. She was angry. *Perfect.* Angry fucking was even better. I began to rub her clit, my fingers sliding in between her legs easily.

"You fucked me bare." It was an accusation I had no way of denying because I'd wanted to fuck her bare from the start.

"And you felt like heaven coming on my cock." I slid a finger into her drenched opening.

Writhing, she added, "You could've given me an STI."

"I'm clean."

She put her free hand on my bicep, squeezing. "You could get me pregnant."

"You're on birth control, and I've had a vasectomy."

She tried to shove me away. "How the hell would you know I'm on birth control?"

I pressed her back against the wall. "Call it a hunch. You like being in control, but there's a part of you that wants to lose it, to cede it to someone else. To me. That's why you keep coming to find me. Seeking me out. Give me your pleasure, Chantelle."

The use of her name made her undulate against me, rubbing like a cat in heat.

A groan bubbled up from my throat. I was going to have her.

I stilled when I heard a car horn. We were in public. Yanking my hand from her panties, I took her by the hand and dragged her to my car. Opening the door, I pushed her into the passenger seat then jogged around the other side.

The engine came to life with a roar.

"Where are you taking me?" she asked breathlessly.

I glanced over at her. Some of her hair had come free from the tight bun she kept it in, and I reached over to tuck it behind her ear. "Back to my place where I can fuck you until you can scream your throat bloody."

Not waiting to hear her protests, I put the car into gear and drove home, the smell of Cox's arousal perfuming the car.

BY THE TIME I SHUT THE FRONT DOOR BEHIND US, I WAS fucking primed for sex. My cock was a steel length behind the zipper of my slacks, and when Chantelle's eyes dropped to my groin, it kicked in anticipation.

"What do you want?"

"I want to stop wanting you," she replied. Coming closer, she ran her hands up my chest. "I want to stop thinking about how you fucked me against the wall outside the restaurant. I want to stop getting flashbacks about how you felt when you filled me."

With a growl, I picked her up by her thighs and pressed her

against the closest wall. The heat of her pussy against the front of my body was torture, and I knew the last thread of my self-control had frayed. Lowering her to the floor, I tore at her blouse, sending the buttons flying, then gave her slacks and panties the same treatment.

Turning her around, I placed my palm in between her shoulder blades and gave her a little shove into the living room just off the entrance.

"Bend over the couch," I commanded, pulling the tails of my shirt from the waistband of my pants then unbuttoning it slowly.

Chantelle placed her palms on the top of the leather and spread them wide, lowering her upper body down at the same time. She was still in her heels and bra. Resting her face against the cool leather, she stared back at me with anticipation shimmering in her gray irises.

Shrugging the shirt off my shoulders, I kicked off my boots and took off my slacks, leaving me completely bare to her. I took a step closer, and she whimpered. Smoothing a hand over her ass, I warmed up her skin then dipped between her legs.

She was soaked.

For me.

"You like the anticipation, don't you?" I asked. Skimming my fingers through her pussy once more, I spread all that arousal around, over the tight opening of her ass too. She jerked away a little at the contact, her eyes widening.

I hushed her. "Not today. But soon, *cara*." Stroking my dick, I imagined what she would feel like. "I'm going to take you bare again."

"Yes," she whispered.

"Good girl." I ran the head of my dick through her folds,

letting her body lubricate mine. She was so ready for me that I slid in easily.

When I reached the end of her, I waited for a moment, feeling her inner walls clenching tightly around me.

"Jesus, you're tight."

She made a small mewling sound but said nothing. I eased back, dragging my dick out of her slick channel until just the head remained inside her. Shutting my eyes, I told myself to last. This wasn't like last night, where I just wanted to mark her as mine. We had time, but I found I was too keyed up to wait.

Thrusting my hips forward, I slid back into her, her inner walls gloving me tightly.

"Fuck," I barked.

Dropping to my knees, I widened her stance a little more, propping one leg up onto the back of the couch. Her glistening cunt was exposed to me, wet and pink and so fucking ready for me. I licked a long line between her legs, running the tip of my tongue around her clit.

"Jesus, Dagger," she breathed, her hands curling into the leather cushions. "Yesss."

I licked my lips, tasting her. She tasted like honey down the back of my throat. "Like that, *cara*?"

"Yes."

"Grind that perfect pussy against my face then. Let me make you come." Pressing myself against the back of the couch, I placed my whole mouth over her cunt, letting her grind and rub and writhe against my lips, tongue, and chin until she was coming hard. I latched my mouth onto her clit, sucking and licking until I was drunk on her taste.

Chantelle's legs became loose, and I stood up to catch her. She leaned her head back against my shoulder, her eyes heavy-lidded and glazed with satisfaction. In one easy movement, I scooped her into my arms and took her into my bedroom.

I still wanted her from behind, so once I had her in position, I slid inside her. A mini orgasm ricocheted through her and clenched around my dick.

"Fuck, fuck, fuck, you feel good, *cara*. Better than anything."

My fingers flexed into her waist with such force that her skin dimpled. Forcing myself to ease off, I focused instead on the feeling of going in and out of her. I was drowning in this woman. Like a siren, she called me, and I went to my death willingly. My gaze became fixed on where my body pushed into hers, that deep burrow in, then the torturous pull out.

She tried to follow my movement, chasing my cock to keep the hard length inside her longer. I tightened my grip to stop her from doing that because if she moved as well, if she provided me that friction, then I was going to fucking come too soon.

Reaching out, I yanked the hair tie from her bun, sending her blonde hair tumbling around her bare shoulders. Grabbing a handful, I twisted my fist around it, pulling it taut. She lifted off the bed, her hands coming to rest on my forearms, holding herself steady. Releasing her hair, I snaked my hand around the front of her throat, wrapping my fingers around it, covering as much as I could.

"Oh, *shit*," she whispered just before her inner walls started to clench around my dick. I echoed her words, unable to stop myself from following her into the abyss of pleasure. I came. Hard. Pumping into her, I let the pleasure wash over me in a crescendo that left me temporarily deaf and blind.

Chantelle fell forward, and I released my hold on her throat, planting one palm on the bed. I collapsed on top of her, pressed against her back. Rolling to one side so I didn't crush her, I waited until my breathing returned to normal.

"Jesus," I muttered. "Fuck, Chantelle."

She turned her head to face me. This close, I could see blue flecks in her gray eyes. Her cheeks were flushed, her swollen mouth parted slightly as she calmed her pulse.

"Why do you go by Dagger instead of Tony."

I heaved out a breath, chuckling. "You been doing some digging, *cara*?"

"I needed to know who I'm selling myself to."

Propping myself up on my elbow, I stared down at her. "What else did you find out?"

"Your military record is sealed, so not much." Her gray eyes had gone smoky clear. "Which means you were involved in something more than top secret."

I gave her my flat stare. I didn't talk about what I used to do.

"Why the nickname Dagger?"

I rolled over only my back and stared at the ceiling. "Can we talk about something else?"

"Fine. How about what the *hell* you were thinking fucking me outside the restaurant?"

"I already told you. To stake my claim on you." Rolling my head to the side, I looked at her. "Why were you following me this afternoon?"

"I wanted to see if you went anywhere interesting."

I gave her a cold stare. "And?"

"Who was the kid?"

"A cousin."

"You have a lot of cousins."

I didn't bother to give her an explanation. Instead, I asked her a question of my own. "Did you fuck that guy?"

She sat up, scooting to the edge of the bed. Her voice sounded hollow when she spoke. "Who?"

"Your *date*." My voice was a snarl. I wanted to fucking bury the other guy for getting to spend time with her. "Last night."

"No."

I balled my hands into tight fists then released them with a harsh breath. "Did you want him to fuck you?" I stared at her, willing her to say no, she didn't. How could she let another man touch her after I had?

"No."

Tension I didn't even realize was being held in my shoulders, eased. "I don't want another man touching you."

Her spine straightened, but she didn't turn around. "You don't get to tell me who can and can't touch me."

"If you want to keep your job you do."

Was that a bastard of a thing to say? Yeah, it was. But I was a possessive bastard.

16

Cox

ANOTHER FUCKING MURDER. ANOTHER *FUCKING* KID. As I pulled up to the house on Carlin Street in West Adams, I blew out a breath. About a dozen marked cars lined the street, the red and blue lights strobing across the surrounding houses. I got out of my car and approached the police line. The tape was raised before I even got within six feet of the thing. Ducking underneath, the cross around my neck swung free of my blouse, catching and reflecting back the flashing lights.

"Detective Cox," a masculine voice said.

I turned at the sound of my name. "What do you want, Bridey?"

The other detective walked toward me, a smug smile on his face. "How's the case going?"

"Fine." I folded my arms across my chest, making my jacket inch up a little.

"Getting any closer to figuring out who is making all these hits?"

"It's my case, Bridey, which means it's none of your business."

He smirked like he knew he was getting under my skin. "And how was dinner at Rivera on Monday night? Did you have a hot date?"

I blinked at him, suddenly too stunned to speak. "I wasn't at Rivera on Monday."

"I saw you, Cox. My wife wanted to eat there. She'd been begging me for months."

Keeping my face completely blank, I said, "Yeah, I had a date. What of it?"

"Did you have fun?"

I frowned at his line of questioning. "If you've got a point to make, I suggest you make it." Irritated didn't really begin to explain how I was feeling.

"Well, I guess I just wanted to know how often you let your date fuck you against the wall outside?"

I froze, a terrible stillness settling over me. Bridey already thought I was a dirty cop—and he wasn't far off it—but if he saw that it was Bane's right-hand man who'd pressed me to that wall and taken me so hard and so thoroughly that I hadn't been able to think straight afterward, well, then I'd be up shit creek.

Swallowing past the lump in my throat, I decided to play it cool. "He's an exhibitionist. Likes to fuck in public places."

Bridey's brow winged up. "Which would mean you're into it too?"

Was that fucking anticipation in his voice? I glared at the man, giving him my best dead stare. When he didn't back down— when he only stared back at me with the corner of his mouth curving up—I knew I was fucked. "I try not to deny my lovers what they really want."

His blue eyes darkened, and I could practically see the man's thoughts flash across his face. They said they saw me as more than a simple professional rival. Now, he saw me as a piece of ass. "Maybe you shouldn't deny me what I want then?"

I gave him a cold look. "And what might that be?"

He stepped closer, lowering his face to mine so it looked like we were discussing something sensitive in nature. "I saw who you were fucking. Rivera's man, Tony Harrison." Reaching out, he ran a fingertip over my collarbone, but I jerked away before he could drop any lower. He smiled. "If you're willing to let a criminal fuck you in public, maybe you're willing to let a fine, upstanding detective fuck you too."

Pulling back a little, I stared at his face. "You're married. You have a six-month-old baby at home."

"And my wife still won't let me into my own bed."

I was stunned into muteness. This couldn't be happening.

Bridey licked his lips. "Let me come over later, and I promise to keep my mouth shut about you screwing a suspect in a murder investigation."

"You're blackmailing me?" My mouth flexed into an empty smile. "Wow, Bridey. And you thought *I* was a dirty cop." I turned to walk toward the house.

"You won't get a second chance to say yes to this," he called out.

Glaring at him over my shoulder, I shouted back, "And you won't get a second chance to say anything like that to me ever again."

With my anger riding me, I stepped onto the small porch and

snapped some gloves from the box. I slid them on and walked inside, turning my head to see that the locks had been broken. Whoever did this, had to force their way in. Movement to my left caught my eye, and I pivoted in that direction to find our vic sprawled on the floor in the living room, one arm behind his back, the other lightly gripping a Sig Sauer.

He was a skinny kid. He hadn't filled out yet through the shoulders and chest, and now he never would. His wavy dark hair was longer in the front than it was in the back, hanging a little over his forehead. His eyes were shut like he was merely sleeping.

I had a stunned moment of recognition as I looked at his face. Shit. I knew who this kid was. Dagger had met up with him yesterday afternoon—Hugo Ramirez.

Two neat bullet holes decorated his chest while another single shot gave him a third eye.

"God*dammit.*"

Ellen approached me. "Things are escalating."

I nodded. At this rate, we'd be scraping blood off the alley walls in a few weeks. "The message is getting more and more punctuated." I scanned the room. "Any drugs found?"

"Some on the body. I'm talking a dime bag of coke, if that. I haven't checked the rest of the house."

"Did you ID him?"

"Hugo Ramirez. Seventeen-years-old. High school drop-out."

"Who called it in?"

"The kid's mother. She's in her bedroom with one of the unis, giving her statement."

Jesus *fuck.* "I'm going to search for the drugs I know we'll find then go speak to her." I jerked my chin in the direction of the

Sig. "Test that for residue and whether it was fired recently."

Moving out of the living room, I walked down a small hallway that was filled with photographs of Ramirez at different points in his life. Most of them were shots of him as a baby or toddler with fewer and fewer of him into his late teenage years. It was the sad fucking reality that there would never be pictures of him with his own child or on his wedding day to add to that collection.

Franklins was standing beside a door in the hallway, and he straightened a little as I approached. I nodded at him before looking into one of the other rooms and confirming it was Hugo's. Stepping past the jamb, I went to his closet first, figuring that would be where he'd hide a stash. I ran my hands up on the high shelf, patting my way across it until my fingers thumped into something hard. I felt around the shape then brought it down. It was a brick of coke—just like all the others. Flipping it over, I searched for the crown. It was there, in the corner. Reaching up again, my hand bumped into another hard object, and I retrieved it, staring at another brick. Once again, there was a crown stamped onto the wrapping.

These dealers were Bane-fucking-Rivera's, and I was going to nail his ass to the fucking wall.

"Franklins!" I called out.

He appeared in an instant. "Yes, Detective?"

"Get Murdoch in here and grab some evidence bags." I gestured to the coke. "We need to process this."

He disappeared from the room, and I waited until he came back with Ella, a photographer, and another member of the team to record the find. I left Ella in charge, moving down to the next bedroom.

Hugo Ramirez's mother was sitting on the edge of her bed, hugging a pillow to her chest. In her hands, she worried a string of wooden rosary beads, the repetitive motion seemingly calming her. The whole room was filled with religious iconography from large gold crosses to rosaries on every flat surface to a painted depiction of Jesus in what looked like a gilt frame.

A sudden whimper brought my attention back to Mrs. Ramirez. Taking a knee beside the bed, I said, "Mrs. Ramirez, I'm so sorry for your loss."

She blinked dark doe-eyes at me and nodded. "Thank you, but that won't bring my boy back."

I licked my lips. "Mrs. Ramirez, I know this is hard, but would you mind telling me what happened tonight?"

"I've already told the other officer what happened."

"I know, but I'd like to hear it from you if you don't mind?"

With a quick nod, she began to speak. "The doorbell rang, and Hugo said he'd get it. I heard him speaking quickly to someone, and when I called out to see if he was okay, he told me to stay in my room." She drew in a large mouthful of air. "I knew what my son did to earn enough money to put food on the table. I had to look the other way." She gripped my hand tightly. "I *had* to. I can't work. I can't..." A sob broke from her throat, and she begged me with her eyes to understand.

Placing my other hand on top of hers, I gave it a reassuring squeeze. "I understand that life can be tough sometimes."

She blinked, tears streaming down her face, but her expression was still a little unsure. "You do?"

I let her have a peek behind my cop exterior, let her see some of my pain. "Yeah, I do."

We had a moment of understanding then. I knew her pain

because for a few years, that was all I had left of my daughter. Mrs. Ramirez had just lost her son, but the pain was the same.

"Do you know who Hugo dealt for?"

Her nose crinkled. "I didn't ask. He didn't tell."

"What happened after he told you to stay in your room?"

She took in a deep, shuddering breath. "I heard four shots."

"Four?"

"Yes."

"You're sure?"

"Yes."

"Okay." Three shots were accounted for, but the fourth wasn't. Maybe Ella would find that the kid's Sig did get used tonight, and if it had, did that mean we had a perp injured with a GSW or were we going to have to look for a slug lodged in a wall or door?

"Franklins," I called again.

"Detective?" he asked, appearing from one side of the door.

I relayed the information to him and told him to tell Ella.

"Yes, Detective."

I refocused on Mrs. Ramirez. "What happened after you heard those shots?"

"I rushed out to find the door open and my Hugo on the ground, dead. I called the police after that."

I patted her hand. "I appreciate you going through that again, Mrs. Ramirez. Thank you, and I really am so sorry for your loss."

As I rose from my crouch, she grabbed my hand and squeezed weakly. "Catch the man who killed my son."

"Man? Why are you so sure it's a man?"

"The other voice I heard was too deep to be a woman's."

She didn't release her grip on me until I nodded, and I walked out of the bedroom.

"Find out anything interesting?" Ella asked me when I met her exiting the other bedroom.

"Aside from the four shots fired? Mrs. Ramirez said she's sure it was a man who was the shooter. I'm going to put out a BOLO for gunshot wounds at hospitals in case our perp goes for some medical attention."

"You got it, Detective."

AN HOUR LATER, I WAS WALKING UP TO THE DOLLHOUSE. Flashing my badge got me past the security guard at the door, but as I stepped inside, I was blindsided by seeing Dagger.

"What are you doing here?" he asked in a dark voice, looking nothing like the man who had taken me back to his place yesterday.

"Police business." My words were clipped. I was getting tired of attending murders of kids. "Move out of my way."

He placed a hand in the center of my chest, keeping me in place. "Remember our deal, *cara*." He'd meant it as a warning, but all I could think of was how much I didn't want to enjoy giving myself to him.

To disguise the shot of lust that thrilled through me, I asked, "Is that a threat?"

"A warning. Bane stays out of this. He's not behind the killings."

"Whoever said he was?" I retorted and pushed him away. He let me go, but he so could've easily held me there instead.

Making my way to the other side of the bar, I entered through the staff door and went up the stairs. When I reached Bane's office, I took a deep breath and knocked.

"Yeah," Bane snarled through the wood. He sounded pissed off, which I thought could work in my favor.

Opening the door, I strolled inside. His dark eyes traveled the length of my body before returning to my face.

"Fuck, what do you want?" he snapped, cinching his fingers shut around the whisky glass in front of him.

"Nice to see you too, Bane."

He glared at me, his mouth twisting into a sneer. "I don't have time for this shit, Detective, so tell me what you want to say, then we can move this night right along."

I wondered briefly what had gotten him so wound up. Maybe I could needle him a little more, make him slip up. "You know I've been keeping an eye on your club."

"If you wanted a job here, all you had to do was ask," he baited. "You'd be a nice addition to my Dolls."

Fucking asshole.

"You know, you shouldn't knock it until you try it. There's something rather thrilling about liberating a man of his hard-earned money." He glanced down at my hand. "And a good-looking, single woman like you would fucking clean up down there." He gestured to the club below.

"Unlucky for you, I'm married to my job on the force."

"Well, if you change your mind, I'll keep a spot open for you."

I folded my arms over my chest. "I didn't come here to discuss job opportunities."

"Oh? Why did you come then?"

A smile tugged at the corners of my mouth, and he frowned. "Did you know Hugo Ramirez was killed today? Shot in cold blood. Two in the chest. One in the head. When we searched his body, he had coke on him. His bedroom was full of coke too… almost five pounds worth. He was only seventeen-years-old."

His face remained blank as he shrugged. "What does this seventeen-year-old punk kid have to do with me?"

The fucking cocksucker! I slammed a fist on his desk, rattling the pens in their holder. "Because he was one of your dealers, Bane."

"I'm not sure what you're talking about. I don't have any dealers unless you count my Dolls? They deal in sex, but it's one hundred percent legal as you're well aware."

"You know, I hate men like you."

"Men like me?"

I pushed away from the desk and turned to face the wall of glass, looking down at women milling around in barely nothing at all. Women who sold themselves to anyone who would pay for them. "Men who exploit women for their own gain. Men who think everyone should be on your payroll." When I turned back to face him, I tried to hide my disgust, but I suspected hatred flashed in my eyes. "Men who break the law repeatedly but are so squeaky clean that shit won't stick."

He simpered, "You say the sweetest things."

I wasn't buying the no-fucking-big-deal act. His dealers were being decimated, which meant his hold on his turf had to be slipping too. "One day you'll fuck up, Rivera, and I'll be there when you do."

"If that's what helps you sleep at night, then, by all means, you think that, Detective Cox. But I have no idea why you keep bringing me news like this. I'm just a businessman… a businessman who pays his taxes, treats his employees fairly, and who goes to church on Sunday."

I sneered. "I'll be in touch."

"I can't wait. And if you do want to get out of the law enforcement game, my doors are wide open."

"Fucking egotistical *fuck*," I muttered under my breath as I left his office. I was down the stairs and out into the club a few moments later, turning ideas over in my head. If Bane wouldn't talk to me, maybe his employees would. Digging into my inside jacket pocket, I pulled out my business cards and began handing them out to the girls dressed in lingerie.

As I passed, Dagger was on the phone, his expression shutting down as he looked my way. No doubt Bane had called to tell him to remove me from the premises. Holding my head high, I stalked past him and out onto the sidewalk.

I needed to break this case.

17

Dagger

IT HAD BEEN THREE HOURS SINCE I'D WATCH COX leave the club, and the sensation of ice in my veins still lingered. The news of Hugo Ramirez's murder had flawed me. I'd only spoken to the kid yesterday afternoon.

I shook my head. Getting attached to dealers was always a bad fucking idea. They were employees, and I had to treat them like that, but sometimes I slipped back into my role as Master Gunnery Sergeant, but instead of fellow Marines in the ranks, I had Bane's dealers taking their places. It was fucking stupid, and now I'd learned my lesson.

Ducking into the staff corridor, I walked down to the end of the hall and opened the door that led into the cleaning hall behind the private rooms. Velvet had her head in the supply closet, while Sierra made them both a cup of coffee. Both girls were wearing all black—the unofficial uniform for the back-of-house staff.

The smell of the French press overrode all the other scents back there, temporarily erasing the fact that they were essentially housekeepers for kink.

"Dagger!" Sierra beamed. "You want some coffee?"

"I'm good, Storm."

She wrinkled her nose. "Storm?"

Velvet pulled out a couple of rolls of paper towels, shoving one under her arm so she could grab another. "Dagger calls the girls he *really* likes by their last names," she said, smiling.

Sierra blinked her wide eyes. "What does he call you?"

"Trouble," I replied for her.

Velvet stuck out her tongue, but smiled. "He just calls me Velvet. The last name I have, I don't want, so I'm going with a one-name-only kind of thing. That doesn't mean he doesn't like me, though."

"Were you just checking up on me?" Sierra asked, caution hovering at the edge of her voice.

"Just doing the rounds. Everything okay back here? Need me to restock supplies?"

"We're all good," Velvet replied. "Just trying to keep Sierra awake. She's not used to working the night shift like this."

"It takes some getting used to." I glanced up at the inset lights above the doors. None of the red lights were on, so they were either still in use or were clean and ready to go for the next couple or group. "Any problems here?" I gestured to the five doors on the opposite side of the hallway.

"None. The Dolls keep things pretty tidy for us."

"Good. If there's nothing else you need, I'll catch you later."

"Bye, Dagger," Sierra said.

Velvet gave me a finger wave.

"Little punk," I mumbled under my breath and exited the space. I went into my office next but didn't take a seat behind my desk. Pulling out my phone, I dialed Fox Wolverton's personal number.

"Master Guns," he answered, sounding tired.

I glanced at the time. "Sorry, it's late."

"It's fine. What's up?"

"Have any intel on Sanderson or Manzetti yet?"

"Manzetti isn't ordering these hits. Sanderson is."

"You're sure? Got the proof?" Bane would never take a drastic step without proof first.

"A hundred percent. I can get it to you. Sanderson has been paying hitmen to take out your dealers. He's trying to weaken Bane's hold on No Man's Land."

"That fuck," I mumbled.

"What do you want to do about it? I can take care of it if you want?"

"No. This shit is personal. I'll take care of it. Thanks."

Hanging up the phone, I drummed my fingers on the desk. I was fucking wired—to wired to work. What I needed was sex. Sex I could get in a second. All I needed to do was go out onto the floor and pick someone I hadn't had before, but the only woman who could stir my body now was fucking Chantelle Cox.

I wanted to go to her, but that wasn't possible while Bane was still here.

But I could call her.

"What do you want, Dagger?" she asked when she answered the phone. "It's past eleven."

"I want you naked and pleasuring yourself while you listen to my voice."

There was a pause, then the sound of rustling sheets. "We're not doing this," she bit out. "We are *not* fucking doing this."

"Yes, we are. Where are you right now?"

"I'm hanging up, Dagger."

"No, you're not. You're going to stay on the phone while you give yourself a fucking orgasm, and I get to listen. Unless you want to get kicked out of vice?" I gave her a moment to think. When she said nothing, I added, "Now, where are you? Right. This. Minute?"

"In my bed," she whispered. Her self-loathing foamed around the edges of her voice, but there was something else there too. I knew she liked giving up her power to me, so it had to be relief that I could hear.

I leaned back in my chair. "Good. Lie back in bed. Tell me what you're wearing."

"You're a sick bastard."

"I know. What are you wearing?"

"Pajamas."

"What kind of pajamas, *cara*, and don't fucking lie to me."

She blew out a frustrated breath. "How would you know I'm lying?"

"We could be FaceTiming right now. Or if you're really feeling rebellious, I could come around to your apartment and see for myself. It's up to you."

"Fuck you, Dagger. I'm wearing a white tank top and panties."

My mouth curved into a smile. "Good girl. What color are your panties?"

"Black."

"Cotton?"

"Silk."

I stood abruptly and locked my office door before sitting back in my chair. My dick was semi-hard and growing.

"Are your nipples hard?"

"I'm not answering that."

"I want you to touch them through the shirt. Rub your nipples. Make them hard. Pretend it's my mouth on them… *cara*? Do it. Now."

There was a pause, then a sharp inhale of breath.

"Tell me how hard they are?"

She gasped, air whistling through her teeth as she exhaled. "They're hard, Dagger. So hard."

A small, frustrated growl escaped my throat. This was fucking torture. Listening to my woman pleasuring herself was driving me insane. Tearing the fastening of my slacks, I wrapped my hand around my cock and groaned at the sensation.

"Pinch them harder, *cara*. Let me hear your breathing get sharper."

There was a soft mewling, and I knew she was doing just as I'd asked. Knowing she was taking my directions made lust shoot through me. Made my dick twitch against my palm.

I licked my lips. "Put the phone on speaker then skim your free hand down to your cunt." I waited a beat, then asked, "Have you put the call on speaker, *cara*?"

"Yes." It was an echoey whisper, but it was there.

"Good. Now, your hand. Glide it down your body and rub your fingers against your pussy but only through the fabric." I gave her a moment to do as I asked, then said, "I bet it's soaked. Tell me it's soaked, *cara*."

"Fuck, it's soaked, Dagger."

Now that she had her hand just where I wanted it to be, I began to stroke myself, running my palm up and down my length.

"Slide your hand into your panties and touch your pussy. Imagine that it's my hand touching you. My fingers sliding into all that slick heat. My fingernails scraping your skin because to not touch you with every part of me is fucking torture."

"Oh." An inarticulate word. "Ohhh." She drew the pleasing interjection out. "Yes."

I moved my palm faster and faster against my cock. Precum was already beading there, and I wanted Cox to be on her knees in front of me instead of over the phone.

"Slide a finger into your drenched opening. Spread your honey all over yourself and rub your clit."

"Fuck. Dagger." The words sounded dragged from her tongue. Like she didn't want to admit that she was enjoying this.

"Yes, *cara*."

"I need you inside me. I need you here with me."

My eyes shut on a shudder, and I had to stop pumping my cock so I could grip the edge of the desk. I couldn't go to her. I had to stay here.

"I know you do, baby, but I can't leave right now."

"Please."

I let out a loud curse, wishing I could give in to her every whim. "I can make you come like this." I gritted out the words. "Give me your pleasure. Shut your eyes and picture me between your legs. My head between your thighs. My tongue spearing through your pussy. My throat drinking down your honey. I would make you come on my tongue twice before I'd fuck you. I'd make sure you were good and ready, wet and glistening for me before I sank my cock inside you. I'd pump into you slowly—"

"Why slowly?" Her question was chased away by a groan.

"Because you make me *insane*, Chantelle. I want you to beg me for it."

"And if I don't?"

"I'd torture you with my dick until you demand I fuck you harder."

"Dagger," she moaned. "I'm close."

Yeah, she was. I put my phone down on the desk, noticing for the first time that my breathing was ragged. I was losing fucking control. I should've been bothered by that, but with Chantelle's labored breathing on the other end of the phone, my brain blanked the fuck out. My palm glided over my cock faster and faster until I felt my balls began to tighten. I was close to coming, but there was no fucking way I'd shoot before she came.

"Fuck, *cara*, I'm close."

"Fuck. Dagger… oh… oh… yes, I'm coming!"

As her groans and moans filled my office, I came in a rush of cum. It jetted out all over my hand, onto my desk, and on my slacks. I kept coming because for as long as Chantelle was riding her pleasure, I was riding mine. Pleasure that I thought I could only feel with a knife in my hand and a willing body beneath me coursed through me, making me temporarily deaf to the world.

When my hearing came back, I blinked at the mess I'd made as I listened to Cox's panted breath.

"Dagger," she whispered, an edge to her voice like she'd been screaming her release while I'd been out of action. "Are you there?"

My phone *pinged* with a message. It was from Bane. He was leaving for the night. A quick glance at the top of the screen said it was just after midnight.

"I'm here. I'm coming over so we can do that again in person."

WHEN I POUNDED ON CHANTELLE'S DOOR TWENTY
minutes later, I'd showered, changed, and was fucking primed
and ready to go for round two. It took a few minutes, but she
opened the door and let me inside. When I turned back around
to face her, I found her blonde hair unbound and tousled from
sleep—or from writhing against her pillow. Yeah, I'd bet it was
from all the writhing. My gaze skated down her body, seeing her
white tank top and black panties.

She had her arms wrapped around her torso, her expression set
somewhere between anger and longing.

"Strip." It was a command, and I waited to see if she would
fight me on it. Would her anger win, or would her desire to have
me between her legs again be too strong to deny?

For a moment, she did nothing. Simply stared at me—that
strange mix of emotions playing over her face. Eventually, her
arms loosened and fell away from her chest. My mouth parted
when I saw her nipples pressed against the fabric. They were
dark shadows under the crisp whiteness of the cotton, and I
wanted to have my mouth all over them.

Forcing myself to stay where I was, I curled my hands into
fists and waited. Running her hands under the hem of her tank
top, she lifted it over her head. Her body was lean—not overly
muscled, but you could see the strength there. My gaze was
transfixed on her breasts, her nipples distended and begging for
my touch.

Unable to remain in place for a moment longer, I went to her,
cupping both breasts in my hands. I liked how big my hands were
on her body. She was nearly as tall as I was, but her body was

smaller—slimmer. I fucking enjoyed dwarfing her. I rubbed both nipples with my thumbs, making them grow harder.

A lot like my dick, which was pushing against the fastening of my slacks.

Lowering my head to one breast, I licked and nipped at her skin, drawing sharp gasps from her throat. Threading her fingers through my hair, she held me to her as I suckled, drawing as much of her into my mouth as I could.

I jerked back when her free hand wrapped around my dick through my slacks. "I want this," she murmured above me.

Glancing up, I found her top teeth dimpling her bottom lip as she chewed it.

"I want this. Give it to me."

Releasing my hold on her body, I stepped away then motioned for her to lose her panties.

"What are you going to do with me?" she asked breathlessly.

"You're going to suck my cock until you're choking on it. Then I'm going to drop to my knees and eat your pussy until you come on my tongue. After that, I'm going to fuck you hard until you're left bruised and sore."

A little shiver racked her body as she nodded and dropped to her knees, ready to take my cock between her lips. She guided it into her mouth, sucking it down to the back of her throat.

I stared down at her through half-lidded eyes. "Put your arms behind your back and keep them there."

She did it without hesitation, sliding her hands around to the small of her back. Gathering her hair together, I tightened my grip and held her head immobile while I fucked her mouth. Small noises of pleasure vibrated from her tongue and through my shaft. God*dammit*, this felt so good.

Thrusting in, I drove myself as far back as I could get, until she was choking on me. Her tightening throat around my shaft made me drive in another half an inch before I released her. She gasped, saliva dripping from her mouth in thick strands. My dick was soaked from her mouth.

I stroked her jaw. "Sore?" I asked.

She shook her head. No.

With gritted teeth, I guided myself back into her mouth and released her hair, giving her space to rock back and forth on my cock. She worked me close to my breaking point, but always pulled back before I could warn her. She seemed to understand my body and what it needed.

"Fuck," I barked out, pulling out of her mouth. Her lips were swollen and red, and the knowledge that my cock was responsible for that made lust shoot through me. I needed to taste this woman. I glanced around the room. Good. We were more or less in the living room.

"Sit on the edge of the couch then lay back."

When she was in position, I dropped to my knees, pushing myself between her thighs. Her cunt was glistening. Pink. Without warming her up, I slid my tongue through her wet folds, making her hands convulse where they clung to my shoulders. The pain of her grip only added another layer to the pleasure of eating out my woman. I lapped at her, ignoring the way she both pushed me away and pulled me closer at the same time. Her brain was fucking addled by my touch.

Stabbing my tongue into her opening, I pressed my thumb into her clit, applying just the right amount of pressure. One minute she was writhing against my face, and the next she was coming hard and long against my tongue.

I licked at her, drawing out her pleasure just like I'd told her I would. When her hold on my head finally eased, I sat back on my heels and stared at her. From this angle, she looked like a woman who was well fucked, but that wasn't exactly true.

At least not yet.

I WOKE THE NEXT MORNING TO THE SUN STREAMING in through the window opposite the bed. It was one of those double-wide, double-height fuckers that let so much light into the bedroom that it was impossible to ignore.

For a moment, I didn't know where I was, but as I looked around the white-on-white bedroom, I remembered.

I was in Chantelle's bed.

After I'd eaten her out, we'd fucked—slowly like I said we would. We'd both fallen asleep in her bed until I woke her a couple of hours later. I'd entered her from behind, wrapping an arm around her upper chest and pinning her to the mattress. She came with a scream, biting into the pillow to stop the sound from carrying.

Turning my head, I looked to see where she was, but her side of the bed was empty. I frowned, listening to the sounds of the apartment. There was water running in the bathroom. I eased back into my pillow and relaxed just as Cox's phone began to vibrate on the nightstand. Leaning over, I swiped it up and saw there was a text from someone called Dante. Who the fuck was Dante? Who *the fuck* was this guy and why was he texting my woman?

"What are you doing with my phone?"

I shifted my gaze from the screen to the woman who had a

stronger hold on me than I thought she did. With a white towel wrapped around her body and water still beading on her skin like she'd hauled ass out of the shower, Cox stood there with her anger flowing off her.

"Who the fuck is Dante?" My words came out in a dark crawl. "Who the *fuck* is he?" I demanded again when she remained quiet.

"He's nobody." She held out her hand, her expression settling into blankness. Her gray eyes had grown cold, like a nuclear winter. "Give me my phone."

"Nobody, huh?" I asked.

"That's right." Stepping forward, she yanked the phone from my hand and folded her arms over her chest, hiding the device from view. "Get out of my apartment, Dagger."

"What?"

"You proved your point, okay? I'm fucking drawn to you and what you can do to my body, but beyond sex, I don't want you in my life."

Her words were like bullets slamming into my chest. The fact that they hurt me simply meant that I had given too much of myself over to her. Too much power. Too many fucking emotions.

I got out of the bed, buck naked, and her eyes dropped down my body to my groin then back again.

"Get out," she said in a softly quaking voice. "Get out before I stop threatening you with a bullet and actually pull the damn trigger."

"I'd like to see you try that, *cara*." I scooped up my clothes and left the bedroom, then her apartment.

18

Cox

AS SOON AS I HEARD THE APARTMENT DOOR SLAM shut, I opened up the message from Dante. I read it twice, then hit the call button. I didn't know whether he'd be able to answer. I hoped he did.

I was on the verge of giving up when the call connected.

"Seren, what is it?" he said in a low voice.

"Is it true? What you said in the message?"

He blew out a breath. "Yeah, it's fucking true. Kavanaugh is in talks with the president of the Savage Hunt MC."

"Which means, what?"

"I don't know yet. The Hunt are into guns and flesh. Kavanaugh might just be looking to restock his weapons cache or looking for something in particular to arm his men with."

I swallowed. "Or he's getting into the flesh trade."

Each year, it was estimated that almost half a million women were sold. Sex trafficking was big business, and the thought of it made my stomach turn.

"Or he's getting into the flesh trade," he agreed reluctantly. "Either way, it's just one talk so far. No deals have been made."

The *yet* was left unsaid.

Knowing Aidan as I did, sex trafficking wasn't beyond him. In fact, I was surprised he hadn't gone into it sooner. Perhaps having Sloane in his life had made him rethink things. But if there was one thing I could bank on, it was that Aidan would always make sure he came up on top—no matter who he had to sacrifice to get there.

"Is there anything else I need to know?"

"Not right now. I have to go."

He hung up, and I stared numbly at the quickly fading screen. If Aidan was getting tangled up in MC business, he was either getting cocky, or he was desperate. I didn't want to think about which one it was. I had no control over Aidan's actions, but there was something I could control here. In LA. I could find out who the fuck had been killing these kids.

Dropping the towel, I got dressed and made my way to the precinct to put in some time on the case before I went to pay Bane another visit.

SIX HOURS LATER, I PULLED UP OUTSIDE THE DOLLHOUSE, finding a parking spot on the street. When I stepped from the car, the heat was oppressive and immediate, making sweat bead on my brow. Walking up to the front entrance, the security guard on the door stared at me impassively. I flashed him my badge, then had to wait while he radioed someone else. As I stood there, I scanned the people in the line. It wasn't even lunchtime on a

Thursday, yet there were already men waiting to get in.

"Dagger says for you to wait at the bar," the guy on the door eventually said.

I scowled at him, but stepped into the club. The hypnotic thrum of music wrapped around me like a velvet caress. Girls were dancing on the poles while some perched on the edge of leather armchairs, pushing their barely-covered breasts up against the men who were sitting in them.

"Can I get you anything?"

I turned to find a woman with raven-black hair standing behind the bar. She was wearing a black teddy, the thin straps a stark contrast to her pale skin. There was a lot of makeup on her face, and I knew she was hiding a black eye.

"I need to speak to Bane Rivera."

"I'm Rachel. Are you here to interview for the job?"

"Interview?"

She cocked her head to the side. "Yeah. The position for a Doll?"

"No. I'm not here for a job."

Her brown eyes drifted down my body then back to my face. "Too bad. Some men love the strict schoolmarm look. You could totally be a Dom and rake in the cash."

I was tossing up whether to put this woman back in her fucking box when I caught sight of Dagger coming out from the doorway that led to Bane's office. He was wearing a navy blue three-piece that just flat out did it for me. He turned his head as if he could feel my stare, his green eyes as hard as emeralds.

Rachel turned to follow my gaze before she walked down to the other end. He said something to her but didn't take his eyes off me. I felt him like a tangible weight. Goosebumps broke out on my skin, but I refused to back down from this. Rachel got busy making him a drink, and he stalked toward me.

Everything about this man turned me on. I was becoming addicted to the way he made me feel, and that was bad. One man should never have that kind of power over me—never again.

"What are you doing here, *cara*."

I lifted my chin. "I can't discuss an ongoing police investigation with you."

"He's not involved." His voice was low—a warning. "I've told you that a number of times already."

"Forgive me if I *don't* take the word of a criminal. Dealers are still getting hit, and it's my job to find out why."

He glanced around before bringing his green eyes back to my face. "I have it from a reliable source that Peter Sanderson is the one giving orders."

"The art dealer?"

"It's a front, Detective. He's behind it. Trust me."

I had the strangest impulse to tell him that I did trust him, but I shook my head before the words came out. My trusting someone who essentially did all the dirty work for a man like Bane Rivera just didn't seem like the smartest thing to do.

"I trust you have proof."

He stared at me. Hard. Expecting me to back down.

"Your drink is ready, Dagger," Rachel called.

"Give me a minute, Rachel," he called back without looking away. "You don't want to keep pushing him."

"Why?"

"Because it might end with a bullet in your skull."

Out of instinct, I reached for the butt of my gun. Dagger's eyes flickered down, watching the movement. "You going to shoot me, Chantelle?" he asked in a soft drawl. "You going to shoot the man whose tongue you came on last night?"

I glared at him. "If I have to. You threatened me."

"I also gave you the best fucking orgasms of your life."

"Moot point."

He stepped closer, his strong hand closing over mine where it lay over the gun. "I'm telling you what you need to know. Bane isn't the kind of man you push without repercussions."

"And what would those repercussions be?"

"I already told you. A bullet in your skull."

I blinked at him. "Would you be the one to pull the trigger?"

"If that's what Bane wanted, yes."

I suddenly felt cold. "Just like that?"

"If I was ordered to. Yeah." He turned and picked up the glass of whisky Rachel had left at his elbow. "Give him ten minutes to fucking cool off and gather his thoughts." And with that, he turned and walked back the way he came.

"How about a drink while you wait?" Rachel asked.

I looked at the woman. "Who hit you? Was it Rivera?"

She startled then touched the black eye hidden underneath the makeup. "No. Mr. Rivera would never lay a hand on me."

"Who did it then?"

"An ex-boyfriend. Bane helped me out by giving me more shifts so I could get my own place." As she spoke, she picked up a bottle of vodka and started to pour some into a squat glass.

I shook my head. "I'm on duty."

"On duty?" she asked, then her eyes became large. "You're a cop?"

"Yeah."

"Jesus, I'm sorry about the assumption that you were a dancer.

You just had a look about you."

"It's fine."

She glanced down, looking at the number of mixers in bottles lined up in front of her. "Would you like some juice then?"

"Sure." My gaze went to the office overlooking the club. "I'll be waiting here for a little while."

She poured me a glass of orange juice. "What made you want to become a cop?" Rachel tacked on hastily. "If you don't mind me asking?"

"I don't mind. I saw a lot of injustice where I grew up. I wanted to do something to stop it."

Rachel threw down a coaster then placed the glass on top. "Did you grow up in LA?"

"Detroit."

She nodded. "I know about growing up rough. My stepdad beat me. My mom let him. I ran away from home when I was sixteen."

"How did you get off the streets?"

"It took me a few years, but I met a guy who said I could live with him. It was fine for a while." Her eyes got that lost quality. "For a while, it was great. Then he started pimping me out so he could feed his drug habit."

"How did you get away from him?"

"There was an ad for a job at the Dollhouse. I came in for a Doll's position, but Mr. Rivera said he didn't hire anyone under the age of twenty-one."

"How old were you then?"

"Barely eighteen."

"So, what did you do?"

"Nothing. I turned to leave, and he offered me a position as server. Then when I turned twenty-one, he paid for me to go to bartending school. I found out later that he hadn't even needed a server at that time. He'd created the position just for me."

Taking a sip from my drink, I let the sweet, slightly bitter taste of the juice slide over my tongue and down my throat. "Mr. Rivera is a good boss then?"

"The best," she replied with a smile. She motioned to one of the servers who had come to the end of the bar with an order. "It was great chatting with you…"

"Detective Cox."

She smiled again. "Detective Cox."

I watched her walk to the other end of the bar, doing a double-take when I saw Bane walk across the floor to speak to one of the dancers. The man she was dancing on said something back before the woman took his hand and led him into a private room along the far wall. Bane disappeared through a curtain. Finishing off my juice, I followed him in. As I approached, another woman with colorful tattoos covering her arms and thighs sashayed into the room.

That was when I realized that the room had a glass wall with a curtain on the outside. Bane had opened it and had a front row seat to a threesome. I knew exactly what the bastard was doing.

"Mr. Rivera," I said.

He turned to face me, smiling. "I'd say it's a pleasure, but I'd be lying."

Even though I already knew the answer, I said, "Let's go and talk somewhere more private."

"If you want to talk to me, Cox, you'll have to talk to me here while I watch my Dolls fuck a man's brains out."

The bastard. Determined not to be deterred, I took the seat beside him. The sounds of moaning came through speakers set into the wall. It was distracting as fuck.

"You can watch them. That's what they want."

"It's pornography."

"It's better than pornography," he shot back, widening his legs a little more. "It involves all the senses… sight, smell, taste. Just take a look. You might find you enjoy it."

I cleared my throat, my eyes skating over to the window when there was a particularly loud groan. One of the women was draped gracefully over the back of the couch. The other woman had spread her legs wide and was eating her out. The same woman giving oral had her ass in the air, the perfect angle for the man to enter her at the same time. I flushed, not because of what I was seeing—although that was part of it. I flushed because I remembered how Dagger had pushed his broad shoulders between my legs and licked between my thighs until I came.

"I know what you're doing," I murmured. I forced myself to keep watching the scene in front of us. "You think this will make me go away and not ask the questions I need to ask."

"Is that why I'm doing it? Maybe I just like watching people fuck."

I turned to face him finally. "Your words and actions won't deter me."

He shrugged. "What do you want then?"

"We have a witness." It was only half a bluff, a plot to get him talking.

"Good for you."

"A witness who can place your man, Tony, speaking to Hugo Ramirez."

"He prefers the name Dagger."

He glanced at me, and I saw every single inch of malice in that look. "And you're full of shit."

"He's willing to testify in court to it. Once they nail *Dagger...*" I sneered, "... it's only a matter of time before your ass is nailed to the wall right alongside his."

"You have a very active imagination."

I gave him a cold smile. "Give it time, Rivera. I will have your ass in jail, and I'll tear down this house of sin."

Turning to face me, he let me see past his civilized mask—the businessman mask. "Listen here, you fucking zealous little *cunt*, it'll be a cold fucking day in hell when that happens. In fact, I can guarantee it will never happen, so stop fucking sniffing around here like the bitch you are and go solve these murders. And here's a hot fucking tip... I have nothing to do with them. Why would I need to kill drug dealers?"

When he sat back again, his hands curled into fists on top of his thighs. That outburst had cost him, and it revealed something to me. He was taking these deaths personally. Dagger had said Sanderson was behind the hits, and maybe he was right, but I wasn't prepared to let Bane off the hook just yet.

I stood, my eyes gravitating back to the threesome for a moment before turning to the curtain. "Rivera?"

"What?" he barked.

"Your time will come."

"Fuck you."

With a smile curving my lips, I walked out the front door of the Dollhouse and made my way back to my car. I checked my phone before starting the engine and saw that I had a few missed calls from Dante. I called him back.

"Seren, I've found out why Aidan has been meeting with

Kaash. They've been working together to set up international skin auctions and sex slave procurement. There's a private skin auction, their first. Exclusive guest list. I'm talking Russians, Chinese, Italians, Albanians, the Irish. All the major players are attending. He's auctioning off six girls, all aged between fourteen and eighteen. Virgins. He could get upward of two hundred thousand a piece for them."

"Shit," I said.

19

Dagger

CHANTELLE LEFT THE DOLLHOUSE AFTER TALKING TO Bane, and as much as I wanted to go after her, I planted my fucking ass in my office chair and continued to stew about the fact that some *cocksucker* called Dante was calling and messaging her.

I was ready to commit murder—violent, bloody murder. It wasn't an idle threat, but one with real possibility as I remembered seeing *his* name flash onto the screen of Cox's phone. I wouldn't share my woman, and I sure as fuck didn't let this kind of shit go. I needed to know who Dante was, but without Cox making a call to him, or receiving one from him, there was no way Devil and his team could get a hit on his location.

Was it an invasion of her fucking privacy to track her calls?

Yeah, but fuck it. I protected my woman.

My phone rang.

It was Devil.

"Thank fuck. What have you got?"

Devil laughed. "Nice to talk to you, too, Master Guns."

"Just get to it," I snarled.

With humor still lacing his voice, he told me, "Hex tried to trace a call your detective made about fifteen minutes ago."

Tried? "Where? Where the hell is this cocksucker?"

Jesus *fuck*, I was a possessive asshole.

"Michigan."

"It's a big fucking state, Devil. Over fifty-eight thousand squares. *Where* in Michigan?"

"That's the thing. Hex had trouble triangulating the exact location. It looks as if whoever this Dante guy is, he's scrambling his position. He pinged off of five different cell towers during their call, all thousands of miles away from each other."

Was this Dante guy her ex-lover? Ex-husband? And why in the hell was he reaching out to Cox? I pulled my phone away from my ear when I heard a beep. Bane was calling me.

"Devil, I have to go."

"We'll keep an eye on it. Let you know if we have any updates."

He hung up, and I answered the other line.

"Wren's apartment is on fire."

I was up and out of my seat a moment later. Outside my office, Bane was already waiting.

"Where's Andy?"

"He was at her apartment. He called me just before he went in."

"Fuck."

Together, we exploded out of the club's rear door and hustled over to my car. I drove like the devil himself was chasing me, pulling up to the apartment block in Boyle Heights twenty minutes later. Thank fuck it was late, otherwise we would've been fighting traffic along the way.

Multiple fire trucks as well as some police cars were already at the scene. The whole top half of the building was alight, the heat and flames extraordinarily fierce. Thick, black smoke boiled into the night sky, obscuring the stars. Firefighters were running in and out of the building, the ones coming out helping residents to safety.

Beside me, Bane made a noise in his throat that sounded like a wounded animal. I understood then that this woman Bane had been spending so much time with wasn't just another piece of ass for him. She meant something to him, and that fissure in his heart she'd created would be his downfall too.

A racking cough drew our attention. Andy was sitting in the back of an ambulance, his face and clothes covered in soot. The smell of smoke coming off him was cloying. Surrounding him were empty bottles of water.

"Where is she?" Bane demanded, his eyes wide as he took in the scene. "Where the hell is Wren?"

"Ambulance took her," he said in a raw, rasping voice. Opening the lid of a water bottle, he drank half the contents, wincing a little as he did. "About ten minutes ago."

"Was she okay? Tell me she was fucking okay!"

"Minor burns to her forearms." Another gulp of water. "Otherwise, fine."

I felt Bane's relief hit me like an invisible force. He was in fucking deep with this woman.

"They took her to Cedars-Sinai."

Bane looked about ready to bolt, but he said, "What about you?" He gestured to the bandages on both of Andy's forearms and on his left hand.

"The EMTs say they're first-degree burns. I soaked a blanket in water and threw it over me before I went in to get her. I'll be okay."

"Thank Christ you were there," Bane told him, taking the other man by the shoulder. "Thank you."

And that was when I knew. I knew unequivocally that Bane was in so fucking deep with Wren Montana that there would be no coming back. And if he did? He'd be a tormented shell of who he used to be. Women had that power over a man. Some didn't want to acknowledge it. Most would deny it was even happening, but that shit was real.

"Ready to rock and roll there, big man?" an EMT asked Andy in a genial voice.

"As ready as I'll ever be."

Bane asked, "Where are you taking him?"

"Cedars-Sinai for a quick check-up. He should be released in a few hours." She smiled at Bane then refocused her attention on her patient. "You all right to get into the back by yourself?"

"I got it," Andy replied, taking a water bottle with him. Once the doors were shut, Bane turned to me.

"I need to see her." His voice was raw. "Now."

I nodded, and we walked back to my car.

"Think this was just a fucking coincidence?" I asked, gesturing to the building that was burning more fully now.

Bane turned his tortured eyes to me. "I don't give a fuck about the building. I need to see Wren. I need to touch her and know she's okay."

BANE HADN'T LEFT WREN'S ROOM SINCE WE'D ARRIVED at the hospital, and I hadn't left the hallway outside her room since then either. For the last fourteen hours, my ass had been going numb as I waited to be dismissed.

I sat up, though, when Cox walked down the hall toward me. She was dressed in a dark gray pantsuit with glossy black heels. Her hair was pulled into a severe bun at the back of her head.

"What are you doing here?" I asked.

"I'm a detective with the LAPD. I'm investigating the fire."

I narrowed my eyes. "You're vice. You don't investigate fires."

"I do when they involve your boss's girlfriend."

"Don't fucking poke this ant's nest, Cox." I jabbed my finger at her. "You don't want to know what Bane will do if you go near his woman."

Her gray eyes sparked with knowledge. "Actually, that's exactly what I want to do."

As she brushed past me, I grabbed her by the arm. She stopped, looked down at where my fingers wrapped around her bicep, then back at my face.

"What are you going to do, Dagger?" she asked in a low purr. "Hmm? You can't fuck me into submission out here." Her words were bitter, her mouth twisted.

I took a look around at the nursing staff who had stopped to watch us. Fuck, fuck, fuck. I released my fingers and flexed my hand into a fist a couple of times. With one final smirk, she pushed into the hospital room.

I hadn't even gotten the chance to warn Bane.

Pacing outside the room, I waited for Cox to re-emerge, wondering what kind of hell she was raising in there. Bane was vulnerable right now. Wren was injured, and Cox coming in to poke around was going to set him off.

If she pissed him off enough, I knew what the next step would be. Me.

It was another fifteen minutes before she stepped out of the room, the word 'cunt' screamed as the door shut.

"I see you were your usual charming self," I drawled.

She left without a word, and I watched her go. Dammit, I watched her go as my dick got hard while she did it. I didn't understand the attraction I had to her. I didn't understand why I couldn't stay away, but whether or not I understood didn't mean a goddamn thing.

I wanted her.

"Go back to the club." I turned at the sound of Bane's weary voice. "She's asleep. Hawk is coming by to visit her. I'll call you when I need to be picked up."

"Yes, boss."

IN MY OFFICE AT THE DOLLHOUSE, I SHOWERED AND changed, then set my blades on my desk, along with metal oil, rags, and newspaper. My anger battered against me. Normally, it felt like a storm raging inside me. Tonight, a hurricane was a better comparison. The rage was focused on one thing and one thing only—Cox.

One of these days, she was going to say something to Bane—suggest at something—that he'd take for the threat it was. After that happened, I would be ordered to take care of the problem.

I dropped into the chair and picked up the first knife, checking the cutting edge to make sure there weren't any nicks or warping in the metal. Placing a few drops of oil onto the rag, I started to clean. Cleaning and oiling my blades always brought me a small measure of calm. It allowed me to get out of my head for a little while, to focus on one task.

If Bane asked me to take care of Cox in the permanent sense, I didn't know whether I could go through with it. This woman was growing to mean something to me, and I hated how that was starting to jade some of my thoughts. Things that were simple before were now becoming a lot less clear-cut. If Bane wanted a competitor beaten but still breathing at the end to retell the tale, then I would do that. If he wanted me to find him staff who were willing to show their appreciation on their knees, I would do that too. Although this morning, before Cox had come to the club looking for Bane, I'd had the opportunity to get my dick sucked by more than one woman, but I'd turned them all down. At the time, I'd told myself it was because I wasn't feeling it, but sitting here now in my office once more, I knew it was because I didn't want to fucking upset the applecart. I didn't want to do that to Chantelle.

Snatching a clean, soft cloth from the table, I buffed the steel to a high shine.

My childhood was normal—well, as normal as a military brat could have, at least. My father was in the Marines, my mother stayed at home to look after my sister and me. My father loved my mother deeply and with all his heart, and was soft with her, but firm with my sister and me. My father's legacy to me was a strong sense of right and wrong, and the drive to become a Marine like him.

I did join, but after seeing the horrors that only war can manifest, my moral compass became a little more flexible. It was how I was able to work for Bane. He may have been ruthless, but there was a valid reason for everything he did. Bane still worked on what was right and wrong, but his scope had shrunk down to involve him, his sister, his businesses, and now, Wren Montana.

Did that make him any weaker? No. If anything, it made him stronger.

He knew where the hard lines were. Cross one and as far as he was concerned, that person would be paid a visit.

By me.

Despite knowing this and seeing this, I still couldn't shake the promise I'd made to myself after my mother's sudden death. I saw what became of my father after her passing. Gone was the strong, vibrant man he used to be. In his place was a broken shell.

After seeing the man I idolized as a kid reduced to nothing more than a blubbering old man pining for his dead wife, I told myself I wouldn't let one woman lead me around by my cock...

... but that's exactly what Cox was doing to me.

"Fuck!" I got out of my chair and went to the liquor cabinet on the adjacent wall, pulling out a glass from the cupboard below. There was a bottle of bourbon on the counter. I unscrewed the cap and poured myself a double shot. The bottle went down, the glass came up, and I swallowed. Winced. Poured myself another shot.

As I stared into space in my office, I tried to remind myself once more why I didn't need a woman.

Love made you weak.

Love gave your enemies something to threaten you with.

Love would kill something inside me—some kind of ruthlessness that I wanted to keep because that ruthlessness helped me do my goddamn job.

I poured another double shot then took the glass to the table.

Picking up the knife I'd been working on, I checked it over one last time, seeing my face reflected back at me in the blade.

It couldn't be love. Cox was prickly and a fucking difficult woman to read. She was fierce, but there were moments where her softness shone through. It wasn't when I was topping her. It was more in the quiet moments, right after I'd made her come that she looked at me in a certain way. It wasn't the usual burning hatred she showed everyone. It was something else. Something I thought might only be for me to see when she let all her walls down.

I set the knife down on the sheet of newspaper I'd spread on the table then picked up the next. I went through the same process again.

Checking the blade for faults.

Cleaning it.

Buffing it until it shone.

Everything else inside me was conflicted, except for this. I knew how to use these weapons. I knew they would save my life, and many of them had.

I took another sip of my bourbon but set the glass on the table and swiped up my phone when it started to ring.

It was Bane.

"Boss?" I answered.

"Cox is threatening to bring you in for questioning."

And there it was. The final insult to Bane. Swallowing down on the lump in my throat, I made sure my voice was even when I asked, "Want me to get rid of her?"

Read: *Do you want me to put a bullet in her skull and dispose of the body where nobody would ever find it?*

"No. If she goes missing, they'll know something is up. I think this witness thing is bullshit but look into it."

"You got it. Anything else?"

"Just tell me we're locked down tight on this."

"We are."

He blew out a breath. "Okay. Call me if you need me. I can be down at the club in ten."

"We're all good, boss." I hung up, tossing the phone back onto the desk. It did two revolutions across the glossy surface before finally coming to rest against a manila folder.

I frowned.

I didn't use fucking manila folders. I didn't even have a fucking filing cabinet in here. Reaching out, I placed my hand on top of the folder and dragged it closer. There was nothing on the front to tell me what might be inside. Taking one of my daggers, I slid it under the flap and lifted. My eyes widened.

Inside, there were surveillance photos and what looked like screen grabs from CCTV cameras of Sanderson meeting with men who I recognized as mercs. I rifled through the papers and found transcripts of phone conversations between Sanderson and the guys he'd hired to take out Bane's dealers.

There was a sticky note on one of the photos that read 'Evidence as requested, D.'"

Devil.

He had fucking come through.

20

Cox

AS I STOOD IN THE MID-AFTERNOON SUN BEHIND A restaurant in Van Nuys that had been closed for renovations, I covered my nose with the back of my hand and tried to keep the tears at bay. They were stinging the corners of my eyes, but I refused to let them fall.

Harper's naked body had been left behind the dumpster, hidden from casual view.

I frowned, trying to recall the last time I'd spoken to her. It had to have been Monday morning—after my run. Maybe if I'd sent the cops over to her place, she would still be alive.

Shaking my head, I tried not to fixate on things that were out of my control.

I had to focus on the evidence so I could find Harper's killer.

She had been stabbed multiple times, although just how many times we wouldn't know until the coroner picked her up. I crouched beside her head and slowly reached my gloved hand out to touch her blonde hair. I'd always assumed the color had come from a bottle, but it was too soft to be anything but real.

"You all right there, Detective?" Ella asked, suddenly appearing beside me.

I jerked to my feet like someone had pulled my strings. Wiping my free hand over my eye, I sheared away the tears and said, "No."

Her shrewd eyes darted from the body, then back to me.

"You know who she is." Not a question. A statement.

I nodded. "Her name is Harper Stephenson. She was a prostitute and one of my informants."

"You're sure it's her?"

I gestured to the tattoo on her chest—the cursive name of her first-ever boyfriend and pimp. "Yeah. I've never met anyone else with that kind of ink." I wiped away another tear quickly. "She was only twenty-five."

"Jesus, I'm sorry, Cox." She touched me briefly on the arm—a bare touch then gone. If I hadn't seen her do it, I would've wondered whether she'd reached for me at all.

I straightened my spine. "It's fine."

Ella nodded and got to work, ignoring the way I was reacting to the death of this young woman. It wasn't that we were friends, but she had the same sort of tragic life as Lucy had had. Despite having an abusive father, who passed her around among his friends, and instead of falling apart, she'd picked herself up and done the best she could with her life.

"My initial count is forty-six stab wounds to her chest, neck, and torso," Ella began. "The attack was frenzied, which would indicate a level of familiarity to the victim." She gestured to some bruising around her thighs. "I'd suggest getting a rape kit done just in case."

"Maybe we'll get a hit on DNA," I murmured. I hoped like hell we did. I had every intention of bringing down this John.

"Do you know if she had any enemies?"

"Not that I knew of. Harper and I kept our arrangement under wraps. Nobody knew…

I stopped, because that wasn't right. *Somebody* knew—or at least I suspected they knew. That morning on the phone when she'd told me her John had come to her apartment covered in blood. He could've overheard at least some of our conversation.

"Detective?"

I blinked and refocused on Ella. "Sorry."

"You thought of something?"

"Just my last phone call with Harper. There was a man with her, and I got the sense that she was scared."

"Do you know who it was?"

"She didn't say." And now I wished I'd forced the issue.

"When did you last speak to her?"

"Monday morning."

Ella looked at Harper's broken body. "I'd say she was only dumped here in the last eighteen to twenty-four hours."

"Find out, Ella." Then I was going to fucking pay a visit to the bastard who thought to lay a hand on her.

I made myself look at Harper one last time. Committed her broken and defiled body to memory. I would live for the rest of my days with the knowledge that she had died because of me. Just like Lucy had died because of me.

AFTER I LEFT THE CRIME SCENE, I RETURNED TO THE OFFICE

to start on the mountain of paperwork I had on my desk. I got lost in the monotony of it, glad that I could stop thinking for a little while.

"I heard one of your whores was found dead this morning."

My eyes drifted up to Tom Bridey, who was standing in front of my desk with his hands on his hips and a smug smile on his lips.

I sat back in my chair. "You're a real asshole, you know that, Bridey?" Shaking my head, I looked back at the report I was writing.

"How the hell are you going to catch the dealer murderer now?" he mocked. "I guess you'll actually have to do some fucking work. For once."

Blowing out a breath, I mentally counted to ten as I inhaled a cleansing breath. "I know you think I pay informants for information with things other than money, but you're goddamn wrong about Harper. She was murdered for helping me. Not for financial gain, but because she knew what right and wrong were."

His smug grin turned into something a little more sinister. "Was she fucking you? Is that what you demanded as payment for your protection? Too bad you couldn't even hold up your end of the bargain."

I was out of my chair before I could think clearly. Rounding the desk, my hand already curled into a fist, I hit the bastard in the nose. Because we were around the same height, I connected right where I'd wanted to. Cartlidge crunched beneath my knuckles. Blood spurted from his nostrils, and he went down—bending at the middle.

He wasn't hurt enough yet, though. Bringing my knee up, I went to ram it into his nose when I felt strong hands wrap around my upper body, pinning my arms to my side, and I was pulled backward. I let out an inarticulate scream, bucking against the arms that held me while tears started to stream down my face.

"Put me down!" I yelled. "Put me the fuck down. Nobody fucking manhandles me!"

"I'll put you down once you calm down, Cox."

It was James Ward. He was strong, and I hadn't realized I'd not noticed it before. Ward was a good cop—solid and dependable in a situation that called for calm.

"Put. Me. Down." I bit out the words, hoping Ward would see that I was serious about fucking Bridey up.

"How about we go sit down for a while?" he suggested, although I wasn't sure why. He simply removed me bodily from the room and into the captain's office. Captain Holt was behind his desk, watching carefully. Ward dropped me into the seat, and I leaped up. Ward shut the door and stood in front of it with his hands up.

"You don't want to do this, Cox."

Calm.

He was so fucking calm.

"Yeah, I do. Bridey has been insinuating things for months now."

"So? Let him."

My jaw clenched. "I can't. You don't know what it's like for a woman on vice."

"Sit the fuck down, Cox," Holt said.

I tore my gaze from the window and looked firstly at the captain then at Ward.

The captain looked calm—almost nonplussed.

Ward said, "I know what it's like to be a cop who's just

responded to a case that hit too fucking close to home.'"

I glared at him, daring him to take back the words. "Why would you think that?"

"I see you didn't deny it."

I held his gaze, waiting for him to flinch. Back down. Something. Instead, he met my stare with a steady patience I wasn't aware he had.

Slumping into the chair, I cradled my head in my hands and said, "She was one of mine. I was supposed to protect her."

"A friend?"

Maybe not in the traditional sense, but... "Yeah."

"You couldn't save her."

I turned my head to look at him. "I didn't know..." Shaking my head, I drew in a shallow breath through my mouth. "She was in trouble, and I knew it, but I was too fucking caught up in my own shit..."

"We all get busy with our own lives. Did she ask for your help?"

"No, but the last thing she did was help me. And now she's fucking dead."

Ward crouched down in front of me—not touching—but close enough that I could see the sincerity in his eyes when he told me, "I think you're getting too close to this case."

"I'm not." Jesus, I even sounded petulant to myself.

Holt interjected, "Jesus Christ, Cox, don't make me order you to take the rest of the day."

I began to shake my head and said to Holt, "I can't."

"You almost killed Bridey."

I blinked at that statement.

"The knee shot would've driven bone fragments into his brain. You broke his nose with the first punch. If you'd kneed him in the nose like you'd wanted to, he probably wouldn't have survived it."

In the moment, I'd wanted him dead. I didn't say that. Instead, I said, "I have to get out of here."

Ward rose to his feet, drawing my attention. "Can I drive you anywhere?"

"No. I got it." I brushed past him but stopped at the door. Turning back to him, I said, "Thanks for talking me off the fucking ledge, Ward."

He gave me a gentle smile. I knew he was a new father, and in that moment, I knew his little girl would want for nothing. There was kindness and compassion in him that so few men had.

Then to Captain Holt I said, "I'm sorry for my conduct, Captain."

He acknowledged my apology with a nod of his head. "Take a couple of days, Cox. Get your head on straight."

Our gazes held for a moment, then I left the precinct.

Getting into my car, I started the engine and got the air conditioning pumping. I sat there for a long time. I didn't know where to go. I didn't know what to do, but for the first time in eighteen years, I knew I didn't want to be alone.

21

Dagger

IT WAS EARLY ON SATURDAY MORNING. I'D GOTTEN to the club before Bane, figuring he wouldn't be in before mid-morning on account of Wren and her recovery from the fire. After I'd dropped them off at his apartment on Thursday night, I sensed Bane needed breathing space and time to work through his anger.

I knew I would have if it was my woman who had nearly died.

I started going through the information Devil had left for me, reading through the transcripts, studying each of the photos to see where the meets had taken place. My eyes ratcheted to my phone when it *pinged* with Cox's location.

"Shit."

I rose from my chair, the holster with my Browning snug against my ribs. I hesitated for a moment before shoving all the papers back into the folder and dumping it into the top drawer.

Cox didn't need to see it.

In the hallway, I turned to the external exit a few feet from my door and opened it. Chantelle stood there—for once not looking like her usual ball-busting self. Dressed in yoga pants and a hoodie, which she'd drawn over her head, it had taken me a moment to recognize her. Her gray eyes were like smoked glass, her jaw set, her emotions locked down. I stared at her and knew something was up.

Whatever the fuck it was, we couldn't be having this conversation outside in plain sight.

"Come into my office."

She stepped into the club, her shoulder, hip, and thigh brushing past my body. Shutting the door, I followed her into the office. She circled the space, looking at the bare walls and even barer desk. I closed the door behind us, locked it, then folded my arms across my chest.

Even though it shouldn't have been possible, she looked like a caged bird in my space. Delicate. Fragile. As I waited her out, I stared at the expanse of her runner's legs and her firm ass as it peeked out from underneath the oversized sweatshirt when she moved.

When she finally turned around to face me, she drew back the hood from her head, determination glinting in her eyes. "This will never happen again."

I pushed off the wall I'd been leaning on. "What won't?"

"This." She gestured to the office. "Why I'm here. What I'm about to ask you for."

I raised a brow. "And what is it you're about to ask me for, *cara?*"

She took in a deep breath and let it out. "I need you to make me forget."

Forget? Then I saw it. I saw every ounce of pain in her face. "Jesus, who hurt you?" I demanded, stepping forward.

"Nobody hurt me. But I am hurt." She let me see the anguish, the tears already welling in her eyes. Her gaze skated down to my hip. "Make me forget. Please."

She wanted me to use my knife on her.

"Cox," I rasped, my dick already getting hard at the prospect of taking a blade to her perfect skin again.

"Please." She gripped my forearm, digging her nails into the muscle. "Please."

I should've told her hell no, that this wasn't the right time or place to do it, but I didn't. I saw the achingly bare and hauntingly raw vulnerability in her gray eyes and knew. Knew it had cost her to come here. It was costing her still to ask me to top her—to make her forget so completely if only for a little while.

"If we do this, I need you to trust me. I don't want to hurt you."

Her eyes became hollow like she was losing herself to a memory. "I don't care if you do."

No, that wasn't how this worked. "You need to trust me, just as I need to trust you'll tell me when to stop. This is important. Nod if you understand what I'm saying to you."

I waited, my skin vibrating with energy.

She finally nodded, and I released the breath I hadn't known I was holding.

"Take off the sweatshirt." My tone had shifted—become more dominant—and she responded.

There was a subtle change to the set of her shoulders as she gave herself over to me. Holding my eyes, she took her sweatshirt off carefully, revealing a spaghetti strap tank beneath.

I fingered the thin fabric holding it onto her body. "Are you attached to that?"

"No." It was a bare whisper.

Unbuttoning my shirt, I undid the cuffs, then shrugged it off my shoulders. Her eyes dropped to my chest then back to my face. Reaching down, I pulled out the dagger strapped to my hip and brought it up to her face.

I pinned her with a hard look. "Trust me." It wasn't a question, but a command, and one I hoped she heeded. Sliding the tip of the blade under one strap, I sliced through the fabric with very little effort. I repeated the action on the other side, watching the thin cotton straps fall away from her shoulders.

With my free hand, I hooked my finger into the front of the tank and dragged it down, pulling the cotton away from her breasts. My eyes feasted on them for a moment, enjoying the way her nipples hardened into taut peaks in the cold rush of air.

Bringing up the blade, I laid the tip against one breast—the sharp edge toward her nipple. Her pulse pounded against the steel, reverberating up into my hand.

"I can feel your heart thudding through the steel." My eyes flickered to hers. "You're scared."

Licking her lips, she nodded.

"But you're not afraid that I'll cut you."

"No."

This fucking woman. Although it took all the strength and fucking willpower I had, I stepped away from her, dropping my arm to my side.

"Strip."

There was a brief hesitation before she hooked her thumbs

into the waistband of her yoga pants and dragged them down and off her legs. She kicked off her panties and rose to her full height once more—staring at me. Pleading with me to continue.

I took my time looking at her naked body, already picturing her skin marked up with my knife. Her breathing was coming in shallow pants that I knew had nothing to do with fear and everything to do with anticipation. I took all of her in. Her bared breasts, which moved gently with the rise and fall of her chest, her slightly concave stomach, the flare of her hips, the slice of heaven between her legs, her athletic thighs and tapered calves.

Gripping her jaw, I forced her to look at me. "I want you to give your pain to me."

She shook her head. "I don't understand."

"You want me to top you… to make you forget. I can do that, but I need you to let me take up the space in your mind."

"Okay."

My answering grin was fierce. "There are rules. This is consensual. If you want to stop something, say *red*. If you're unsure of something, but want to continue, say *yellow*. *Green* means you're okay with what's going on and you're enjoying yourself. Understand?"

She nodded.

"Using knives in edge play can be dangerous. Don't jerk or move unexpectedly.

After the scene is finished, I'll make sure you feel okay. There is just one more thing I ask of you."

Her gray eyes widened. "What is it?"

Releasing her, I opened up my closet and pulled out a black tie. I showed it to her.

"I want to blindfold you."

For a long moment she said nothing, and I thought I'd maybe pushed her too far—too fast.

"Yellow," she eventually whispered.

Relief settled over me.

She was so strong-willed that I wasn't surprised she was being cautious.

"I've got you, *cara*."

Stepping forward, I secured the tie in place, knotting the back. A small tremor rocked through her body as she stood before me, but I didn't think it was fear that made her shiver.

With her eyesight gone, the effect would be immediate. All her other senses would take up the slack. She would be able to hear the whisper of my clothing as I moved around her. She would be able to smell the metal oil I used on my blades. She would be able to taste my anticipation. But most of all—she would be able to experience everything.

I took her by the wrist, feeling her resist against my grip almost immediately. Placing my mouth to her ear, I said, "I need to get you in position."

She swallowed, opened her mouth to protest, then shut it. Her muscles unclenched, and I took her closer to the desk.

"Bend over, hands out. Press your palms against the desktop."

Lowering herself down, she rested the top half of her body on the desk, while her ass remained in the air.

Hovering over her body, I whispered into her ear, "Are you ready?"

After waiting for her nod, I caressed her shoulders, her back, her ass. The long, languid strokes would bring down her heart rate and ease her breathing. When I was sure she was ready, I began to move the knife. I started at the top of her back, running the dull edge of the blade over the ridges of her spine. The metal undulated over each protrusion until I reached the top of her ass. Leaning down, I licked the path the knife had taken, making her suck in a sharp gasp. Her skin tasted of salt. And of sorrow.

Placing the dagger at the top of her shoulder blade this time, I outlined the flat bone as it curved close to her spine then drew it down her side. She whimpered a little with that but didn't use the safe word. I did the same on the other side, hearing her sigh. Trailing the dull side of the tip across her ass gave her a visceral response—goosebumps breaking out on her skin in a frenzied rush. Down the backs of her thighs, red lines formed in the wake of the steel.

When the back of her body was decorated with red marks, I helped her stand and turned her around. Her nipples were hard peaks, and I leaned down to take one into my mouth. She moaned, her hands flexing at her sides like she wasn't sure she could move them.

Drawing her other nipple into my mouth, I bit down on the sensitive flesh then licked away the sting.

"How are you feeling?" I asked.

"Green."

"You're sure?"

When she nodded, I rested the flat of my blade against her breast then ran the tip very gently around her nipple. Her responding gasp went straight to my dick. I was so fucking ready to impale her with my body, but I didn't mix knife play with sex at the same time. If there were ever a time you could fuck it up, it would be then.

Trailing the tip between the valley of her breasts, I circled the other aching bud then lowered the knife between her thighs.

Skimming the dull edge along the inside of her thighs, I reached that perfect spot on a woman, where her leg finished and her pussy began. Chantelle shivered when I ran the steel against her, moaning, but not moving.

"Good girl," I praised quietly, dropping a kiss to the edge of her mouth. "You look fucking beautiful covered in my marks, *cara*. Do you know that?"

Biting her lip, she nodded. From underneath the blindfold, a single tear escaped. Seeing that one droplet felt like a kick in the fucking guts. I set the dagger down.

"Chantelle?" I asked, pulling the blindfold down and revealing her clear gray eyes. Usually, they were filled with determination and drive, but now they were filled with tears.

I scooped her up into my arms and cradled her against my chest, trying to ignore how good it felt to have her there. "Did I hurt you? Talk to me, Chantelle. Did I *hurt* you?"

"No."

My shoulders slumped in relief. I strode around the desk and lowered myself into my office chair. She squirmed in my arms, but I tightened my grip. "If I didn't hurt you, then tell me what's wrong. Tell me who to kill, *cara*, and they're dead."

"Nobody hurt me," she replied in a deceptively soft voice.

I scowled. "Then what the fuck happened?"

She fixed her steely gaze on my face as she tried to wall up her emotions once more, tears still drying on her cheeks. "Let me up."

"No."

Glaring, she tried to wiggle free again. But I didn't let her. "Dagger, let me up."

Her bare breasts pressed against my chest. "No."

"You aren't going to let it go, are you?"

"No."

She stared ahead at the wall, refusing to meet my eyes. "One of my informants was found murdered yesterday afternoon."

"Okay."

"Will you let me up now?"

"No. Keep talking."

Inhaling deeply through her nose, she continued, "She was only twenty-five years old, and I knew she was in trouble. I *knew* it but I was so wrapped up in the case that I didn't see it in time..."

She dragged in a deep, rattling breath, like she'd been bottling this up and now that there was a chink in her armor, it was all flowing out. I'd thought Cox was a heartless bitch who enjoyed torturing people, but I was seeing a glimmer of something else here. A sliver of humanity that I wasn't sure I still had in my possession.

"I... I... Lucy..." she moaned. Tears started streaking down her cheeks again, and I couldn't take it anymore. I repositioned her so she was straddling my hips and held her while she cried—her face pressed to my chest. She wrapped her arms around my body, clinging to me as she fell apart. Like I was her safe harbor. Like I would stop her from floating away on this sea of grief.

Her whole body shook as she cried for the death of the woman, and I held her against me like I could protect her from everything the world could throw our way.

After ten minutes, her body started to lose some of those shaking jerks. After fifteen, the crying had slowed. After twenty, she blinked up at me with red-rimmed eyes. Snapping some tissues from the box in my drawer, I handed them to her.

She blew her nose and wiped the last of the tears away,

scrunching the used tissue in her palm.

"How long was Lucy your informant?" I asked, my voice hoarse.

She stared at me. "Lucy wasn't my informant."

"But you said her name was Lucy."

"No…" A frown. "No… her name was Harper."

I filed that name away. Maybe Devil's guys could find out who Lucy was to Cox. "All right. How long was *Harper* your informant?"

"I don't want to talk about this, Dagger."

"What do you want to do?"

The look in her eyes made my cock twitch. "I want to forget. I want you to fuck me so hard that I forget this pain."

"*Cara,*" I said in warning. She'd emotionally broken apart in front of me. As much as I wanted to give her what she was asking for, I didn't think sex was the answer, until she said…

"Please."

I couldn't say no to my woman when she was begging me. I growled low in my throat, then pressed my mouth to hers. She opened for me, groaning. We kissed so fiercely that our teeth clashed, our tongues dueled, each of us trying to dominate the other. Her fingers tightened against my neck while she pushed her chest against mine.

"Grind your cunt against me," I said against her mouth.

With a small moan, she did just that. Rolling her hips, she pressed the softest part of her against the hardest part of me. I was thick and long behind my zipper, and she writhed against all that hard length.

"I need you inside me," she whispered. "Fuck me, Dagger. Please."

I grabbed her by the hips, a guttural 'fuck' bubbling up from my throat. Lifting her off my lap, I placed her on the edge of the desk so I could get my cock out. She watched me so intensely that I wished she was still dressed so I could tear the clothes from her body.

Taking her by the waist, I settled her back onto my lap, my cock pressing against the heat of her hot, glistening pussy. I stroked her clit with the pad of my thumb, making her throw her head back. Leaning forward, I licked up the column of her bare throat, inhaling the scent of her skin.

She raised her body above my hips, gliding the head of my cock through her pussy lips. She was drenched, and when she lined me up with her entrance, I flexed my hips and entered her in one strong surge.

"Dagger," she gasped, sitting back down, taking all of me into her warm, wet body.

Wrapping one arm around her waist, I snaked the other up her spine and wrapped my fingers around the back of her neck, controlling her movements. A stiffness that had been in her body was suddenly gone as I took control of the sex. I pounded into her body, the slapping sound of naked flesh filling my office.

"I want to hit the end of you," I told her, standing and kicking the chair back toward the wall. "I want to mark my goddamn territory." What I didn't verbalize was the reason. I wanted to mark her so that any other man who got access to her sweet cunt would know I was there before him. Even the thought made me want to commit murder. But there was one place that hadn't been explored yet, and I was going to make it mine.

She wrapped her legs around my waist, our bodies still connected. When I made it around to the other side of my desk,

I was forced to slide my way out of her slick channel while I turned her around and placed her hands on the desk. Taking a step back, I looked at the perfection that was mine.

Fuck.

She was a feast for the senses, from the smell of sex to the soft mewling sounds she made in the back of her throat.

"Show me that cunt of yours, *cara*. Spread your legs a little wider."

With a small whimper, she widened her stance. I stroked one ass cheek then the other before dipping my fingers lower into all that sweet honey. My fingers were damp with her juices, and I brought one finger up to that tight bud I hadn't explored yet.

I worked the tip inside her, feeling her muscles tense around me.

"Relax," I murmured. "I'll make you feel so good. All you have to do is give me your pleasure."

Like a good submissive, she relaxed against my probing finger, and I was able to push in to my first knuckle. I wondered if she knew that's what she was—a submissive. Not full-time, but in the bedroom, her pleasure belonged to me.

"God," she gasped, pushing back against me.

I smiled. She was eager, and the knowledge made my cock jump. "I won't fuck your sweet ass today, but soon. For now, you'll take my finger, won't you, baby?"

She moaned a 'yes,' and I stepped closer. Lining my cock up with her entrance, I worked my way inside. I shoved all the way in until I could feel the end of her body like a physical barrier, then withdrew slowly, dragging my cock over that spot inside her. At the same time, I worked my finger deeper inside her ass, feeling the twin contractions of her inner muscles.

Reaching around, she clawed at my arm. "Faster. More."

Flexing my hips forward, I gave her what she wanted, slamming into her quickly before pulling out slowly. She writhed as I moved into her, then clamped down as I tried to withdraw.

"You're greedy for my cock, aren't you? Say it, *cara.* Say you want my cock."

Her words came out in a rush. "I want it. I want your cock."

Leaning over her, I dropped saliva onto her ass and spread it around with my index finger. Now that she was better lubricated, I was able to work my way into her body a little more—to my second knuckle.

"Dagger!" she gasped.

There was something about my name on Chantelle's lips that flat out did it for me. I pumped into her with my cock and finger, feeling her body beginning to tighten around me.

"I'm close," she whispered. "So close. So close. So close."

I thrust into her more deeply, feeling my balls draw up, the orgasm coming quickly.

"Come with me," I rasped. My pace was frantic, the sound of our slapping flesh loud in my office. "Come now. Now!"

She screamed her release, her orgasm milking my cock until I was coming inside of her too. We chased each other's orgasms, every spasm of her inner muscles drawing another jet of cum from me.

I collapsed onto her back—one hand planted next to hers on the desk. Our breathing matched. Both a harsh wheeze. Both labored. Drawing my hips away, I stumbled back a step. I stared at her, still bent over, wondering why she had this power over me.

Before I could think about it anymore, my phone rang. Scooping it up from the desk, I answered, "Boss?" My voice was even, not betraying how winded I was.

"What the fuck happened in four?"

I frowned, having no idea what he was talking about. "Boss?"

"Get your ass down here." He hung up. When I looked up, Chantelle was pulling on her hoodie and yoga pants, barely looking at me.

"Where are you going?"

"Home," she replied sharply. "I got what I needed."

Coldness settled over me. "You just needed a dick?"

"Yeah." Her gray gaze flickered my way quickly then away. "All I needed was a dick."

"Bullshit."

"Look, I don't have time for this." She moved to the door, but I stopped her.

"Bullshit, Chantelle. You were really hurting when you came in here. You came to me for comfort."

She turned on me, hitting me with the full force of her intelligent eyes. "Yeah, I did." She laughed, and it was a harsh sound. "I don't fucking know why. I don't know why I expected you to be able to offer me comfort. You're the bodyguard to a criminal. You know nothing about comforting someone."

She was pulling away from me, and my anger flared. "Cox," I ground out—a warning that the violence I was feeling was stripping away my civility.

"It's Cox now, is it?" She barked another humorless laugh and shook her head. "Of course, it is." Unlocking the door, she yanked it open and stepped from my office.

Goddammit, I wanted to go after her, but my loyalty was to Bane.

Throwing on my clothes, I hustled out into the Dollhouse

where I found Bane standing in front of room four. He gestured to the open door, and I stepped inside. The leather chair had been tipped over onto its side and the seat slashed, the cupboard with the floggers, paddles, shibari ropes, and whips in disarray. Even the drawer where the condoms and lube were held had been upended. *What in the actual fuck had happened?*

"It wasn't like this at closing last night."

"So, when did it happen?" he demanded in a sharp tone.

Digging into my pocket, I pulled out my phone and clicked into the club's log system. All the Dolls had access cards to get into the rooms. Each time they swiped to gain entry, it got logged with a time stamp.

"This morning. According to the system, the room was accessed by Veronica at ten o'clock." The same time Cox had come to the back door. Fucking hell.

"Get her in my office. Now!" he bellowed. "And fucking get this room cleaned up." He stalked away, and I called Veronica.

"Veronica? Dagger. Bane wants to see you."

"I'm about ten minutes away," she replied softly. "Do you know what this is about?"

"You'll find out when you get here."

I heard her swallow before I hung up. Walking to the back of the room, I opened the door that led into the cleaning corridor and found Velvet reading a magazine on the couch. She had a pair of headphones on, her head bobbing to the beat of whatever she was listening to.

"What are you doing here? Your shift doesn't start for another four hours."

She turned, her cheeks flushing with color as she pushed the speakers from her ears. "Shit's going on at home. I couldn't stand to be there."

I had to find out what was up. But for now… "Come and help me."

She slid off the couch and entered the room, her eyes widening. "What the hell happened in here?"

"That's what we're trying to find out. You didn't hear anything?"

She took the headphones from around her neck. "No."

"I need you to clean up while I source some more furniture for the room."

Stepping back into the corridor, I opened another door which functioned as our furniture closet. We'd discovered that the private space furniture needed to be changed often so we ordered more than one of everything. Identifying the chair I needed, I retrieved it from the industrial shelving unit and returned to the room.

Velvet had most of the unbroken furniture righted and was putting away the toys. I took out the ruined chair and brought in the new one. When it looked as it did last night, I thanked Velvet and went to wait at the bar for Veronica.

The Doll came through the staff entrance a few minutes later, her makeup a little heavier than normal and sporting a cut on her lip. Her eyes stayed on the floor as she said, "Is Mr. Rivera mad at me?"

I tipped up her chin so I could see her face properly. "What the fuck happened to you?"

"I got mugged last night after my shift," she replied in a hoarse voice.

"Let's go and speak to Bane."

I escorted her up to his office, where he gave her the same twenty-questions routine as I had.

He paced across his office, his hands curled into fists. "Tell me everything again."

"I take the bus home from the club, but the stop is about a block from my apartment. That's when it happened."

"Jesus *fuck!*" he shouted.

Veronica flinched, edging back a step. I placed my hand on the small of her back, keeping her in place.

Bane rolled to a stop. "Are you okay? Any other injuries beside the shiner and the busted lip?"

"Fine, physically."

"What did they take? Did you get a good look at them?"

"My bag was stolen. I tried to snatch it back, and my phone fell out. I grabbed that and dialed 911. They were long gone by the time the cops got to me."

"Was your swipe card in there?"

She bobbed her head. "Yeah, and all the tips I made last night."

"How much did you make?" Bane asked, reaching into his wallet.

"About three hundred."

He pulled out five one hundred dollar bills and handed them to her.

She bent her head over the money. "This is too much, Mr. Rivera."

"The extra is to get yourself some makeup or some shit to cover that black eye. I can't have you working here with a split lip, though. You'll have to take some time off to heal. I'll pay you even though you aren't coming in."

"Seriously?"

He nodded. "I look after my Dolls, Veronica."

For a moment, she didn't do a thing. Then she walked over to

Bane, dropped to her knees, and reached for his belt.

Bane caught her hands. "What are you doing?" he asked in a hollow voice.

"Thanking you."

Instead of taking her up on the offer like I thought he would, he helped her stand and turned her around, shoving her in the direction of the door. "You can thank me by healing and getting back here as soon as you can. Call Dagger if you need anything."

After the girl stumbled from the room, Bane focused on me.

"I need you to fucking find out who accessed that room, Dagger. Go through the footage. And when you find out who fucked me over, I'm going to fuck *them* over."

"Yes, boss."

I RETURNED TO BANE'S OFFICE AN HOUR LATER TO show him the surveillance footage of Syndy entering the club. Since the bitch had been fired and her swipe card confiscated, she had to be the one who mugged Veronica. Bane would have the girl's head for this. As I entered the staff area, a feeling of unease prickled at the back of my neck. Even though I couldn't hear anything, my senses didn't lie. Something was wrong. I hustled to get to Bane's office door. Pushing inside, I scanned the scene in two seconds then pulled out my Browning, holding it level with Syndy's head as she stood there, unmoving.

In a deceptively calm voice, Bane said, "She set the fire at Wren's apartment. She's also the one who mugged Veronica and stole her access card."

I slid my finger off the guard and onto the trigger. "Want me to get rid of her?"

"Please!" Syndy begged, all the color draining from her face. "I just wanted you to see that we are meant to be together."

"Not here," Bane replied. "Take her somewhere nobody will *ever* find her."

"Please. No. *Please!*" Syn begged as I removed her from the room.

"Shut her up. We don't need people hearing her scream."

Nodding, I brought the butt of the gun down on her temple, knocking her out. Before I left, I said, "Top drawer of my desk. There's something that will interest you in there."

What I didn't say was that I needed him to have his head back on business before I showed it to him. Now that Wren was recovering well, it was time to share what Devil had found out.

Bane nodded.

Throwing Syndy over my shoulder, I walked down the stairs and out into the alley behind the club. After zip-tying her wrists and ankles, gagging her, and shoving her into the trunk of the car, I went into that place inside my head where there was nothing but white noise and a numb coldness. Murder was something I did. *Did it play on my conscience?* Probably not in the way most people would think.

The act itself didn't bother me. What bothered me the most was that it *didn't* bother me. I was okay with snuffing the flame of another person. I could only blame that on my training, but sometimes it made me wonder whether I was simply a sociopath with a proclivity for taking life.

I drove down to the docks where I did all the wet work for Bane. The warehouse was set up under a dummy corporation within another dummy corporation, so if anyone were to discover it, they'd be chasing their tails trying to find out who it really belonged to.

Arriving at the warehouse, I parked inside and took Syndy from the trunk. She'd woken up on the drive over. She screamed around the gag as I pulled her from the back of the car and dragged her over to the large blue tarp that was always laid out.

"Nobody can hear you," I told her, pulling my Browning from under my suit jacket and attaching the suppressor.

She tried to crawl away from me, but with her wrists and ankles bound, there was no way she could move freely. She eventually gave up, falling onto her back so she was staring up at me.

Standing over her, I stared right back—into her wide eyes. "You crossed the wrong man, Syndy."

Before she could make another sound, I put two bullets into her skull. She slumped to the tarp-covered floor, blood pouring from the neat holes between her eyes. Unscrewing the suppressor from the muzzle of my gun, I tucked it back into my pocket then put up the weapon. Pulling out my phone, I hit the second number on my speed dial.

"I need a clean-up," I said when the call connected.

"The usual spot?" the woman on the other end replied, her Eastern European accent thick.

"Yes." I hung up. There were twin sisters that I only knew by the names Wicked and Death, who were known for their proficiency in cleaning up murder scenes. Bane had them on retainer, which meant they dropped whatever else they were working on to attend our scenes. Neither of us had ever seen the pair in person. They were ghosts.

I took my car through a carwash on the way back to the club, making sure I cleaned out the trunk space. When I was sure no evidence of Syndy could ever be found in there, I returned to my office to get rid of my clothes and shower. Shucking the shirt and pants, I shoved them into a trash bag that I would take with me when I was done for the night. They were destined for an incinerator, which I kept in a shed in the back garden of my place.

Turning on the water, I didn't bother waiting until it got hot before stepping in. I hissed as the cold spray hit me, but soon relaxed under the punishing pressure of the water. My shoulders held a lot of tension—more so when I was doing wet work. If the cops knew how many people I'd killed under Bane's orders, I would be serving enough life sentences to know I'd never be getting parole.

Once I washed my hair and body meticulously, I got out, snapping a towel from the railing. I dried myself quickly, splashed bleach on every inch of the shower stall and walls, then got dressed.

As I climbed the stairs, I realized Bane's door was cracked open, the sound of a curse then ringing, like a call on loudspeaker filtering through. When the call rang out, it was followed by another curse and another dial.

"Everything all right, boss?" I asked as I strolled into his office.

"Yes. No. Fuck." Uncharacteristically, he ran his hands through his hair. "I don't know. I can't get a hold of Andy."

I leaned against the jamb, folding my arms. "What was he supposed to be doing?"

"Dropping Wren off, but that was an hour ago."

Jesus fuck. The tension in the room was suddenly suffocating, like Bane's admission had been the catalyst for the fucking pressure. "I'll follow it up."

I got back into my car and headed over to Bane's apartment

since that's where the woman was staying.

Maybe Andy was still there, but as I navigated through the dense LA traffic, a fucking horrible thought squeezed my chest. Andy always followed orders. Always. If Bane asked him to check in, he would do it. The fact that he hadn't meant one of two things.

His phone was dead…

… or he was.

I was a block away from Bane's penthouse when I saw the ambulances.

"Fuck," I muttered, double-parking, and flipping off the guy who honked his horn at me. Marching up to the nearest EMT, I demanded to know what happened.

"There's nothing to see here." He spoke without looking up from the clipboard he was writing on. "Move along."

Andy was being loaded into an ambulance a few feet away.

My jaw tensed. "What the hell happened?"

The EMT looked at me, recognition flashing. He swallowed. "Gun shot. In the chest. He's going to be all right. The bullet missed his heart, but looks like it may have nicked his lung. They won't know until they get him to hospital."

"What about the other passenger?"

"Other passenger?"

"A woman. In the back seat?"

He shook his head. "There was only one person in the car when we arrived." The EMT wandered away, leaving me looking at the scene in front of me and wondering how in the hell I was going to tell Bane that Wren was missing.

WHEN I GOT BACK TO THE CLUB, I FOUND BANE IN HIS

office, pacing the floor like a caged wild animal. Hearing what I had to tell him wasn't going to make him any less enraged, so I ripped the Band-Aid off.

"There was an accident. Andy was shot and taken to hospital. Wren wasn't in the back of the car."

"I know," he replied, drawing to a stop. "I just got off the phone with *fucking* Sanderson. That bastard has her."

I stilled. "What?"

"He told me he's been picking off the dealers one by one… not that we didn't already know that thanks to your intel."

"What else did he say?"

"He said he was the one who sent Cox our way in the first place."

I licked my lips. "What does he want from you?"

When Bane cursed and balled his hands into fists, I knew whatever he was going to say next wasn't going to be good. "He wants me out of No Man's Land. And if I don't get out of No Man's Land, he's going to kill Wren." He bit out each of the words like his anger and irritation were ratcheting up with each syllable.

"How are we going to get her back?"

"He texted me an address, and you wouldn't believe where he's set up the meet."

"Where?"

"Our main supply warehouse."

My eyes widened. "At the wharf?"

Bane confirmed my question with a tense nod.

"What are we going to do? We show up there, and he's going to put a bullet in her brain."

"I know. That's why I'm going to call Cox."

I made sure to keep my expression passive, even though inside panic gripped me. "Why?"

"We can't go in there without putting Wren at risk. But she fucking can. If we're lucky, Sanderson might even take the cunt out for us."

22

Cox

I HAD JUST DRIFTED OFF INTO A FITFUL SLEEP WHEN my phone had rung. Groggy, I reached over and answered it.

"Cox," I said, prying my eyes open to look at the time. It was a little before eleven o'clock, which meant I'd had a grand total of thirty minutes of sleep. I had to blame my lack of shut-eye on one thing, and one thing only—Dagger.

There was only breathing on the other end of the line, so I barked, "Who is this?"

"It's Rivera."

That woke me up. I sat up in bed, letting the light sheets fall away from my chest. "Mr. Rivera. What can I do for you?"

"We need to talk."

"Talk?" I replied. "About what? Or are you ready to confess?"

I could've sworn I heard his molars grinding together over the line. "I knew this would fucking happen," he muttered more to himself than to me.

I let him go through the mental gymnastics for a bit longer before saying, "Rivera, it's late. I'm tired. Why the late-night phone call?"

"I need…" Another pause. A curse then a thump like he'd just placed a whisky glass down too hard on a surface. A deep inhalation. "I need your… help with something."

"Can you repeat that? It sounds like you need my help."

"Fuck you, you condescending, cocksucking cunt," he snarled.

"My, my, you have a temper." I was baiting him—I knew that—but this could be the break I needed.

"Peter Sanderson has Wren."

"Wren Montana, the same woman who was in that apartment fire? The same woman you're fucking?"

Grind. Grind. Grind. "Yeah."

"Why would Peter Sanderson have her? I assume you're talking kidnapping rather than over for dinner."

"Because he's fucking punishing me."

"Punishing you for what?" I knew what I was doing—asking him to admit out loud that he was a drug lord, and they were his dealers getting hit. That he had somehow pissed off Sanderson so much that now there was a turf war brewing.

"Are you going to help me or not?" He ground the words out like they were something solid.

"I haven't decided yet. You haven't told me anything other than Wren is with Sanderson."

"Why do you have to be such a cunt about all this?"

I smiled, but there was no humor to it—no warmth. "That's the second time you've called me that in a matter of minutes. What's got your dick in a twist?"

He blew out a breath and this time, it simply sounded resigned.

"If you help me now, I'll agree to a deal."

I swung my legs off the side of the bed and stood, starting to pace. "What kind of deal?" My voice didn't betray an ounce of the eagerness I felt.

"I don't fucking know, but we'll figure something out."

"I want intel about criminal activity in Los Angeles."

He seethed. "No."

"I need something, Rivera. I don't do things out of the kindness of my fucking heart."

"That's because you don't have one," he shot back, his voice low and threatening.

I let that comment slide. "Give me another option then."

"I'll owe you one favor to be decided at a later date. *After* Wren is back and in one piece. What I won't grant you is the names of any of my associates, specific dates, or deals."

"That gives me nothing."

"If you're smart, you'll take this deal."

I blew out a breath. Having the biggest dealer in LA with possible links to the mafia in my pocket was an unexpected boon. "There's a multi-story parking garage on West 6th Street. Be there tomorrow morning at nine o'clock. Level six."

"No. I need to see you tonight. It's important."

"Sorry."

"She'll be dead tomorrow morning at nine," he ground out, like that one confession had cost him. And it had. He had finally showed me his hand. This woman was his weak spot and his blind spot, all rolled into one.

"Fine. Meet me in twenty minutes."

NINETEEN MINUTES LATER, I WAS DRIVING INTO THE parking garage on West 6th. Normally at this time, the place is a ghost town, but it was a Saturday night and people were out, so the place was almost completely full. When I crested the final ramp onto the top level, I saw a solitary car parked at the far end. I pulled in beside it, shut off the engine, and opened the door.

"Mr. Rivera," I said when I slid into the passenger seat of his vehicle. "I must say… your phone call has me intrigued."

"I hope it's intriguing enough that you'll do everything in your power to ensure Wren Montana's survival."

It was. It was the break I needed. It also guaranteed my arrest rate for however long I could draw it out. Having Bane as a one-time informant was like having a goose that laid the golden egg. "It is. But to be sure, tell me everything again."

He ground his molars together, making the muscle in his jaw flex violently. "Peter Sanderson has Wren."

"Why?"

"She's being used as leverage against me."

"Why?"

Grind. Grind. Grind. "I've been stepping on Sanderson's toes for ten years. I guess he's had enough."

I blew out a frustrated breath. "Stepping on his toes, *how*? All you're giving me are cryptic statements, Rivera."

He slammed his hand against the steering wheel, saying angrily, "I don't know what you want me to say."

He was so close to pulling away, but I couldn't afford for him to run now. Not when I was so close, so I decided to change tact. "You know… I looked up Peter Sanderson. Aside from being an art collector, the guy is squeaky clean."

He turned his head to face me. "Then you need to look a little harder."

"How about you tell me what pies he's got his fingers in, then we'll go from there."

"I'm not a fucking rat, and I'm not about to start now."

I smiled. "You are a rat, though. The only reason I came here was to get information from you. You mentioned something about those dealers getting killed. Are they yours?"

"I have no comment on that. Even if they were, you don't have a fucking thing to tie it to me."

"Lying by omission is still lying."

"Lying by omission is the only way to stay breathing," he sneered, cutting me with a sharp glare. "The dealers that have been hit. I can tell you who's been giving the orders."

I shook my head. That wasn't enough. "I want more. I need proof."

He handed me a manila folder. Keeping my eyes on him, I flipped open the top then looked down at the five-by-eight color photographs inside. It showed Sanderson with some known hitmen.

"You'll find more proof waiting for you at this address." He handed me a piece of paper, folded over once. Opening it, I glanced at the address. It was down at the wharves.

"Nine o'clock tomorrow morning. Be there, and you'll get all the proof you need."

I refolded the paper and held his gaze. "Is this legit, or are you sending me on a wild goose chase?"

He shrugged. "I guess the only way you'll know is if you go tomorrow. Now get out of my fucking car."

I popped open the door. "Always a pleasure, Mr. Rivera."

OVER THE LAST FEW HOURS, I'D GONE THROUGH THE folder Rivera had given me, pouring over each picture and each word of the transcripts. Sanderson had been a very busy boy.

"Are you ready, Detective?" Ward's voice crackled through the police radio attached to the dash of my unmarked car.

I picked up the speaker-microphone and pressed the button on the side to speak. "Ready."

Even though Captain Holt had told me to rest for a few days, when I'd brought him this information, I'd said the only reason I was sharing it was because I wanted in on the raid, and I got to choose the team. Reluctantly, Holt had agreed.

I was riding at the back of the convoy with Ward and his partner in the vehicle in front of me. That was another one of the caveats Holt had placed on me—I could go to the raid, but I couldn't be first into the building. Biting my tongue had been difficult, but I'd done as he asked.

Dust was flying into the air as the half dozen squad cars ahead of me entered the wharf and past the chain-link fence that was erected around the warehouse Rivera had revealed to me. *Did I know what the hell I was going to find?* No. Except I hoped that Rivera's woman was still alive—if she was there at all. Trusting the bad guys not to fuck me over was getting easier and easier, and I only had Dagger to blame for that.

Ward came to a stop about sixty feet from the entrance to the warehouse, and I pulled in beside him. Getting out, the oppressive sun was hot on my face and neck, making me sweat in an instant. Ahead of us, officers were out of their cars and taking up positions, falling into organized ranks just like they were trained to do.

"What do you think we'll find?" Ward asked.

I spare him a glance. "Hopefully, our hostage still alive. That's all I can hope for."

"And if she's not?"

"Then whoever the fuck harmed her will be getting a visit from me."

Ahead of us, one of the officers peeled away from the cover of the building and kicked in the door, the other men following him in. From this distance, they looked like ants swarming the ant hill. Once they were in all, I braced for gunfire, letting out a breath when one cop stepped from the doorway and waved me over.

"Cox, come and see this."

Ward stuck to my back as I walked toward the building. Stepping into the warehouse, I had to wait a minute for my eyes to adjust, then I saw it.

The girl was tied to a chair in front of a shipping container that had its doors wide open.

"Ward, get her out of here and call in the EMTs on standby."

He went to Montana's side, and I focused on what was inside the container. Row after row of cocaine bricks. Shit. The street value of it would easily be in the billions.

"Is it pure?" I demanded.

The officer who had called me over, pulled out a switch blade from his pocket. I eyed the knife as he slid the tip into one of the cellophane bags and withdrew it with white powder on the edge of the blade. Licking his pinkie finger first, he dipped it into the powder then rubbed it into his gum. He spat the substance out and said, "As a virgin Columbian."

"Who does it belong to?" another officer asked, inspecting the bricks. If it had a fucking crown on the wrapping, I was going to nail Rivera's ass to the wall.

"The packaging is clean."

"I need to get the paperwork on this warehouse. Find out who the fuck owns it!" I screamed, my voice ricocheting around the vast space. Turning, I retreated from the warehouse to get some fucking air. The wail of ambulances was close. Ward came out with Montana, helping her toward his car. She'd been beaten badly enough that I hardly recognized her as the young woman I'd seen in the hospital.

From a distance, I watched Ward get her settled into the seat of his car, then looked back at the warehouse. What the hell had happened in there? Who had beat this poor girl? Was it Sanderson himself or did he have one of his lackeys do the dirty work? Sanderson simply didn't seem like the kind of man who would get blood on his hands.

"Out! Everyone out!" someone screamed from the warehouse.

I'd just turned my head to see what the problem was when I was blown backward by an explosion. Heat licked at my face and bare arms, singeing the fine hairs on my forearms as I landed hard on my back. The blow shoved all the air from my lungs. Desperately, I tried to suck in the oxygen I needed.

My first thought was my men.

Some of my men were still in the building when it blew.

Getting to my feet, I staggered toward what remained of the warehouse, coughing to clear my suddenly tight throat.

I couldn't have anyone else's deaths on my hands.

I refused.

Shielding my face from the heat, I watched as flames licked the sky, angry orange and yellow. Black smoke ballooned into the atmosphere, the scent of chemicals and burning plastic chasing it. The ground was littered with metal and other identifiable objects that had once belonged to the building.

As I stumbled closer, I scanned the ground, seeing parts of bodies that should never be separated. How many men had I lost? How many families were destroyed because they'd volunteered to come on this raid with me. I wasn't sure my guilt could take another hit.

There was a gasping sound, and I saw I was standing next to a man who was still alive—but not whole. Dropping to my knees, I moved chunks of rubble from his partially covered body. The sharp edges of metal and concrete soon broke my fingernails and cut up my hands, but I ignored the pain. My pain wasn't important.

"Briggs, it's going to be all right," I told him, glancing down the length of his body to check for injuries. I swallowed hard when I found that one of his legs had been blown clean off. I wanted to scream that it wasn't fair, that it shouldn't have ever happened. But mostly, I wanted to step back in time and not come. Never agree to come here. Never agree to meet Rivera in the parking garage. No amount of information could be worth this sort of carnage and loss.

Pushing the bloody hair stuck to his forehead away from his face, I whispered, "We're going to get you out of here. You're going to be all right."

Behind me, ambulances tore into the destruction, getting as close as they could until they couldn't navigate the minefield of debris anymore.

"Come and help me, goddammit!" I yelled. "Help!"

One set of EMTs got out and hustled in my direction while the next two teams spread out and looked for survivors.

I stepped away from Briggs and collapsed back against a chunk of concrete, my eyes beginning to sting with unshed tears.

23

Dagger

I TOOK BANE TO THE HOSPITAL FOUR HOURS LATER.

Four. Fucking. Hours.

I thought Bane was going to lose his ever-loving mind.

After I dropped him off, I parked in the multi-story lot nearby and pulled out my phone. Bringing up Cox's information, I stared at the digits and her name on the screen and told myself to grow a fucking pair of balls. Grow a fucking pair of big hairy ones because Cox wasn't the one in hospital right now.

But she had been hurt.

The memory of her struggling to her feet, soot covering her face and her ripped and torn clothing had broken something inside me. I'd had wanted to go to her, and it had taken every ounce of my self-control not to. She'd staggered around the blast sight, looking for any men who were still alive. I figured the explosion would've had to have killed about a half dozen men, and for the first time in my life, I felt a twinge of guilt about that.

I didn't like the idea of Cox hurting. Of causing her pain.

And I hadn't liked seeing her desperately clawing through the rubble, looking for survivors.

I needed to know she was okay. I *needed* to touch her again, but I didn't know whether she would take my call. My thumb hovered over the call button for a few seconds before I stopped being such a fucking pussy and dialed her number.

It went straight to voicemail.

My free hand curled into a fist and I redialed.

Voicemail. Again.

I hung up and tried one more time, finally leaving a message.

"Cox, I know you're fucking screening my calls. Call me back."

Drumming my fingers on my thigh, I waited for the phone to ring. And waited. And waited. I snatched up the device and threw it onto the dash. I needed to hear from her. I was going *insane* from not knowing.

Lunging forward, I grabbed the phone and dialed her again, completely aware that I was acting like a fucking pussy-whipped punk.

"Stop calling me, Dagger," she said after answering on the sixth ring.

Hearing her voice loosened something in my chest. "You're okay."

There was a beat of silence, then she asked in a low voice, "Why wouldn't I be okay?"

I couldn't tell her the real reason I was worried.

"You were there, weren't you?" she asked slowly as the pieces fell together. "At the dock. You were there."

Fuck. "Bane had to know you got his woman out," I admitted.

"So, I was just used as a fucking stalking horse? Did you know the warehouse was going to explode? Did you know there were drugs in there?"

"Who does the warehouse belong to, *cara*? Did you find out?"

"You know who it fucking belongs to."

"Say it."

"Sanderson. It was Sanderson's fucking warehouse, and it was Sanderson's fucking coke in there."

A wave of relief coursed through me. "Have you arrested him yet?"

"We have an APB out on him right now, but we haven't been able to..." She hesitated. "Fuck, why am I telling you this?"

Because she wanted to share things with me. Because she *needed* someone in her life to vent to. I didn't say that to her, though. The truth can be a bitch to look in the face. Instead, I said, "Were you hurt in the blast?"

"No. Superficial cuts and a few bruises but nothing serious. I can't say the same thing for some of my men."

Guilt stabbed at me once more. "Where are you now?"

"At home. Where I want to be left alone."

My free hand curled into a fist on my thigh. I didn't want to leave her alone. I needed to be with her.

As if sensing where my thoughts were heading, she snarled, "Don't come over here," and killed the call.

I was about to call her back when the phone started to ring once more. It was Bane.

"Boss? How is she?"

"Fine, no thanks to her fucking brother."

"Her brother?" I asked.

Bane laid it all out for me, how Hawk had borrowed money

from Sanderson to pay him back. Clearly, the bastard had also negotiated so much more than that because he became Sanderson's attack dog too.

"What do you need from me?" I asked. If I couldn't see Cox, I needed something else to keep my mind occupied.

"I need you to drag Hawk down to our usual spot and keep him conscious until I get there."

"It's done."

Dropping my phone onto the seat beside me, I started my car and went out looking for Hawk Montana. I started at the kid's apartment, figuring the dumb shit wouldn't know where else to go. As I crept along the hall, I heard the sound of moaning coming from his apartment. I guess he figured he was going to die anyway. Might as well get a quick fuck in. Pulling out the Browning from the holster under my arm, I brought it up then kicked in the door.

I scanned the apartment quickly, fixing my eyes on Hawk, who was sitting on the couch with his pants around his ankles and his hand on his cock. Porn. He was watching porn.

"Couldn't find a woman to suck your dick one last time?" I asked, stepping into the room.

Hawk got to his feet, pulling up his pants and stuffing his quickly deflating dick back inside. His eyes darted to the table, where a Colt 1911 was lying. His fingers twitched, and I brought my Browning up in a two-handed grip.

"Don't even think about it." I took another step forward. "You can either do this the easy way or the hard way, Montana. As much as I want you to choose the hard way, I think you should take the easy route today. I'm in no fucking mood for heroics."

He licked his lips. "Where are you taking me?"

"It doesn't matter."

"Sanderson will come for me."

I shook my head, watching the hope leave his eyes. "No. He won't. Sanderson doesn't give a fuck about you. He used you, made you beat your own sister, and for what?" I took another step closer. "Keep your fucking hands where I can see them and step away from the couch."

For a heartbeat, I wasn't sure he'd comply. I thought he was not going to take my advice and try to put up a fight, but then he shuffled his feet away from the couch, away from the Colt, and closer to me.

"Turn around."

Shoving the muzzle of the Browning in between his shoulder blades, I marched him from the apartment. As we moved down the hall, curious residents peered out from behind their doors. When they saw me, though, they retreated, locking themselves inside.

I stuffed Hawk into the trunk then drove him down to the same warehouse where I took Syndy. Keeping the kid in the trunk, I went inside and dragged over an oil drum, positioning it under the hoist chain in the ceiling. Back at the car, I opened the trunk, where Hawk looked at me with fear in his eyes.

"Finally figured out you should be scared?" I taunted softly. "Good." Taking a bundle of rope from one of the compartments, I secured Hawk's hands and feet together then jacked the kid up over my shoulder. Returning to the warehouse, I lowered the sling hook down then secured it around the restraints on his feet. Raised over the old oil drum, Hawk pulled against the bonds, but they didn't budge.

I called Bane, told him Hawk was ready, then grabbed my H&K

from the back seat.

TWENTY MINUTES LATER, BANE STROLLED THROUGH THE warehouse doors, casting me a look that said he wanted to be in control of this one. I nodded and stepped back, leaning against an oil drum. Hawk's eyes widened when he saw Bane moving toward him, his body jerking and twitching as he tried to get away.

Bane pulled out his Glock and shoved it into the kid's mouth.

Hawk's blue eyes widened.

"You signed your death warrant when you agreed to be Sanderson's bitch," he snarled into his face. Bane eased back enough with the gun so Hawk could speak. "Have anything to say?"

"I did it to protect Wren," Hawk gasped.

"You did it to *protect* Wren?" Bane repeated incredulously.

I could tell from the set of Bane's shoulders that he was ready to put a bullet in the kid's skull right now, but he wouldn't finish it before he had all the information.

Hawk continued, "Sanderson was going to kill her outright, then leave her dumped outside the club to remind you who was boss."

Bane's jaw was tight. He flicked his fingers to tell him to continue.

"I convinced him that this was a better plan."

Bane snapped. "Beating and leaving her in my own goddamn warehouse?" he barked, shoving the muzzle of the gun into Hawk's temple this time. His finger hovered over the trigger.

"He would've killed her and waited for you to find her body,"

Hawk said quickly. "I convinced him to kill her in front of you instead, to let you live with those memories."

"Because you're generous like that." Bane's words were like acid.

Bane glanced over at me, searching for my reaction to what I'd heard. I gave him a blank face in return. This wasn't my vendetta. This was Bane's. *Did I think the piece of shit deserved to die for this?* Absolutely, but I wouldn't be the one pulling the trigger.

Not this time.

Bane shoved the gun harder into Hawk's temple for a second then dropped his arm to his side.

"Why did you go to Sanderson for that money?"

Hawk closed his eyes and took in a deep breath. "Sanderson approached me. He told me he'd give me the money, but I had to work for him. If I didn't, he'd destroy Wren and her business."

"To get to me, right?"

He nodded, the motion making him swing a little. "He wanted you to suffer."

"I wanted *you* to realize what a fucking mistake you'd made," a dark voice said behind us.

Tensing, I spun around to find Sanderson standing a few feet inside the doorway of the warehouse. I hadn't even heard him come in. Three men hung back past the door, and I recognized all of them from the surveillance photographs Devil had acquired. These were the fuckers who had killed our dealers.

I unfolded my arms and reached for the H&K slung across my body. Sanderson's gaze flickered briefly in my direction—dismissing me—then returned to Bane.

"You couldn't have just left shit alone, could you, Rivera?" He strolled casually into the space. "If you had, none of those kids would've died. They would've been working for me instead of you, but you had to flood No Man's Land with your cheap coke and cash in."

Bane shrugged. "I'm a businessman, just like you. There was a hole in the market."

The other man ground his teeth. "No Man's Land was something Manzetti and I agreed on. That territory put an end to decades of fighting between us, to bring *peace* back to the community, then you swan in and start dealing, start taking *our* dealers from us."

Bane barked a laugh. "You're whining to me like I give a shit. I don't, Sanderson. I don't give a shit that I've stepped on your toes. You think I'm some punk-ass bitch who doesn't know what he's doing? I know *exactly* what I'm doing. I'm building a fucking empire, and you and Manzetti are standing in the way."

His lips peeled back from his teeth. "You're a little kid playing in the big boys' sandbox."

Bane shook his head slowly. "I hope you've got all your affairs in order, Sanderson."

"If I don't come back from this meeting, Manzetti has orders to bring you fucking down, to burn your *empire* to the ground."

Bane barked a humorless laugh. "I'm not talking about killing you, you egotistical fuck. I'm talking about the cops arresting you for drug possession, intent to distribute, and the murder of three Los Angeles police officers."

"What are you talking about?" He narrowed his eyes. "That was your warehouse. Your coke. Your fucking C4." Laughing, he added, "You fucked yourself up the ass with that stunt today."

Bane shrugged. "Maybe I lost myself some cash with those drugs going up in smoke, but I'm happy with that decision because it wasn't my name on the deed to that warehouse. It was yours."

I watched as Bane's words hit home and rage took over Sanderson's face. "You motherfucker, I'll fucking end you."

He reached into his jacket and pulled out a Glock at the same time that Bane dove to the floor, taking cover behind the oil drum beneath Hawk. Bringing up the submachine gun, I started firing, spraying the fucking place in a wide arc as Sanderson's men ran into the fray.

From the corner of my eye, I saw Bane leaning around the barrel and squeezing off his own rounds. There was a grunt of pain, then Bane was suddenly sliding in beside me. A hail of bullets *pinged* against the metal.

"Are you good?" he asked me, wiping blood from his face.

I nodded. "I'll take out the other two. You focus on Sanderson."

Bringing up his gun, he gave the signal with the jerk of his chin, and we both stepped free of the drums. I easily mowed down the first of what remained of Sanderson's men, whose weapon had jammed on him. He fell to the warehouse floor in a tangle of bloody limbs.

I raised my muzzle to the remaining guy. He did the same, and we both pulled the triggers. Whether it was bad luck or fucking fate, we were both out of ammo. I didn't think about what to do next. I worked on instinct, on years of military training.

Stripping myself of the machine gun, I brought my hands up in front of me and engaged. I'd done enough mixed martial arts to know how to hit and where, but this guy had to have had martial arts training. He slammed his foot into my liver on multiple occasions, always dancing out of the way afterward.

"Fucking enough," I growled, pulling a knife from my hip

sheath and launching myself at the other guy. I managed to get him on the ground, but somehow, a knife magically appeared in his hand too. He was much faster than I anticipated with the knife and slashed at me. I grunted when I felt the blade bite through my skin, but the adrenaline dump was too much—too strong—so I kept fighting.

Bane joined me then, and I took a moment to see that Sanderson's brain was leaking out onto the ground. Bane had had his revenge.

Together, we circled the last man standing. The fucker's brown eyes darted around the warehouse, looking for a way out.

"The only way out of here is in a body bag," Bane growled.

Flipping the dagger in his hand, Sanderson's man changed grip and came at Bane, slashing. Bane missed each arc of his blade, giving me my opening to attack. I sank the tip of my blade into the man's throat, driving the steel through the flesh where his shoulder and neck met. Blood spewed from the wound, gushing down to the dusty warehouse floor. He weaved on his feet for a moment, clutching at the wound like that would stem the flow. Staggering toward the door, he reached the handle and pressed it down.

I looked over at Bane, who simply shook his head.

There was no way he was walking out of here.

Sanderson's man took a lurching step before falling face-first into the dirt. Blood pumped from his neck, pooling on the ground in a macabre black puddle. Turning around, I looked at the carnage, then at the corpses that weren't there fifteen minutes ago.

Exertion from the fight finally crashed over me, and with that exertion, came the pain. Clutching the side of my stomach, I walked over to Bane, whose serious eyes slid down my torso.

"Did you get hit?" he asked, and I heard the fear in his voice.

I stared at him for a moment, before my knees gave out. Bane caught me under the arm before I hit the concrete with my entire body weight behind me. He eased me down, my world moving in slow motion. I blinked up at him as he moved my hand to lift my black shirt out of the way.

"Fuck!" He rose, wiping my blood onto his pants. Pulling out his phone, he made a call. I couldn't keep track of the conversation, my hearing growing dimmer by the minute. For a second, I thought he called Andy, but the bastard couldn't be in any condition to help us.

There was a sharp pressure on my stomach, and I came to with a gasp. I had passed out, and not even realized it.

"Andy... hurt," I rasped.

Bane shook his head. "He's okay. Nothing major hit like they thought. He discharged himself against medical advice an hour ago." He pressed a little harder into the wound, and the pain was too much.

Pain and darkness and surrender beckoned to me.

And that was the last thing I knew.

24

ONE WEEK LATER...

AS THE LAST OF THE NINE SHOTS WERE FIRED INTO the air by the Honor Guard at the joint funerals of the three men who'd lost their lives in the raid last week, I stared out at the sea of deep navy-blue suits and white-peaked caps. The turnout had been big—not that I was surprised. Whenever a police officer was killed in the line of duty, others came to pay their respects.

Because it was the right thing to do.

We were all doing this job, knowing the risks we took every damn day.

When it was all said and done, we were one family.

A hush fell over the crowd of mourners as a moment of silence was observed. When this was over, I could try to put this fucking disaster behind me. The guilt I felt for the deaths of these men had only grown in the week that followed.

I hadn't heard from Dagger in all that time, but with no more hits on dealers, I wondered whether I would ever again.

As soon as the padre presiding over the service made his closing statements, small groups of officers pulled away from the larger pack, their soft murmurs of condolement and hugs the thing binding them together.

I stood separate from all of them.

Someone beside me heaved a sigh, and I turned to find Ward.

"This wasn't your fault, you know."

I looked away. "Maybe not, but the guilt I'm feeling won't go away."

"I understand that, but you didn't force any of these men to go on this raid. You were working on information you'd received from a trusted source."

Was it a trusted source, though? I hardly knew anymore. I knew that trusting Bane wasn't my best decision, but for whatever reason, I trusted Dagger. He had saved my life.

"Maybe," I conceded. I couldn't tell Ward the whole truth. He had a young family, and I didn't need to involve him in this. "I have to go."

I turned and walked away, not looking back over my shoulder at the stoic grief on display. Although, seeing this funeral now, it made me wonder whether Harper had gotten the funeral she deserved, or had she been buried in a budget grave thanks to the city of Los Angeles? I should've attended her funeral.

When I got to my car, I unlocked it then slid into the driver's seat, just thinking about everything that had gone down. There'd been a warehouse fire not far from the explosion site, where five bodies were burned beyond recognition. Even the dental records were of no help. Call it a hunch, but I would've bet my last dollar that the corpses belonged to Sanderson and his crew, and I would've given my life if it wasn't Bane Rivera who had lit that fire.

But I had no proof.

I shifted into gear and returned home to my darkened apartment.

I hadn't opened the drapes in a few days—the cool darkness pressing on me the only comfort I allowed myself. Dropping my phone on the kitchen counter, I pulled a bottle of water from the fridge and drained half of it. For days, it felt as if my throat had been clogged with unspoken and unacknowledged feelings. I knew that if I looked at them too closely, I would break.

I'd just placed the bottle of water down on the counter when a lamp in the living room turned on.

Dagger was sitting in an armchair right beside the lamp.

Flattening my hand over my racing heart, I said, "Jesus, Dagger…" I stopped when I got a closer look at him. "What the hell happened to you?"

"I had an accident."

My eyes darted down to where he clutched at the right side of his abdomen. "What kind of accident?"

He shifted in the seat, wincing. "One where I ran into a bullet."

"What happened, Tony?"

His eyes flared at the use of his name. I'd only ever used it once before, and it sounded strange on my tongue.

"I told you. An accident."

"Are you in pain?"

"Sometimes."

Easing closer, I sat on the edge of my couch. "Will you ever tell me?"

"No."

I folded my arms over my chest. "Did you get hurt in that warehouse fire?"

He stilled.

Sighing, I said in a resigned tone, "I already suspect Bane's involvement."

He cocked his head to the side. "And if I confirmed that involvement? What then?"

"I don't know. Maybe nothing." He stared at me, and I continued, "Let's assume one of the bodies in the warehouse belonged to Sanderson. Would I prefer that justice had been served in a different way? Yeah. He should've gone through all the steps of arrest and trial."

Dagger's expression gave nothing away as he listened to me.

Sucking in a deep breath, I let it out. "But there's a part of me, a dark part, that likes that he got what was coming to him. He kidnapped Ms. Montana to get revenge on Mr. Rivera. I don't know all the details of this perceived slight, but I know that if I had the resources, I would've chosen retribution rather than the legal system."

I was letting him see a piece of me that rarely saw the light of day.

The piece of me that revealed I was once the daughter of a motorcycle club president. I wasn't a stranger to violence. I'd been brought up on a steady diet of it until I left when I was fifteen, but that didn't mean I didn't see it as a means to an end. That didn't mean I didn't *use* it to further my cause.

Dagger's eyes narrowed on my face, like he was unsure about me now.

Licking my lips, I asked, "Now that Sanderson is dead and

the dealers' hits have stopped, does that mean what's going on between us stops? I won't be investigating your boss anymore. Our business is done."

Other than his jaw bulging in agitation, I had no idea what he was thinking. "Our business will never be done." He bit each word out, making them sound like there were exclamation points at the end of them. Then topped off with a bullet.

I frowned. "You'd seriously keep this hanging over my head. Just so you can fuck me?"

Heat filled his gaze. "You're mine now. I don't share, and I sure as fuck won't let you go."

Running my bottom lip between my teeth, I thought about that. "What about a renegotiation?"

Dagger was still silent, watching me with his burning green eyes. Eventually, he said, "I'm listening."

"The agreement before was you get my body in exchange for keeping your mouth shut about how I get my information. Right?"

"Right."

"What if I were to say to you that the new deal would mean you still get to fuck me, but you need to start feeding me information about what's going on in other underworld dealings?"

"You make it sound like I'm benefiting from the fucking favor instead of demanding it," he growled.

"You already showed me your hand, Dagger. You want me. You *claim* me. You won't share, and I sure as fuck won't give my body to a man who's not giving me anything in exchange."

He scoffed. "You sound like a whore."

I knew the words were meant to be derogatory. I leveled him with a flat stare. "And you want this whore. So?" I challenged.

"Choose."

The look in his eyes would've sent any other person running. He looked like he was ready to wrap his hands around my throat and choke the life out of me. I was playing Russian Roulette with him, though. I wasn't one hundred percent sure this was the right decision. Here was a man who was used to getting what he wanted, who intimidated and extorted others for his boss's gain. He was an expert killer, who wore tailored black suits and donned his cockiness like a second skin.

He was also the man who made my entire body light up with pleasure.

He was the man who made me climax with nothing but a knife and hot, filthy words whispered into my ear.

Slowly, he rose from the chair and stalked toward me. Wrapping one hand around my throat and another in my hair, he forced my head into position.

In a low, graveled voice, he hissed, "I want it all with you, and I'm never letting you go."

Then he kissed me.

25

Cox

FOURTEEN MONTHS LATER...

I'D BEEN DREAMING. DREAMING OF A TIME WHERE I wasn't in deep with the second-in-command to LA's largest drug dealer and supplier with the biggest reputation for violence. But, of course, as my eyes fluttered open, that was exactly my life. Dagger was at my back with one muscular leg thrown over mine and his thick arm around my waist—his huge palm cupping one of my breasts. I was caged against the heat of his body. His scent was in my nose and all over my skin.

I wondered what we looked like together—the cop and the criminal. It shouldn't have worked, but somehow it did. At least for now.

Ever since that day over a year ago, we'd slept in the same bed together. Sometimes it was at my place, but mostly it was his. His sprawling house had more room for the both of us. I never thought I'd be so domesticated with a man, but I had soon learned that Dagger was anything but domesticated.

There would be a time where I would have to walk away from him, but as I snuggled a little deeper into his embrace, I hoped it wasn't soon. What had started out as a dirty deal had become something I hadn't known I was looking for. Dagger didn't judge me for my ruthlessness. He didn't sneer when I told him I paid another informant off with drugs. He saw the world, and all the people in it, how I saw it—like something you have to master in order to survive.

The only caveat we had placed on our relationship was that we couldn't fall in love. Love would break us, and neither one of us could afford to be broken.

I glanced up when my phone started to vibrate on the nightstand. Reaching out carefully so as to not disturb Dagger, I picked up the phone and looked at the number.

It was Dante.

It was also four in the morning in Michigan.

Carefully extricating myself from the cage of Dagger's body, I left the bedroom, shutting the door behind me, and padded naked into the kitchen.

"Dante? What—"

"You need to come to Detroit. Now."

I was instantly on alert. "Why? What's happened?"

For the last fourteen months, Aidan had been holding auctions, the events getting bigger and more exclusive each time. I'd been given regular updates, but Detroit was way out of my jurisdiction, and Dante was still building his case against the Savage Hunt MC. So, for now, all we could do was watch the train wreck happen.

"Aidan is selling Sloane in the next auction."

A ringing started in my ears as a sharp, coldness began in

the center of my chest and slowly expanded outward. Like ice freezing on the surface of a lake, I felt every inch of it overtake my body and seep into my veins. And with that cold, came a numbness. I slumped against the kitchen counter and ran a hand through my hair, only to notice my hand shaking.

"Seren, are you there?"

"I'm here." But I needed to be there, with Sloane. I needed to be in Detroit. "When?" I asked in a warbling voice. I'd never heard that sound coming from my mouth before. Swallowing thickly, I asked, "When is this supposed to be happening?"

"I don't know," he replied, his voice strained. "It's soon, though. Within the next couple of days."

"I'll be on the first flight out," I told him. I hung up, the phone falling away from my ear. I needed to go, but I couldn't tell Dagger. He would follow me, and having him in Detroit in the same zip code as Aidan was dangerous.

When I crept back into Dagger's bedroom to find my clothes, I was startled by his rasping voice in the dark.

"Who was on the phone, *cara*?"

An involuntary shiver tracked down my body as I remembered him whispering filthy words into my ear earlier in the night. How he needed me. How he owned me. How I was his.

"Nobody." I looked around the floor, but it was dark, and I couldn't find my bra or panties. Knowing Dagger, he'd torn the former from my body and shredded the latter.

"Don't lie to me, *cara*."

Ignoring him, I found my bra, thankfully still intact. I slid the straps over my arms and fastened it at the back.

He clicked on the lamp as I was buttoning up my blouse. I stared at him, cursing him for looking so damn fuckable. If I had known this was going to be our last night together, I would've made love to him longer. I looked away, my throat closing up around the words I was about to say. "We can't do this anymore."

"Can't do what?"

"See each other."

"Seeing each other would imply we had more than a sexual relationship," he replied casually, rubbing his palm over his short hair. "Why should we stop? Bane doesn't suspect a goddam thing."

"He could find out."

"As long as his business isn't affected, he doesn't care who sucks my dick."

"I'm glad to hear that's all you think I'm good for… *sucking your dick*." I shook my head. "It doesn't matter anyway. I won't be in LA for much longer."

He sat up, the sheet falling away from his chest. "Why?"

My eyes lingered on the linear scars across his pectorals. "That's none of your business."

"Jesus *fuck*, Chantelle." He ran another hand through his hair. "Just tell me."

"Why should I? We aren't in a relationship. This is just *fucking*." I threw the words back at him with a sneer, stepping into my skirt and reaching back to zip it up.

He stalked from the bed, completely naked, and semi-hard. "Where are you going?"

He leveled me with an arctic stare. I could've lied to him, but he would know. He always knew. He also always knew where I was. I suspected he had some way of tracking me, but beyond a hidden app on my phone, I had no idea how he was pulling it off. "Detroit."

His hands curled into fists. "Why?"

"That's none of your business."

"Is it for work?"

"That's none of your business."

He narrowed his eyes, then wrapped his hand around his cock, starting a slow pump up and down his shaft. I watched him hungrily for half a second before I told him in a strained voice, "We're not doing this."

He stepped closer. "Yes, we are." Curling his hand around the back of my neck, he said softly, "If this is it for us, I want to have your lips wrapped around my dick one last time."

I struggled out of his grip, but he had no intention of letting me go. Why was he making this so fucking difficult? Leaving him was hard enough. His refusal to drop it making it damn near impossible.

He squeezed a little harder. "On your knees, *cara*. Now."

"N—"

His mouth was suddenly on mine, his tongue thrusting inside my mouth, demanding I give him everything. As much as I wanted to fall under his spell again, as much as this felt like I was tearing out my own heart, I had to stop this.

I bit him on the lip, causing him to jerk away. I had to make him see that this was over now.

I had to make him despise me. I had to make it so he wouldn't follow me at all.

"I hate you," I seethed, wiping his blood from my lips.

"I have no doubt about that." His words were benign, but his tone was antagonistic. "Tell me why you're going to Detroit."

I glared at him. "Personal reasons."

"How long?"

"You don't *own* me, Tony. And there's nothing you can do to *coerce* me into telling you." I winced when he tightened his grip.

"If you want to keep your career, I do."

I wanted to laugh in his face. As soon as he felt threatened, he threw our old deal back into my face. It didn't matter if he told my captain about what I'd been doing. As far as I was concerned, I was no longer a cop because the things I was about to do would null and void the oath I'd taken to serve and protect.

"There are some things more important than a career." I stepped from his hold, hearing him grind his teeth in response.

"I can find out, you know?" he told me in a low, dark voice. "You have your methods of getting information, and so do I."

I turned toward the door. "Just leave it, Tony. There's nothing you can do to save me... at least not this time."

I left his apartment, driving home too fast. As soon as I was in the door, I hurried into my bedroom, grabbed a bag from the top of my closet, and started to throw clothes inside.

26

Dagger

IT HAD BEEN TEN HOURS SINCE COX LEFT.

Ten.

Motherfucking.

Hours.

I'd managed to refrain from tracking her location for all of twelve minutes, but in the end, my protective instincts flared, and I had to know where my woman had gone.

She hadn't lied to me.

She had gone to the airport. Flew to Detroit.

But what I didn't know was *why?*

What was in Detroit, aside from fucking long winters, car manufacturing, race riots, and corrupt government officials?

Not knowing if she was okay right now was eating me alive. I couldn't focus. Couldn't concentrate on work. And as I walked through the Dollhouse, checking on all the staff, my mind kept tracking back to Cox, her words haunting me.

There's nothing you can do to save me—at least not this time.

My hands curled into fists. It was my duty to protect her, and I fucking would whether that stubborn, infuriating woman would let me or not. Although we both played it like we meant nothing to each other, it wasn't true. We both didn't want to acknowledge that either one of us had grown to mean so much. And in the heat of the moment, I knew I whispered the words to her. She was mine. She belonged to me. She was my reason for breathing.

My phone *pinged* with a new message. It was from Bane, who said he needed to speak to me. With a sigh, I left the floor of the Dollhouse and walked up the stairs to his office.

I found him behind his desk, commanding as always. He'd returned from his honeymoon a few days ago looking tanned and as relaxed as I'd ever seen him. While he'd been away in Hawaii with Wren, shit had gone a little sideways with an attempted break-in at the restaurant, but I hadn't told him about that. He needed to spend time with his new bride—his new *pregnant* bride.

Now, however, he didn't look like an expecting father. He looked like he was ready to commit murder.

"Boss?" I asked.

"Shut the door."

I did.

His expression was tight, his lips formed a thin line. "How much damaged was caused at the restaurant?"

Fuck. He knew. It was probably his sister who had called. "We need a new rear door as well as a new safe in the office. The other was compromised."

A muscle in his jaw feathered. "Anything else?"

"The dumpster out back was set on fire. It did some superficial damage to the back wall of the kitchen."

"Jesus *Christ*." He glowered at his desk, and when he returned his gaze to me, his eyes were dark. "This is the third break-in at Rivera in the last year. Not to mention I've had six attempts on my life, my shipments hijacked in transit on more than one occasion, and one unsuccessful car bomb. I'm getting fucking irritated by the disruptions, Dagger."

"I understand."

"I don't think you do." He blew out a breath. "Manzetti is fucking me up the ass with this shit because Cox has been hounding him for the last nine months. She and her team have wiped out twenty percent of his supply chain and arrested his underboss on some trumped-up tax evasion charges.

"Now I find out he's enlisted the help of the Armenian Mafioso. He's going to have more fucking boots on the ground and more fucking guns pointed at my back. I want to put the bastard back into his box. And to do that, I need all my soldiers well-armed and ready for anything. The thing that really fucks me up the ass is that Manzetti controls the weapons game on the West Coast, and I don't have access to any significant firepower. Which leaves me with the East Coast and the only person who can supply me with what I need is Aidan Kavanaugh."

I felt my brows rise. "You want to make a deal with Hannibal?" I knew Bane had balls the size of Texas, but this was something else. Aidan Kavanaugh had been terrorizing Detroit for the last five years—a truth sociopath—who had once eaten the liver of an enemy after a deal had gone south, hence the nickname.

"I've set up a meeting with him. For Monday next week." Bane continued, "I can't leave Wren right now. This fucking morning sickness is more like all-day sickness and she can't stop vomiting. Bianca's suggested she get admitted to the hospital to go on fluids to help it stop. I'm not willing to risk Wren's life or that of our baby by going away for business deal right now."

Well, color me fucking surprised. Marriage and impending fatherhood had changed the infamous Bane Rivera. "Understood."

Bane stared at me, looking for what, I didn't know. Straightening my spine and squaring my shoulders, I took the scrutiny, feeling as if my skin was slowly being flayed from my muscles.

"Are we still actively feeding Cox information?"

"Yeah."

His jaw feathered. "I want her dead. I want that cocksucking cunt dead." He sat back in his office chair, the leather squeaking softly like even it didn't want to draw his attention. Steepling his fingers in front of his face, Bane stared at me with all the lethal patience of a viper waiting to strike. "She's fucking up my business."

Rage filled my veins like a flash flood, but I tamped down on the urge to explode. Instead of telling him to go fuck himself, I said as calmly as I could, "Understood."

He arched a brow at me. "That's it?"

"What else would you like me to say?"

He sat forward, deliberately placing his elbows onto the blotter and interlacing his fingers. "Maybe a better response would be 'why'?"

"It's not my business to know why. You want her dead. End of story."

He gave me a hard stare. "I just asked you to put a bullet in the head of the woman you've been fucking for the last year, and that's all you have to say to me? '*Understood*'? Come on, Dagger."

I didn't let my shock that he knew about me and Cox show. I thought we'd been careful.

"You're really not going to tell me to go blow myself?" he asked in a low voice, something like wonder in his tone. When I stayed quiet, he rose from his chair and walked to the window that overlooked the Dollhouse.

"I thought Wren did that enough for you," I replied drily.

Bane turned to look at me then barked out a laugh. "My wife does know how to please me." He returned his gaze to the club and asked, "Did you think I didn't know about you and Cox?"

"There is no me and Cox. She's a piece of ass."

The low-banked fire of his rage made an appearance as he roared, "Don't fucking lie to me, Dagger."

I heaved a sigh. "Not a lie. We fuck, but that's it."

He stared at me from over his shoulder. "How did it start?" Bane's voice was low, humming with malice.

Reflexively, my hands curled into tight fists. "I blackmailed her." When Bane only raised his brows, I added, "She pays her dealers off with drugs. I caught her doing it. In order to keep my silence, she agreed that I could have her anytime. Anywhere."

His gaze flickered to me in the reflection. His jaw was tight, his mouth pressed into a hard line. "She's a fucking liability. I trust you with my fucking life, Dagger. Wren's too. Fucking a cop is dangerous, but fucking with me? Well, let's just say that you aren't as indispensable as you think."

I met his eyes in the mirror-like glass. "I'd die before betraying you. Cox is nothing to me. If you'd told me you wanted to poison her dog? I'd do it in a heartbeat. Kill her mother? Yup, no problem." I squared up against him. I needed him to see how fucking serious I was. "You fucking want her dead. It's done."

"Good. That's all I needed to hear." He moved back to his desk and sat in the chair. "Get it done."

I turned to leave, but he stopped me and said, "I don't want to be disturbed for the rest of the night, either."

"Yes, boss."

I walked back into my office feeling like my whole fucking world was about to implode. My boss had given me an order to kill the woman I... the woman I... not loved because we promised each other we could never fall in love, but Cox was more than a piece of ass to me, despite what I'd told Bane. She was smart, sexy, and determined, and her fucking mouth set the blood in my veins on fire. When she let down her walls, her eyes defrosted and adoration shone through them. Vulnerability. Trust...

Fuck, fuck, *fuck!*

I fucking loved her.

And the thought of harming her made me think violent thoughts. But if I didn't kill her, then Bane would send someone else. Jesus *fuck*, how was I supposed to find my way out of this one?

I ducked back into my office to call Devil.

He was breathing heavily. "Master Guns?"

"Did I catch you at a bad time?"

"No. Out for a run, that's all. What can I do for you?"

"The detective you've been tracking for me. Can you see where she is exactly?"

"Hex can hijack a satellite in two minutes and find out."

"Do it. I need her exact location ASAP."

"You got it. Anything else?"

I thought about it for a moment. "Yeah."

Ten minutes later, I hung up.

27

Cox

I WOKE UP WHEN THE WHEELS HIT THE TARMAC AS the plane landed at Detroit Metro Airport. I'd boarded the first flight out of LAX at just after five-thirty in the morning. Almost four and a half hours later, I was in my hometown once more.

The plane taxied to the aerobridge. Everyone too impatient to sit on their asses and wait until the bird had stopped moving shuffled around, opening up the overhead compartments and pulling down their bags.

When the aircraft had come to a complete stop, I had to fight my way off the damn plane, brushing past angry and tired commuters and escaping into the terminal, my bag knocking against my back as I held it over my shoulder. I hadn't been home in eighteen years. It was a long time, but Aidan had given me an exceptionally good reason to stay away.

At the time, I hadn't understood why he'd given me the

ultimatum, especially when his MO involved bullets-in-brains. Perhaps love had been the real reason he let me go, or perhaps he wanted me to find out that our daughter hadn't died at birth, but knowing she was alive would be torture enough.

"Seren."

I pulled up short when I heard my name being called. Glancing around the busy arrival hall, I spotted Dante standing in the crowd. He was wearing a ball cap pulled down tight over his dark hair, shielding his even darker eyes from view. Dressed in a black leather jacket over a black T-shirt, black jeans, and black boots, he didn't exactly blend in.

When I was close, he wrapped one arm around the small of my back and ushered me from the airport.

"What are you doing here?" I asked under my breath.

"Meeting my sister." He shot me a devil-may-care smile I remember from my childhood. "I needed a cover."

"*I'm* your sister?" Everywhere he was dark, I was pale. "We don't look anything alike."

"A sister from another mister, then," he replied.

"Unbelievable," I muttered, batting his arm away.

He chuckled while walking over to a black and silver motorcycle parked up at the curb. Two helmets sat on the seat, and I eyed the seven-hundred-pound deathtrap warily. He threw one of the helmets to me, then jerked his chin at the seat. "Get on."

I brought my carry-on bag up in front of me to show him.

"Put it between our bodies."

Knowing time wasn't on our side, I did as he asked, sliding onto the back of the motorcycle and wedging my bag between us. Thank God I'd packed light.

When we were moving, I asked him, "How did you know I

was on this flight?"

"It was a guess. This was the first one in from LA for the day."

I squeezed him a little more tightly around the waist when he overtook a couple of slow-moving cars, then said, "When's the auction?"

"Tonight."

Tonight? Fuck! "Where?"

"It's being held in the ballroom of the Prism Hotel and Resort."

"Jesus, could they be any more out in the open?"

"The Kavanaugh family run this city now, Seren. A lot has changed since you were last here. With Killian gone, Aidan changed how things operate. He took the mafia out of the shadows and reinvented them."

"What about the cops?"

"Aidan has them *all* on his payroll. You don't join the Detroit Police Department without knowing exactly who you're working for."

"And what about you? You're on the vice squad here."

"And I have been for the last six years. I got in deep undercover before Aidan rose to the level of power he's wielding right now."

"How's your case going?"

"Growing. Kaash, like Aidan, has been building a bigger and bigger power base here in Detroit. His operation is now bigger than Talon's."

I let out a breath at the mention of my brother's name. I hadn't thought about him for so long. Escaping my family was all I could focus on, but I did regret leaving him.

"He's still president of Devil's Chaos?"

"There have been a couple of attempts at coups, but your

brother is one tough sonofabitch.""

I knew that. He always seemed to land on his feet.

"He's got a daughter," Dante added softly. "Her name's Alexis."

My throat was suddenly thick with emotion. I had a niece. I had no idea. "Has she been made into a club whore too?" The fact that I'd jumped to that conclusion first said a lot about the emotional baggage I was still toting.

He shook his head. "She owns and operates an autobody shop. She's a mechanic, and a damn good one too. I keep tabs on her."

"That's good."

"She's got her head on straight… well, *mostly* straight. I can't say she has the greatest taste in men."

Apparently, that made two of us. It must have been a genetic trait. "What do you mean?"

"She went through that rebellious stage and took up with the VP of the Devil's for a while. She soon came to her senses."

He drove us through Detroit, through all my old stomping grounds. It was as if I'd never been away from this place. "Where are we going?"

"I'll take you to my safehouse for now. Aidan has lookouts all over town. One look at you, and they'd know exactly who you are."

"How? I've been gone eighteen years."

He slowed to take a turn into a quiet street, not answering me until he slid into the dark coolness of an underground parking garage. "When you see your daughter, you'll know exactly why."

Dante lowered the kickstand and helped me from the motorcycle. With my bag clutched to me, I followed him into a bright and relatively new apartment building. We took the service elevator up to the fourth floor, and then he was showing me into an equally bright and airy apartment.

"When you said safehouse, I kind of had a picture of a dank, dark little room with no windows and a leaky faucet."

He grinned at me, flashing his straight, white teeth. "Let me show you around." He walked down a short hallway. There was a door at the end, then one immediately to the left and right of it. "This will be your bedroom while you're here." He gestured to the other door. "This will be Sloane's when we get her back."

I peered inside the rooms, trying to picture my daughter in there. The only problem was, I had no idea what she looked like, and since she didn't have a criminal record, there was no way for me to find out either.

Dante indicated the only remaining door in the hallway, and opened it. "Bathroom."

As we walked back down the hall, he told me he'd stocked the fridge with just about anything I could want.

"I've got to head back to the clubhouse. Kaash needs all hands on deck for this one."

I walked him to the door. "Thank you, Dante."

He flashed me that same smile as before and disappeared down the hall. I shut the door behind him, breathing out a long, deep breath. Exhaustion had slowly been creeping up on me since I left LA. I was too wired to sleep, though. How could I when my daughter was going to be sold to the highest bidder by the end of the evening? All I had was a bunch of restless energy bouncing around under my skin and no way to expel it. Normally, I'd go for a run, but I couldn't risk being spotted by Aidan's men, which left me with what?

Fucking nothing.

In the small but neat galley kitchen, I opened the refrigerator and took a look inside. Fruit. Bottles of water. Some chocolate. In the cupboard, there were some bags of chips, but not much else. Dante hadn't shopped like we'd be here for very long. I had to hope he was right.

Grabbing a bottle of water, I cracked the lid and took a long pull. Then my head turned to the side when there was a pounding on the apartment door. My heart instantly started galloping in my chest. Dante had told me nobody knew about this place. Setting the bottle on the counter, I peered through the aperture in the door. All I could see was the convex view of the hallway beyond. Stepping back, I wondered if I was jumpy simply because I was back in Detroit knowing full well that I was putting my daughter's life in even more risk.

"*Cara*, I can hear you breathing." Dagger's dark voice wrapped around me from the other side of the door. "Let me in."

Dagger was here? "What are you doing here?"

"I followed you. Now open the fucking door before I break the fucking lock."

Sucking in a calming breath, I flipped the locks and opened the door wide. Dagger took up the entire frame, his green eyes laser-focused on me. He was dressed in black slacks and a white button-down that was open at the throat so it showed a slice of his delicious chest.

"What are you doing here?" I repeated, stepping back when he advanced through the jamb.

"I could ask you the same thing."

"I told you I was coming to Detroit."

"You did." He kicked the door shut behind him, the noise of it slamming making me jump. "You just didn't tell me that you were coming into Aidan Kavanaugh's territory."

I licked my lips, anxious all of a sudden. "Is that why you're here?"

"Bane has set up a business meeting on Monday."

"With Aidan?"

"Yes." His gaze had an almost physical weight. "Why are you here?"

I couldn't answer that question without endangering Sloane. So I lied. "Visiting a friend."

"And how long do you intend on visiting this *friend*?"

"I don't know yet. Hopefully not long."

He stepped closer, getting into my personal space until all I could hear, smell, and see was him. My eyes fluttered shut when he wrapped one hand around my throat and buried the other into my hair. He tugged the tie out, sending my blonde hair around my face.

Into my ear, he whispered, "You've been gone for half a day too long. I need to fuck my woman. And I need to fuck her now."

"Your woman?" I asked, a part of me thrilling at the claim.

"Yes, my woman. You got a problem with that?" He bit the words out, glaring at me, daring me to deny it. To deny him.

Even though it hurt my heart, I stepped away, forcing him to release his hold. Turning around, I wrapped my arms around my upper body. If shit went sideways in the next couple of days, I didn't want to drag Dagger down with me. "We fuck, Dagger. There can be nothing more between us. We agreed to that."

"Bullshit. Look at me, Chantelle." When I stayed turned away, he barked, "Fucking *look* at me!" When he had my attention, he pinned me in place with his stare. "I've claimed you. You're mine."

"Just because you say I'm yours doesn't mean everything else will be all right."

His brows slammed down over his darkening eyes. "Tell me what's wrong, and I'll help you burn the fucking world, and whoever wronged you, to the ground."

He didn't want to do it *for me*. He wanted to do it *with* me. This frustrating, wonderful man. Why the fuck couldn't he just let me go? Why couldn't he have made this easy and got on with his own life. "Life doesn't work that way, Tony."

Agitation beaded off him. Running a hand through his short hair, he bit out, "It does when my boss ordered me to put a bullet in your skull and make your body disappear."

My heart stopped beating, and our gazes locked. In his eyes, I saw regret. Pain. Resignation. I didn't know what he saw in mine, but it was probably my fear. "What?"

"He wants you dead."

"Are you going to do it?" My voice was barely a whisper, brushing up against the sudden tension in the room. "Are you going to shoot me then dump my body?"

Suddenly, all I could see was Harper's broken body left behind the dumpster. The silence stretched out until I couldn't stand it anymore. Pounding my fists into his chest, I screamed into his face, "Then fucking do it! Kill me! Put me out of my *fucking* misery!"

Wrapping his large, strong hands around my wrists, he stopped me from hitting him and tucked me in close to his chest, his arms around my back. I was caged. Still struggling to break his hold, he squeezed a little tighter.

Strangulation instead of a bullet, then.

Shooting would be easier but far messier.

"I'm not going to kill you, *cara*," he said softly into my ear. I could feel his muscles bunching and relaxing as I tried to break out of the cage of his arms. "I'm not going to kill you. *Chantelle*, I'm *not* going to kill you."

I stilled, his words finally making sense to me. Tilting my head back, I looked at him. "You're not?"

Pushing some hair behind my ear, he searched my face. "How could I kill the woman I love?"

"I don't know!" I yelled. "You've been Bane's attack dog for years. I just figured..." I slowed, thinking about what I'd heard. "Wait, did you say you *love* me?"

He ducked his eyes and said gruffly, "And if I did. What then?"

Ignoring the heat suffusing my body at the revelation, I rubbed at my forehead. "This is messed up, Dagger."

His wary gaze flickered in my direction. "What is? That I'm capable of loving someone?"

"Honestly? Yeah. We promised each other. We promised no feelings would ever be involved."

His expression grew stormy. "Do you trust me?"

I let out a deep breath through my nose. I evaded his question. "There are some things about me that you don't know, Dagger."

"You think I don't know you have secrets? I know everything about you when you showed up as Chantelle Cox eighteen years ago. What I'm not sure about is who you were before that."

For a moment, all I could do was stare. He'd found out. Somehow, he had found out that I'd changed my name, but he had no idea who or where I was before that. If he didn't find that out, there was a chance he could walk away right now.

"But if you can trust me to love you, you can trust me with everything else."

I wanted to. I wanted to so badly my chest ached. But I had learned that trust had to be earned, not given away. If there was no emotional baggage attached to it, it was meaningless.

"I do trust you, but I can't trust you with who I was eighteen years ago."

His voice dropped, and his gaze was intense—drilling into me. "Does it have something to do with why you're in Detroit?"

I blinked at him.

"It is, isn't it? Does it have anything to do with Dante?" He sneered my friend's name. "Is he your ex-husband or something?"

"No."

His top lip curled. "Got a whole other family here? I bet that's it, right?"

"No!"

"Then fucking prove me wrong, Chantelle. Tell me the goddamn truth!" he thundered.

"I have a daughter!" I screamed the words I had hidden inside me for so long. For too long. A sob escaped my throat, and the next thing I knew, I was being wrapped in Dagger's strong arms again. More sobs shook my chest, bubbling out of my mouth. But I didn't know how to stop them. I didn't know how to make them slow. I was being emotionally flayed in front of the man I'd tried to keep my distance from for over a year.

Dagger scooped me up into his arms and settled on the couch. I tried to squirm free. "Let me go. I'm not a fucking *child.*"

"No," he said firmly. "What's her name?"

From my position tucked up against his chest, I glared at him. His blank stare only made me more spitting mad.

"I can wait here as long as it takes," he drawled.

I didn't have all day and night to wait him out. I didn't even have a few hours. Tongue thick, I replied, "Sloane. Her name is Sloane."

"What happened to her?"

I glanced down—away from his piercing eyes—because it felt as if my heart was being hacked out of my chest with a hatchet.

"You can trust me with this. I'm not going to run away. I'm not going to look at you any differently. I'm going to fucking have your back because you're mine."

Rubbing at the spot where pain was flaring along my skin, I finally decided to tell him.

I decided to trust him.

Completely.

He was defying the only man who could control him.

For me.

The least I could do was open myself up a little more.

It took me two tries to speak before any words came out, but when they did, they were like a torrent that had been held back by a dam. There was a crack in the structure of the fortress I kept all my secrets in, and I was powerless to stop them from falling.

"I was born Seren La Croix. My father was Steve La Croix, president of the Devil's Chaos Motorcycle Club. When I was eight, the VP killed my father and assumed the position of President. He also took my mom as his new wife. My brother, Talon, and me were raised in the club. I was learning how to boost cars, pick locks, and sell drugs before I'd hit puberty. As soon as that happened, my stepfather started to pass me around the club. I became their whore.

"When I was fifteen, I ran away from home. I ended up on the streets. I met another girl, Lucy Stern, who was the same age as me. We'd stuck together... protected one another. About a year after living rough, I met a guy. He was older than me by a few years. I didn't know who he was when I met him, but I soon found out.

"His name was Aidan Kavanaugh." I looked at Dagger. "*The* Aidan Kavanaugh. His father, Killian, was the head of the American-Irish mafia. Aidan charmed me and Lucy, offering us clothes, food, a warm place to sleep. We ended up moving into the Kavanaugh estate in New Baltimore. It was an eight-bedroom, ten-bathroom monstrosity of a house with a pool and lake frontage.

"After six months, he began a sexual relationship with me, while Lucy was used as the family whore. She was told which men to fuck, whose dick to suck. More than once, I told her we could leave, but she said she didn't have anything better to go back to. At least there, she had food in her belly and a roof over her head."

I swallowed thickly over the memories and of the last image I had of Lucy on her knees with Aidan's gun pointed at her head.

"I fell pregnant with Aidan's baby. He was as happy as I'd ever seen him, but his behavior had grown more erratic too."

"Jesus, Chantelle," Dagger murmured, tightening his arms around me.

"When I was eight-and-a-half months pregnant, Aidan killed Lucy in front of me. She was on her knees after giving him a blow job. He'd made me watch them because he was a sadistic fuck.

"I ran away that same night, only..." I rubbed at my chest again. It felt like that old wound was starting to flare. "I made it to the bus station, but it was late and the next bus out West wasn't until the next morning. I waited on those hard plastic seats for hours."

The memories had started to surface again, and with them came that soul-crushing desperation and fear. I had to remind myself that memories couldn't hurt me. That was in the past, and this was now. I focused on the feel of Dagger's arms around me, keeping me safe and secure.

"I had placenta abruption, which means the placenta separated from my uterus. There was so much blood on the seat, on the ground, between my legs."

Dagger squeezed me a little tighter. "Jesus, fuck."

Dragging in a deep breath, I continued because I knew that if I didn't get this out now, I would eventually choke on the words. "The security guard at the depot took me to the hospital. He was trying to keep me calm. He told me he and his wife had four kids. He told me all about them." I looked up at the strong profile of Dagger's face. "The youngest was called Chantelle."

"You named yourself after her?"

"I did. Frank Cox had saved my life. If I hadn't gotten to the hospital when I had, I would've died."

Dagger was stroking my arm absently. "What happened next?"

"I had to have an emergency cesarean section. I was put under, and when I woke up, my baby was gone. At first, I thought she was in NICU or something, but then Aidan walked into my room. He told me she'd died... our daughter had *died*... and it was all my fault. Then he chastised me for trying to leave him. He said his father had ordered him to kill me for my disobedience, and that was what I wanted too. My daughter was dead. My life didn't matter anymore. Then, he had a change of heart. He said I could either die right then and there, or I could promise to leave

Michigan and never come back. At the time, I didn't understand his reasoning, but I see it now. I would suffer more knowing I had lost a child. But he was wrong. I suffered a thousand times more because I knew she was alive and living with the monster who had sired her.

"After I left Detroit, I went to LA. I finished school. I became a cop and worked toward detective. I wanted to be able to stop men like Aidan Kavanaugh from hurting other women like he had hurt Lucy and me."

"That explains your hard-on for Bane."

I nodded, my cheek rasping against Dagger's shirt. "I thought Bane was just like all the rest, but I've spoken to some of the girls who work at the club, and they all sing his praises. A lot of the time, he saved their lives."

He grunted. "Don't let the word out. It'll ruin his street cred."

We both fell silent, each of us lost in our own heads, it seemed.

"Why did you come to Detroit?"

I shut my eyes and drew in a deep breath. Dagger's scent was everywhere, and it settled the frenetic thoughts in my head. "Aidan has been doing business with the Savage Hunt MC for the last year. They've gotten into the flesh trade together, running auctions that have grown in demand." I swallowed. "Dante told me that Aidan was selling Sloane off in the next one."

Dagger's whole body tightened. "When is it happening?" he asked in a cold, murderous voice.

"Tonight."

"Do you know where?"

"In the ballroom of the Prism Hotel and Resort."

"I'm going to help you get her back." It wasn't an offer. It was an oath. "And when we get her back, we're going to return to

LA, and you can both live with me."

I jolted away from him, staring into his strong, arrogant face. "What?"

"You're going to live with me, Seren."

The sound of my real name on his lips made my eyes close in pleasure. It had been almost two decades since someone other than Dante had used my name.

"And what if I don't want to live with you?" I asked.

"I can move into your apartment if you prefer, but it'll be too small for all three of us."

Frowning, I asked, "Where is this coming from, Tony?"

"I love you. I love the woman you've become. You might be a hard-headed, cold-hearted bitch, but you're my hard-headed, cold-hearted bitch. But I've also seen what's underneath that tough exterior you show the world. I know what's in your soul. And you don't have to say the words back to me. The fact that you shared this with me *shows* me how you feel." Spinning me around so I was straddling him, he added, "Now give me your mouth."

The kiss started off slow but soon became a fire that scorched the earth. The heat. The need. The desire. The love I was too afraid to verbalize. I let it all consume me—consume us—until we were both breathless and panting. Standing with me still wrapped around his waist, he carefully set me on the couch and dropped to his knees.

"I need to taste you." His rough words were really a rough command. "Strip."

When I was completely naked, I settled back onto the couch and watched as he lowered his face between my thighs. He licked my pussy, humming in satisfaction when my taste hit his tongue.

Then he spread me wide, staring at what was between my legs.

"Your cunt is perfect, *cara*. I fucking love it. And I fucking love you." Growling low in his throat, he dove back in.

Licking.

Sucking.

Tasting.

Grunting.

A feral noise trickled up from his throat as he ate me, devouring every last drop of me like a starving man. "I want to feel you come on my cock," he said, digging his fingers into the backs of my thighs. He pinched my clit, making my breath rush out of me, and penetrated me with his tongue.

I moaned his name, and he jerked back, unbuttoning his shirt quickly and shrugging it from his shoulders. His slacks followed, and then he was standing completely naked before me, his cock hard and long and wide. He looked down at me through slitted eyes.

"I want your lips wrapped around it. Now."

I slid from the couch and to my knees, taking him into my mouth. Sucking him down, he hit the back of my throat, and my gag reflex kicked in.

Dagger groaned as I choked on his cock, fisting my hair in his hand and pulling it taut. My scalp prickled with heat, the pain-edged-with-pleasure lighting up my nerve endings.

"If you keep doing that, I'll come in the back of your throat."

He forced me to rise from my knees, spinning me around and threading one arm over my shoulders to cup one of my breasts while his other hand wrapped around my stomach. His hard length pressed into the crease of my ass, prodding, looking for entry.

A soft mewling sound broke free of my throat as I tried to maneuver into a position where he could slip inside my body.

"Fuck," he hissed, taking us both onto the couch. I ended up on my hands and knees, Dagger arching above me from behind. His large, calloused hands roved my lower back and ass, stroking me. "Tell me you need my cock," he gritted out between clenched teeth. "Tell me. Now."

"I need your cock," I panted.

With one hand on my hip, he guided his length into my drenched opening. He filled me. Completely. Warmth spilled through me, and that warmth turned into molten lava in my veins.

"I'm not going to last, *cara*." He pushed the words out between clenched teeth. "You feel too fucking good. It drives me crazy."

I was shunted along the couch cushions with each of his deep thrusts, his cock hitting the end of me, tearing a little bit more of my self-preservation away. Falling for Dagger wasn't a good idea, but I couldn't seem to stop myself.

"Shit, I'm close," were the strangled words he uttered as he thrust more deeply inside me, brushing the head of his cock against my G-spot on the retreat. I came around his cock, fisting it with my inner walls, making him moan my name.

His thrusts grew quieter as my own pleasure crested and broke on the shores of his presence, and when the last spasm wracked my body, he flipped me over onto my back and began pounding once more.

I wrapped my legs around his waist and dug my heels into his back, arching into his touch. He looked at me with wild eyes, his lower body still pounding against mine. There was something more to this claiming.

When he finally came, he dropped his head, muffling his grunts against the side of my neck. He collapsed on top of me, both of us breathing heavily, our hearts racing in the same frenetic pace. Rolling onto the floor, Dagger dragged me down with him until I was draped across his chest. Inhaling the scent of his skin, I listened to the way his frenzied breathing began to settle.

For nearly two decades, I'd been alone. Alone in the lies. Alone in the secrets. But here was a man who knew everything there was to know, and he wasn't running away. He was embracing me, loving me, wanting to fight with me, but what if that wasn't enough?

"What if we don't get her back?" I whispered the words, not wanting to give them any power.

Dagger's arms banded around me. "We will. You think I came here unprepared? I have backup waiting for me downstairs."

I peered up at his face. "What?"

"I called in a favor."

28

Dagger

AN HOUR LATER, I HAD SPOKEN TO CHANTELLE'S MAN on the inside. Dante was undercover with the club, and he shared as much information as he could about how things were going to play out tonight. With all the facts sitting in front of me, I called Devil, and we devised a plan that would guarantee the least number of casualties and the highest rate of success.

I met him in a nearby parking garage where we would have the privacy we needed. We shook hands, slapping each other on the back. Behind him were his crew. I recognized two of the men—Jax Booker and Wilder Knox. They'd both served in my unit.

"Master Guns," Wilder said, wearing his usual cocky grin. With dark blond hair and piercing blue eyes, he looked like lots of women's wet dreams and fucking knew it. Like Devil, he was tall and broad.

"Ace," I replied, shaking his hand.

"How are you, brother?" Jax asked when I turned his way, clutching at my forearm and bringing me in for a quick embrace.

"I'm good, King. Yourself?"

He shrugged his broad shoulders, and I noticed the dark lines under his green eyes. "I've been better."

"Yeah, I heard about your wife. Sorry, brother."

The guy shrugged. "We're better off without her."

Devil introduced me to the others. "This is Joker, Deuce, and Hex."

I kept my eyes on the man who had been sending me information on Cox for the last year. He was the most clean-cut of the bunch with a pair of rectangular-framed glasses perched on his Roman nose.

"Hex, I wanted to thank you for all your help hacking into government satellites and agencies."

"No problem. Devil tells me you saved his life back in Afghanistan."

I glanced over at the guy, remembering the day we were ambushed and how I had to drag his injured ass out of the line of fire. "Yeah, I did."

"All right, enough of the fucking chit-chat, ladies," Devil announced, clapping his hands together to get our attention. He handed me the floor. "Master Guns?"

I nodded. "There's going to be a flesh auction tonight at the Prism Hotel and Resort on 3rd Avenue. It's being run by Aidan Kavanaugh and Savage Hunt's president, Kaash Silva. Our job is to get the girls out alive before the auction takes place."

"Fucking cocksucking cunts," King muttered, his hands balling into fists. "Men like that should be sent to prison and fucked up the ass."

I couldn't have agreed more.

"How many?" Joker asked in a bass drawl.

"Twelve confirmed. The girls are being kept apart right now so that there can be no communication. My idea is to get them out of the holding rooms before they can be moved to the hotel. Current intel says they're all being held in one location."

Hex asked, "Where?"

"In a six-bedroom house in Lafayette Park. Security is tight. We're talking wired to home base security. Hex, will you be able to shut it off?"

He smiled. "Child's play."

"Guards?" Ace asked.

"At least one on each door of the bedrooms. Two on the front. Two at the rear."

"Ten in total," Deuce mumbled, a smile spreading on his face. "Piece of cake."

I looked over at Devil. "You can decide who goes where."

He nodded. "Hex, you'll stay in the van. Ace, you'll take the front guards. King, the back. Once they've been dispatched, Joker and me will infiltrate the building first, laying down cover if necessary. From there, we'll split up. Including Dagger, there are six of us. One guard a piece once we're inside. Take down a guard then—"

"How clean do we have to be?" King asked, interrupting Devil.

"As dirty as you want," I replied. These men were harboring young girls and women to be sold into the sex trade. No fucking way was I giving them a fucking pass on that.

"Oorah," King replied. The word was echoed among all the men.

"Once the guards are dead, the girls will be loaded into the van

Hex is waiting in and driven away. The rest of us will disperse into the night. We'll rendezvous thirty minutes later in a location I'll disclose to you en route in case one of us is compromised."

Devil stared each man in the eye. "Let's make these motherfuckers pay for their sins."

THE AUCTION WAS SUPPOSED TO START AT EIGHT o'clock in the evening with the plan of moving the girls over to the hotel an hour before. We decided to hit at six. As soon as Hex parked the van, he started hacking into the building's security system. Two minutes later, any alarm system that would've alerted Aidan of a breach was silenced forever.

The two-story, red-brick house was surrounded by a six-foot-high wrought iron fence, an equally imposing wrought iron gate marking the only way in or out. Large shrubs screened off the front of the house from the street, but where I was positioned— behind a car parked on the opposite side of the road—I could see the front door through the gates.

Just like Dante said there would be, there were two guards at the door. They weren't from military stock. These had to be members of the motorcycle club who were playing rent-a-cops for the night. Their hands were clasped together in front of their hips, their stance shoulder-width apart and ready. I couldn't see any weapons on them, but I assumed there were guns at the small of their backs.

I scanned the street, finding signs of Devil, King, Deuce, and Joker. Each were scattered along the front of the building, waiting for my signal. Glancing down at my watch, I raised my hand and counted down from three.

Two.

One.

Pressing my index and first fingers together and raising my thumb to form the shape of a gun with my hand, I ordered my men forward with the flick of my wrist. They moved as one, each of them quiet. Stealthy. Ace and King were the first ones over the fence, moving like ghosts through the garden. I saw King slip around the side of the house while Ace took out both guards with a bullet a piece. He motioned the remainder of us forward. Joker and Devil watched each other's six while Deuce and I teamed up.

I was the last one through the door, shutting it softly behind me. Ahead, there was a grunt then the quick *thwap, thwap* of a gun with a suppressor kicking two slugs into gray matter. King emerged from the hallway above, his whistle sounding to let us know it was him.

When we were one unit at the bottom of the stairs, Devil nodded to Deuce who produced a flashbang from the pocket of his combat pants. Pulling the pin, he lobbed it up the stairs. There was a bright light and a thunderous noise that rivaled the sound of a jet engine powering up. Once the device detonated, Joker and Devil took point.

The gun blast was loud in the confined space, but it was quickly followed by a double *thwap, thwap*. A body hit the floor just as I emerged on the top landing. I turned when there was movement to my right, pulling the trigger on the Browning Devil had given me.

The nine-millimeter slug took the guy in the face, making his brain matter splatter onto the wall behind him. I smiled down at what was left, then cursed when my thigh began to sting.

There was a bullet hole in my BDUs, blood gushing from the wound. Ignoring the pain, I continued on, clearing rooms and taking down the guards. Gunshots were ringing out as I took cover behind a wall. Some of the guards were taking cover inside the rooms with the girls. Others were hiding behind walls like I was.

Another hail of bullets sunk into the wall of the hallway, and I sent up an ascending whistle to make sure everyone was still breathing.

Five descending whistles came back.

We were all still breathing. Fucking fantastic.

More gunfire thundered through the house, and I was sure it was Kaash's trigger-happy members who were doing it. My men wouldn't waste fucking ammunition like that. I waited a beat, counting. After I got to ten, there was another volley.

Across from me was a partially opened door. I waited for the next spray of gunfire to stop, then crossed the hall and entered the room—gun drawn. When I wasn't immediately shot at or stabbed, I checked behind the two doors. One was a closet. The other a bathroom. Empty. I cocked my head to the side when I heard whimpering.

Lowering my gun to my thigh, I followed the sound to under the bed. On my haunches, I peered under the dust ruffle and found a pair of terrified blue eyes staring back at me.

"It's okay," I murmured. "You can come out. I'm not here to hurt you."

The girl shook her head, then cringed back when more shots were fired outside. This time, two shots were popped off directly after and all fell silent.

"Clear!" someone said out in the hallway.

"I'm in here," I yelled back in case they heard movement and thought it was another target. Turning my attention back to the girl, I tried again.

"You're safe. Those guys are dead."

Rising to my feet, I retreated to the door and waited. Now that I was farther away from her, the girl found her courage, and she shimmied out from under the bed.

Dressed in lingerie that looked too mature for her body, she covered her breasts with an arm and her hips with her hand. She was so terrified she was shaking, the tremors running through her entire body.

"What's your name?"

"D-D-Daisy," she stammered.

"Daisy," I repeated, making sure I kept eye contact. "My name's Tony. Me and my friends have come to help you, okay?"

She nodded.

"Where are you from, Daisy?"

"Florida."

Jesus, fuck, how fucking far and wide did Aidan go to get these girls?

"How old are you, Daisy?"

"Seventeen," she whispered.

"I'm going to take you out of this room in a minute, but I don't want you looking around or down at the ground. I want you to keep your eyes on my back, okay? I'll lead you outside, and we'll take you back to your family."

"Okay?"

"Okay." I nodded and took a step toward her. She retreated, the back of her long legs hitting the edge of the mattress. I holstered my gun and put my hands out in front of me. "Hey, it's okay. It's okay. We can go at your pace here."

"Dagger?" Devil said behind me. "You good."

Without taking my eyes off Daisy, I said, "Yep. Me and Daisy here were just talking about how nice it is outside. Weren't we?"

The girl's eyes ratcheted over my shoulder, where Devil just appeared. He smiled softly.

"Hey, Daisy. I have five other girls out here waiting to go home. You want to join them?"

Only five? Where the hell were the other six, and was Sloane one of the girls out in the hall? I wanted to ask Devil, but now wasn't the time.

Daisy worried at her lip. "The others are out there?"

"Sure are," Devil replied. "You want to come out and see them?"

She bobbed her head quickly. I stood off to one side and watched her leave with Devil. A moment later, there were sobs and laughs of joy. I let the girls, led by King, pass by the room and go down the stairs before I brought up the rear with Devil.

"We swept the rooms. Only found five girls, six including Daisy."

"You're sure? My source swore there were twelve."

"I counted them myself and checked each room afterward too."

I looked over the sea of heads ahead of us. "Any of them called Sloane?"

Devil said, "No."

If there were only five girls here, and none were Chantelle's daughter, we were fucked. Maybe she was never here, or she and the other five girls been moved to another location before the auction. We were out of time to figure out where they were being held.

And the only thing we could do now was go to the auction ourselves.

29

Cox

THE GRAND BALLROOM OF THE PRISM HOTEL AND Resort was 14,000 square feet of opulence. The carpet beneath our feet looked a lot like an Australian Aboriginal Dreamtime Scape in ochers, oranges, browns, and white. The walls were wallpapered in a deep apricot, matching the overall color scheme. That was not the atmosphere I was getting. Silk gossamer curtains in violets, dark blue, fuchsia, and indigo hung artfully from the ceiling, making the whole room feel as if we'd stepped back in time to Arabian Nights. Given this place was to be used for the sale of girls, the choice of décor didn't surprise me.

Covered in deep teal tablecloths, over five-hundred round banquet tables that seated eight people were dotted around the back three-quarters of the room. The first quarter, where a dance floor might usually be set up, held a large stage and podium. In front of the stage were Mughal-style low seats stuffed with jewel-colored cushions.

Beside me, Dagger was dressed in a tuxedo, walking with his same confidence that I suddenly envied. I was not ready for this. When it was clear the only way we would be able to reach Sloane was here at the auction, Dagger secured the credentials we needed to enter, along with an invitation. I didn't ask him how, but I suspected it was the same way he knew exactly where I was at all times.

I tugged at the sheer gown draped over my body, regretting the decision to put it on. Reaching for the gun strapped to my thigh was going to be too difficult with the yards of fabric I had to get through first.

"Did I tell you that you look beautiful?"

Dagger's question caught me off guard. "No."

"My mistake then," he growled. "I'll rectify that later."

Heat shot through me, but it did absolutely nothing to chase away the nervous energy that was assaulting my body.

His large palm was suddenly at my back, and he leaned in. "We'll get her back. I promise you."

"How did you know what I was thinking?"

"You're wringing your hands."

I looked down at the offending appendages and smoothed them down my thighs.

Dagger's voice softened. "I've never seen you telegraph your emotions this much before."

"I've never had to rescue my estranged daughter from my psychotic ex as he tries to sell her in an international sex auction before." I took a deep breath and pulled myself together. I had to think of this like any other police case. I had to stay emotionally removed and focus on getting the criminal.

"I swear to you, Seren, we'll get her back."

I glanced up at him. "You called me Seren. That's the second time you have."

"It's your name, *cara*."

It hadn't been my name for a long time. "While we're here, you should call me Chantelle. I have no doubt Aidan will have ears as well as eyes all around."

The room was filling up. Men in tuxedos milled around with flutes of champagne in their hands. There were a few women among them, but it was predominantly an all-male affair. Dagger and I were pretending to be a British power couple. I was a madam of a famous brothel, and Dagger was my husband. I couldn't do accents for shit, but Dagger assured me he had it under control.

I took a flute of champagne from the tray of a passing waiter, holding the glass up to my mouth and saying, "There has to be over a thousand people here," before taking a sip.

Dagger was scanning the room. "Jesus, I can see someone from MS-13 over there, as well as a Bratva *avtoriyet*. This thing is fucking big."

Glancing over in the direction he'd been looking, I memorized the faces of the men. "It also has the potential to go very wrong, very quickly." I could see the Russian glaring at a Latino man. "Who's that?" I asked Dagger.

"Sinaloa cartel. I heard there's a beef between the two right now over a narcotics route."

Jesus, if I had this kind of intel in my line of work, I would be able to do so much good.

The room swelled with noise as more and more people strolled in until the great doors that were the only exit and entry into the room slammed shut.

A man in his mid-thirties with dark hair and even darker eyes stood up at the podium and tapped the microphone. When he was sure everyone was looking his way, he began.

"Gentleman, before tonight's main event takes place, we will all share a meal together in the interest of keeping peace. This is the first time we have brought rival organizations together in order to do business. Mr. Kavanaugh asks that you all remain civil with one another. Any rivalries that you have outside this city will remain outside this city. You are Mr. Kavanaugh's guests while in Detroit. Please show him the respect he deserves."

Well, that explained why there were so many rivals in one room and blood hadn't been shed *yet*.

"You were all assigned a table. Please check the boards to find out where you'll be seated for the first half of this evening."

As people moved around to the large boards propped up on tripods that held the seating chart, I said to Dagger under my breath, "What the hell happens if we're on a table with someone who recognizes you?"

"Don't worry about it, *cara*. It's already been taken care of." With his hand on the small of my back, he led me to a table that was at the rear of the room. Each place setting had a name card above it, along with numbered paddles. I glanced at the names on each setting, not recognizing them.

I hissed, "Who the hell are these people?"

Helping me into my chair, he dropped a kiss onto the back of my hand and whispered against my skin, "My backup."

The men seated around the table all looked different, but there was something about them that screamed *military*. It wasn't that they had the same buzz cut or the same tattoos—although many of them did—but they all had that air of danger to them. A lot like Dagger did.

Dagger took the seat beside me. He nodded to the first guy, who gave me a cocky smile as he lowered himself into his seat. "Ace."

Ace looked to be in his mid-to-late thirties with dark blond hair cut short and eyes the color of a spring sky. He was tall and broad through the shoulders but narrow through the waist so that his tux fit him perfectly.

"King."

This guy looked like he'd just as easily shoot you than smile. He looked a lot like Dagger—dark hair and green eyes—but his cheekbones were sharper and his jaw squarer.

"Joker."

Joker had a beard that any lumberjack would be envious of. His eyes were dark, his shoulder-length hair a dark shade of blond. Through his nostril, he had a silver stud.

"Deuce."

Deuce's hair was long and blond that he kept tied up. The pale color of his hair brought out the green flecks in his hazel eyes. He had ear gauges that added to his overall rugged I-don't-give-a-fuck appearance.

"Hex."

Hex was clean-cut and looked like an accountant. With the rectangular glasses and chocolate-brown hair, he screamed boy-next-door. His dark blue eyes glittered with genuine warmth.

"And finally, Devil."

"You could've started with me," Devil grumbled.

Even sitting down, I could tell he was tall. His tux jacket was straining over his shoulders, so he had to work out at least six times a week. With dark hair cut short on the sides but slightly longer on the top, he had a trimmed beard.

"These guys know what to do if things go to hell."

"And are things going to go to hell?"

"Not if I can help it."

Dinner was served, but I was too anxious to eat. The men, however, laughed and joked—slapping each other on the back every now and then. All except for Joker, who watched the table with stoic intensity.

"You need to eat," Dagger said into my ear. "If you don't look relaxed, they'll know what's up."

I picked up my fork and stabbed at some steamed green beans on my plate. Once I had one on the tines, I brought it to my mouth. It tasted like ash. Giving up on trying to look like I was enjoying myself, I sat back in my chair and glared at the men standing around the room, trying not to look like security guards. I counted them, then again to make sure I'd gotten it right. There were at least fifty.

Dagger's hand landed on my thigh. "What have you noticed?"

"The number of guards," I replied in a whisper.

He looked around casually, like he was trying to spot someone in the crowd, then returned his serious gaze to me. "They won't be a problem."

"But how—"

Leaning down, he slammed his mouth to mine in a possessive kiss. I felt more than saw the rest of the men at the table staring at us. When we broke apart, he said, "Trust me, *cara*. I have a plan."

Even though it killed me to sit there and wait for something to happen, I nodded.

By the time the dessert plates were cleared, I was ready to start climbing the fucking walls. I was just about to excuse myself to the restroom when the MC took to the stage.

"Gentlemen, I hope you enjoyed your meal. First of all, let me apologize in advance. You came here expecting twelve items, but there was a logistical error, and we only have half that number. Worry not. They are the cream of the crop, and I guarantee you will find something you like."

The bastard winked at the crowd like a goddamn game show host.

"Now, let's get down to business. You're all here tonight to bid on something that you won't see again. Mr. Kavanaugh and his associates have been working hard for the last twelve months to secure these extraordinary items.

"They are rare, and they are precious, but there can only be one jewel in the crown that shines the brightest."

As he spoke, two screens descended on either side of the stage. The lights dimmed. An image was projected onto the screens. It was a headshot of young woman, who looked familiar, like I'd seen her in the media.

"This is Leesa Maci. Her father is the CEO of McCallum, America's largest drug distributor."

Another photo. This time the woman was a little older. "Jessica Lowie. Her mother is the head of health insurer, Vitality."

Another photo. "Nova Anwa. Her father is the owner of Energize."

And another. "Maia Stern. Her parents are the founders of Morgan and Stern Financial Holdings."

And another. "Cora Blake. Her father owns all the shipping ports from New York State to Florida."

The final image that flashed onto the screen made my heart stop in my chest.

"Sloane," I whispered, transfixed on the image of a beautiful young woman with platinum blonde hair and eyes the same color as mine.

"This is the jewel of the night. Simply called 'Diamond' she will be auctioned off last," the MC announced, his gaze moving to the back of the room. I turned to find a tall man with shoulder-length dirty blond hair and a beard nodding to the MC.

"Diamond is a code word," I told Dagger softly. "The man at the back just acknowledged it. I think this is already a done deal."

He took his time studying the other man. "I've never seen him before, but Kavanaugh has a lot of enemies in this room. If they knew she was his daughter, they would simply kill her. I think a deal was already pre-arranged before tonight."

"What about the other girls?"

"Decoys, maybe. I don't know."

"Introducing our first item," the MC said, gesturing to the stage. "The lovely Leesa Maci."

There was a noise like a door sliding open and a cylindrical cage only wide enough for someone to stand upright in rose from under the stage. The first girl was in it, dressed in lingerie that showed off her large breasts.

"Do we have an opening bid?"

"Ninety thousand," someone called out from a table closer to the front.

"I will accept ninety, but she is worth way more to her father. Do I hear one hundred thousand?"

I swallowed hard, trying to remain in place. They'd stolen all these girls from their families and were auctioning them off to the highest bidder, all to get a higher ransom, or perhaps something more from the girls' families. How in the hell did Sloane fit into all of this then? I turned and looked at the man behind me once more, only to find him staring at me.

We were suspended there for a long moment, his solemn gaze on my face, and my angry eyes glaring at him. There was no way in hell I was going to let him have Sloane.

"—sold for two hundred and ten thousand dollars."

My attention was jerked back to the stage, where the cage and the young woman with it, disappeared into the floor. There was a pause of five minutes, where the winning bidder was invited into the back to inspect his purchase.

When the next girl came up, the same process happened. Jessica sold for three hundred and eight thousand. Nova for four hundred and twenty-five. Maia sold for the same price, and Cora a hundred thousand more. I was shocked. How could anyone put a price on a human being?

"And now, for the crowning glory. The unparalleled jewel in the crown. Diamond."

The cage lifted onto the stage, and I gripped the table so hard my hands were mottled white. Sloane had on nothing more than a black bra, black lace panties, a matching garter and seven-inch heels.

"Easy," Dagger murmured. "Easy."

I stared at him, wondering how he could be so calm.

"Do I have an opening bid of five hundred thousand dollars?" the MC asked.

For a moment, nobody said a word, until behind me a heavily Irish accented voice said, "Five hundred thousand."

"Five hundred thousand. Do I hear six hundred-thousand?"

Beside me, Dagger stuck up his paddle. "Six hundred thousand."

I gaped at him.

The Irish guy behind me upped his bid again. Dagger countered each bid until Irish pronounced, "One million dollars."

Without missing a beat, Dagger countered. "One point five."

Murmurs broke out among the crowd, and the MC-come-auctioneer looked like he was levitating.

"Do you raise your bid, sir?" he asked Irish.

Turning my head, I looked at him. His mouth was twisted into a snarl as his eyes flashed with anger. Eventually, he shook his head, and the MC pronounced Dagger as the winner.

One of the security guards peeled off from the wall closest to us and approached the table.

"But how?" I stammered. "Where would you get that kind of money?"

"I've been saving for a decade, baby."

Before I could question him further, the guard said, "Come with me, sir. We'll take the payment then you can inspect the goods."

Dagger leaned down to kiss me on the cheek and whispered into my ear, "I told you it would be fine."

AN HOUR LATER, WE WERE BACK IN DANTE'S SAFEHOUSE. Dagger had insisted we blindfold Sloane before we put her in the car just to be safe. Now, she was dressed in a shirt one of the men at the table had taken off his own back and sitting on the couch with her hands bound behind her and her eyes still covered.

It killed a little part of me to see her like that, but her reaction to finding out what had happened could be volatile.

"You fucking wasted your money on me, you heartless bastard," she spat out, her head moving like she was trying to lock her gaze on someone. "I will hunt down and kill any man who tries to touch me." She struggled against her bindings, making pained noises as the sharp-edged cable ties bit into her skin.

Dagger stepped up beside her, then glanced at me. Sucking in a deep breath through my nose, I released it and nodded. He removed Sloane's blindfold but not the bindings from her wrists. Not yet. We had to be sure.

Immediately, she yanked her head around to glare at Dagger. Then spat on him. It landed on his shirt, but he didn't react.

"You're a piece of shit. Couldn't get any pussy on your own, you motherfucking cocksucker?"

Dagger glanced over at me and raised his brows, as if to say, *this is your daughter?*

"And you!" Sloane began, rounding on me. "I thought a woman would have more fucking compassion. How the fuck could you... you..." She frowned at me, then her eyes widened. "I know you. I've seen your photo..." She bit her lip, blinking rapidly. "Mom?" she asked on a croak.

I nodded but held myself in check, staying in my seat even though every part of me wanted to go to her. Tightening my grip on the arms of the chair, my knuckles mottled white as I willed her to see the regret in my eyes.

"You're really my mom?"

"Yes." The word was jagged and broken. "I am."

She looked at me in wonder, like I'd been resurrected from the dead before her expression shuttered—locking down. She was going into protection mode, and I couldn't blame her one bit. Her voice reflected her new sense of self-preservation. "Dad told me you were dead."

"Your father told me *you* were dead."

"Where have you been? Why haven't you reached out before this?"

It was a question I knew she was going to ask, and I was nowhere near as prepared for it as I should've been. "I…" My gaze settled on her arms restrained behind her back. To Dagger, I said, "Cut her loose. I can't stand to see her bound like that."

Dagger did as I asked, then stepped back.

Slowly, Sloane brought her hands around, rubbing at her wrists while she waited for my answer.

I licked my lips. "There's so much to explain."

A frown formed between her eyes and for a moment, I caught a flash of her father in her. "Can you try?"

I owed her that. "I was so young when I had you."

"How young?"

"Your age… barely eighteen."

"Why did you leave?"

Without thinking, I shuffled forward in my seat. I desperately wanted to reach out and touch her. Hold her to me, but I wasn't sure if she'd let me. "It's complicated. Your father is…" I hesitated, stumbling over the words I wanted to say.

"My father is a mobster. Is that what you were going to say?"

I blinked at her, then nodded. She was smart. "Yes."

"And his father before him."

"Yes."

"How long have you known about me?"

"Three years."

"*How* did you find out?"

"A friend of mine saw you. Recognized you."

She cocked her head to the side. "How? How did he know what I looked like?"

"Your eyes are like mine. Your hair is the same. He saw you with your father and knew who you were."

"Why didn't you come for me before tonight?" She was trembling—from fear or rage or something else, I didn't know—but I wanted to comfort her.

I rose from my seat. "Can I hug you? Please?" I asked, knowing that she could say no. She could tell me to go to hell for abandoning her all these years. She could walk out the door right this minute, and I would let her go if that was what she wanted.

For the longest minute, she only stared at me before she nodded.

Holding my arms out, she stepped into my embrace, and I felt it. I felt like whatever the hell had been missing from my life was suddenly found again. More tears fell as I cried into her hair. She clutched at the back of my dress, fisting the material and holding me tight. We were both sobbing and apologizing.

"I'll tell you everything once you're safe, away from Detroit and your father," I whispered into her ear.

She clung to me a little more tightly. "Promise?"

"Promise."

"It's late," Dagger said gruffly, and I peered at him over my shoulder. "We have to be out of here in a few hours so can I suggest we all get some sleep."

I nodded and started to pull away, wiping the tears from Sloane's cheeks with my thumbs as I cradled her face in my hands.

"Where are we going?" She looked from me to Dagger. "And who the hell are you?"

"Your mom is my woman," Dagger announced, giving me a savage look. A look so heavy with possession and wanting that it tightened things down low in my belly. "And Los Angeles. There'll be plenty of room for you at my place," Dagger said, "For both of you."

Sloane's gray eyes flickered between us. "You live together?"

I glared at him. "We haven't discussed this."

"I know what I want, *cara*." Taking me by the chin, he kissed me deeply—thoroughly. "And what I want is you. All of you." Tucking me into his side, he added, "Now, let's go to bed. Sloane, your room is opposite the bathroom. There's a bag of clothes in there for you along with a toothbrush and anything else you need to freshen up."

He steered me down the hallway, leaving me craning my neck to keep my eyes on Sloane. She stared open-mouthed for a moment before smiling and giving me a little wave goodbye.

Dagger shut the bedroom door and threw me onto the bed, covering me with his body completely. I gasped when I felt his cock pressing insistently between my thighs.

"Move in with me," he said.

"Are you asking me or telling me?"

He palmed one of my breasts through the dress. "Telling you because you're a hard woman to convince."

"What about Bane? His order for you to kill me?"

Dragging the fabric away, he leaned down and sucked my nipple into his mouth. "I've already taken care of it."

Moaning, I pressed my lips together. I didn't need Sloane to hear us.

Dagger turned his attention to my other breast, suckling at it and making me writhe beneath him. Running his hands up the inside of my thigh, he shoved the dress out of the way so he could touch more of my skin.

Although Dagger's mouth was driving me insane, I managed to ask, "How? How did you get him to cancel the hit?"

"I told him you were my woman. That you would never do anything to jeopardize us or my relationship with him." Against my breast, he repeated, "Move in with me."

Running my fingers through his short hair, I said, "Give me one good reason."

He plunged a thick finger into me, making me cry out. "I'll fucking give you five right now. Sloane will live with us. We can be a family. Get a fucking dog if you want one. I'll fuck you every night and every morning. You won't find another man who can satisfy you like I can. I fucking love you."

Another gasp escaped me.

A family.

I had waited so long for that.

"That was six," I managed to say, feeling the pressure building inside me.

With a growl, Dagger bit down on my nipple, sending me over the edge and scrambling to ride my pleasure. I was temporarily deaf as my orgasm overtook me. When I finally came back down, Dagger was whispering 'I love you. Move in with me,' in my ear, over and over.

"Tell me again."

"Move in with me."

I held his green gaze with mine and said, "Okay."

EPILOGUE

Sloane

AS I LAID AWAKE AND STARED AT THE CEILING OF THE
apartment my mom—my *mom*— was staying at, I finally let out
the breath I'd been holding. The tension in my shoulders didn't
ease, though.

That may have had something to do with the fact that my
own father had tried to sell me at auction like a dairy cow. Last
week, I'd been at home, studying for my SATs, dreaming of
the day I could escape Detroit—escape *Michigan*—and go to
college like any normal eighteen-year-old. My father had been
against the idea, of course, and had flown into a rage over the
mere suggestion that I go to an out-of-state school.

He told me it was too dangerous, that too many people
would try to harm me. Little did I know, that harm came from
someone a lot closer to home.

My dad was the one who told me my mom had died giving
birth to me, but when I found a photo in the bottom of a

drawer one day when I was twelve, it hadn't been him who had told me the truth. It was our housekeeper, Monica. She said she'd just started working at the house when my mom and another girl came to live there. They were barely sixteen.

It wasn't spoken about, but they were supposed to be playthings for my dad—a distraction. But then my mom got pregnant with me, and she changed from being a plaything to a liability. It had always been my father's plan to kill her once he grew bored of her, but the pregnancy had stopped that from happening.

Monica had helped to raise me, and it hadn't taken me long to realize my father and grandfather were both extraordinarily bad men. When I was six, I was placed in kindergarten and came home crying because another girl had told me I couldn't have a playdate because my dad was in the mafia and killed people.

Aidan hadn't denied it.

He had told me that this was the life I was born into. Family was everything, and when people fucked with our family, they ended up at the bottom of the lake with cement shoes. I grew up as a lonely child, wishing for the mother I had lost.

I heaved a sigh and turned onto my side, staring out the window opposite the bed. I could see the starry night beyond and the tip of a tree moving with the wind. I sat up, though, when the silhouette of a man skimmed past the glass.

There was a creak beside the bed, and I spun in time to see a man emerge from the shadows. Dressed all in black and with a mask over his face, he placed his finger to his lips in the universal sign for 'keep quiet.' Never one to follow the rules, I opened my mouth to scream instead, but the sound was snuffed from my throat when something hard and sharp was pressed against my neck.

"Who—" That was all I managed to get out before the darkness came.

MY EYES FLUTTERED OPEN, AND I DIDN'T KNOW WHAT had woken me. I was moving—rocking gently from side to side. On my back, my head was resting on something hard and warm.

"Don't scream," someone said above me in a thick, Irish brogue. "I mean you no harm, lass."

I turned, opened my mouth, and screamed. The man shoved his hand over my mouth and glared at me with icy-blue eyes. "I said *don't* scream. If you can't behave, I'll make you behave. Blink once if you understand."

I blinked once, and he removed his hand.

I screamed, and with a growl, the man stuck me with a syringe. As I drifted off into the dark haze of indifference, I asked, "Who... are you?"

"Name's Grayson, lass. And I'm taking you to my boss."

Thank you so much for reading Little Secrets.

If you want to find out what happens to Sloane, you can read her and Grayson's story in 'The Warlord', book one of the Mac Tíre Mafia series.

MAC TÍRE
MAFIA

THE
WARLORD

USA TODAY BESTSELLING AUTHOR
KALLY ASH

I'M A PAWN IN A VERY DANGEROUS GAME.

I was kidnapped and sold to one of the most dangerous mafia groups in Ireland - the Mac Tire Clan.

I've been entrusted into the care of a man known simply as The Warlord.

He watches me like a wolf stalking his prey.

He stares like he wants to devour me.

The scary thing is, I think I might want him, too.

little
SECRETS

A DARK MAFIA ROMANCE

USA TODAY BESTSELLING AUTHOR

KALLY ASH

Lightning Source UK Ltd.
Milton Keynes UK
UKHW010728170622
404574UK00001B/131